THE MORALS OF A MURDERER

An enthralling crime mystery full of twists

(Yorkshire Murder Mysteries Book 4)

ROGER SILVERWOOD

JOFFE
BOOKS

Revised edition 2019
Joffe Books, London
www.joffebooks.com

First published as "The Importance of Being Honest" 2005

Please join our mailing list for free Kindle crime thriller, detective, and mystery books and new releases.
www.joffebooks.com/contact

ISBN: 978-1-78931-239-3

CHAPTER ONE

London, UK. 17 April 2003, 2pm.

A dark blue armoured security van criss-crossed its way through the busy traffic along City Road into DeLisle Street and stopped outside the Bank of Agara. The driver and guard got out of the cab. The driver pulled back his elbows to stretch his back. The guard took out a partly smoked cigarette from behind his ear and lit it. They strolled round to the rear of the van. They glanced round the busy street at the unremarkable pedestrians and motor vehicles purposefully pursuing their destinations. The guard tapped a code on the door and it was promptly opened from the inside.

Then all hell was let loose!

Four men in street-clothes wearing black masks and waving handguns appeared: two from behind pillars on the bank steps, one from behind a newspaper stand and a fourth out of an office-block doorway There were gunshots. Men shouted and women screamed. Two of the men climbed on to the top of the van. It set off and weaved its way into the stream of traffic. As it gained speed, the men on the roof climbed down and jumped off. A big black car came from nowhere with doors wide open. The men dived into it while it was still on the move. The doors closed and the car dissolved into traffic immediately behind the van.

In the gutter, a man lay still. Blood trickled through the jacket of his blue uniform across the silver buttons. The other two guards kneeled down by his side, one of them speaking urgently into a mobile phone.

Two men in traditional Arabian long white robes, head-dresses with black surrounds, rimless sunglasses and sporting black moustaches and beards rushed out to the top step of the bank and looked anxiously around.

Police sirens wailed their two-tone racket in the distance.

*

Imperial Distillery, Slogmarrow, Near Bromersley, South Yorkshire. UK. 4 April 2005 9 a.m.

A small grey-haired man came through the large door smartly embellished with the words BOARD ROOM in gold leaf upon it and shuffled on to the landing of the old mill building.

'Andrew. Andrew!' he called in a Scottish twang down the stone stairway to the floor below. He dug his bony hand into the trouser pocket of his Reid & Taylor suit and pulled out a handful of coins; he held the clenched fist against the gold watch-chain hanging in an elegant sweep across his tartan waistcoat. 'Andrew!' he called again impatiently. He opened his hand, peered at the coins and slowly turned them over one by one with the other hand.

A young man in a cream blouse and kilt, came running up the stairs.

'Yes, Mr Fleming.'

'Ah, there you are. Ah, Andrew, when you go into Bromersley next, will you go into the sweetie-shop for me?'

'Yes, Mr Fleming.'

'Ay. I want you to get me — mmm — a quarter of those Grampian humbugs. I'll give you the right money. Just a minute.' He turned the money over again, and made a selection

2

of coins. 'Mmm. No, better make it two ounces. Here's eighty-two pence. Yes. That's right. Tell Miss Millington I want those in the quiet wrappers.'

'Yes, Mr Fleming.'

Andrew rushed off.

The old man turned round and, stooping slightly forward, his lean arms hanging limply by his side, shuffled back into the boardroom.

A log fire crackled in the big hearth, and an illuminated crystal chandelier hung from the high vaulted roof. The floor was carpeted with the McFee tartan, and the walls had a thistle-pattern wallpaper covering. Above the mantelshelf, pinned to the wall, was the blue-and-white flag of St Andrew.

Three bald men were seated in high backed chairs at the long polished table in the middle of the room. Mr Finlay, the financial director and, at seventy years of age, the youngest of them, was speaking.

'I am quite determined to tell the chairman that I am simply not able to serve the company any longer. I must take my retirement now. I will not be put off again.' He took out an inhaler from his pocket, screwed off the top and stuffed it up one blue craggy nostril.

'I agree,' Mr Menzies interjected, rubbing a painful, arthritic thumb-joint.

'This has been brought up at every annual meeting since young Duncan McFee became chairman, I can tell you,' added Mr Reid, director of Human Resources. 'But nothing will be done, you'll see.'

Fleming took his seat at the head of the table.

'There was the difficulty with the wars.'

'The war's been over nigh on sixty years!'

'I know. I know.'

'It's like talking to a brick wall,' Menzies said.

The grumbling and maundering continued awhile.

The antecedents of these worthy gentlemen and most of the other people working at Imperial Gin had originated in the Western Isles of Scotland and had drifted south, bringing their skills at distilling, to provide work to the masses of the Yorkshire unskilled labour market in the 1920s.

When unemployment was rife throughout Scotland, in April 1863, Hector McFee came to Yorkshire to the big house and estate at Slogmarrow on the eastern slope of the Pennines in Yorkshire, and founded a small distillery specifically to produce gin.

Over the succeeding 139 years, the Scots ventured out of their estate to the nearby village and cattle-market at Tunistone and the market town of Bromersley, some six miles away. They married local folk and some found employment in Bromersley or further afield, many retaining their Scottish traditions, some still regularly wearing their kilts.

The present chairman of Imperial Gin, Duncan McFee, who was the great-great-grandson of Hector was visiting Slogmarrow this day and the four senior directors were assembled, awaiting his arrival.

The sound of an engine, the crunching on gravel as the vehicle swerved, and then the squeal of brakes, followed by the slamming of two car doors disturbed the quiet.

Four heads popped up. The bickering stopped.

'Ah!' Fleming said. 'That sounds like him now. Take a wee look, Mr Finlay, will you now?'

The youngest member of the quartet put the cap back on his nasal inhaler and thrust it in his pocket. He pulled the lightweight deck-shoes on to his uncovered, ill-shaped feet, pushed back his chair and shuffled over to the small window to peer down to the courtyard. A big man in a tartan cloak and a deer-stalker hat was getting out of a Range Rover, being assisted by a younger man.

'Yes, gentleman,' Finlay said. 'It's McFee.'

The men pushed back their chairs and made their way to the landing. Finlay was the slowest, shuffling along in his soft shoes. They peered down the stone steps at the arched double door that led into the building from the courtyard. It opened and the big man walked in. He looked up at the reception committee on the landing, smiled warmly, waved a hand the size of a frying pan and made straight for the stairs, followed by the young driver carrying a leather briefcase. He overtook McFee and carried on up towards the boardroom.

'Ah, my friends,' the big man said with a generous smile as he pulled on the handrail. Eventually, he reached the top of the stairs and, breathing heavily, repeated: 'My very dear friends.'

He shook hands with each one in turn.

'Mr Fleming. Mr Menzies. Mr Finlay. Mr Reid.'

They smiled, nodded and muttered: 'Mr Chairman,' as, in turn, they clasped his hot hand.

Then McFee strode purposefully into the boardroom followed by the four directors.

When the driver had left the room and closed the door, McFee began:

'How good to be back with you all. Let us get down to business. Everything appears to be going very well. I will do the tasting this evening as usual.'

Fleming coughed, then said:

'Chairman, on behalf of the board, I have something I would like to discuss with you about our pensions.'

The other three elders nodded and muttered: 'Yes. That's right.'

McFee waved an impatient hand.

'Gentlemen. Friends. Let us get the balance sheet out first. It is only a month away. We are having an excellent year. When we see the exact figures, we may feel that we can vote ourselves an even bigger bonus than last year, and that was a record, wasn't it. Don't you agree?'

Finlay already looked defeated.

'Ay, well, the chairman has a point there.'

Reid said: 'But time is going on.'

Menzies said: 'Time is moving inexorably on and it is time it was settled. I believe I am the oldest here and — '

'I'm the oldest' Fleming said.

'Only by two months. What's that.'

'Gentlemen. Friends,' said McFee. 'Please. I suggest we postpone the decision about our pension allotments until after the year-end figures are out. Agreed?' He looked into the board-members' faces.

They sat stony-faced.

He smiled expansively. 'That's it. You know it makes sense.'

'Very well,' Fleming said grudgingly. 'If that is the majority view. Put it in the minutes, Mr Reid.'

The chairman nodded enthusiastically.

'Good. Good. Now let's move on. I have called this meeting for a very special reason. A personal reason. You four are my closest friends as well as being long and loyal servants of Imperial Gin plc. Tomorrow is my birthday. I will celebrate fifty years: half a century. Now I know I come from a family of survivors who have a boringly enviable reputation of longevity. My grandfather lived to be ninety and my father ninety-four. I might die this very afternoon or I might live another fifty years. I know that only God knows the time. But fifty is something of a landmark, isn't it.'

The old men nodded, uninterestedly.

'Tomorrow I am having a celebration dinner and I invite you all to attend.'

The dinner never took place.

*

Six miles from the Slogmarrow distillery was the South Yorkshire town of Bromersley. Once renowned for coal, now it was infamous for public houses, banks and supermarkets. On the road north out of the town was a forecourt with thirty or so cars, polished and gleaming, bearing huge price-tickets, red on white, stuck on their windscreens, awaiting the inspection of walkers aspiring to become drivers and willing to take a gamble! Next to the forecourt was a large barnlike building with big doors wide open, packed with more cars, old and older, in different states of roadworthiness. In front of that was a tiny two-roomed red brick office building.

In the office, at his desk, was Evan Jones, a slim, wiry man, with white, silky hair, immaculately dressed in a light-grey suit, white shirt and a red bow tie. Opposite him was Olivia Button, a smartly turned out thirty-year-old, fair-haired woman in a cream trouser-suit, with the figure of a Michaelangelo statue. The two were leaning forward, over the desk, looking into each other's eyes. He smiled and she sighed. Then he sighed and she smiled. He held her soft, responsive hands, and in a low musical voice, was ardently promising her the world with treacle on it.

No one wanted to kick a tyre or dispute the mileage on a clock, so what more pleasant occupation was there for Evan Jones than to spend a little time with his new-found girlfriend?

They sighed.

After a minute, the jangle of the telephone broke the spell.

'Oh,' he moaned in a dreamy, Welsh musical cadence. He loosened the tender touch of one of her soothing hands and, still looking into her big eyes, reached for the phone. 'Hello, yes? Evan Jones speaking,' he said distantly. Then his voice suddenly hardened. 'Oh, yes. I said two grand … All right, seeing as it's you, eighteen hundred — cash.'

Olivia Button gazed closely at his lips as he spoke animatedly into the telephone, fascinated by the up-and-down movement of his pencil-thin, forties'-style moustache.

'Right,' Jones said firmly. 'Thank you very much. I'll have it ready for you. With a full tank of petrol … Goodbye.' He replaced the phone. 'Sorry about that, Olivia, my darling,' he said as he reached out to take her hand again.

Her gaze left him briefly as out of the corner of her eye, through the window, she saw a woman determinedly advancing through the line of cars on the forecourt straight for the office door.

'Oh. I think you've a customer, Evan.' She pouted. 'A woman.'

He jumped up, releasing her hands.

'Have I? Oh. Ah. Right, love. Must get on. See you tonight then.'

She stood up and put her arms round his neck.

'Oh, Evan,' she whined.

He leaned forward and kissed her gently on the lips.

'You must go, Olivia,' he said, unravelling her arms from round his neck. 'Use the back door, love.'

She smiled at him through half-closed eyes, picked up her handbag and slung it on to her shoulder.

'Bye.'

He straightened his coat-sleeves, adjusted the gold cufflinks, tweaked the dicky-bow and glanced towards the window.

As the back door closed, the front door opened.

A woman with a set of big teeth, an ill-fitting brown coat and a blue headscarf entered, banged the door shut, and stood there, feet apart, staring imperiously at him. Evan Jones's face whitened beneath the tan.

'Oh. It's you,' he said, pulling an unwelcome face. 'What are you wanting now, Amy?' He spoke in that up-and-down musical delivery the Welsh have.

The woman swaggered up to the desk, dragged the headscarf downwards, and shook her head to allow a mop of red hair to fall out. She plonked down on the chair recently occupied by Olivia Button.

'To collect what you owe me, and no nonsense,' she sneered in the local vernacular. 'Have you got a cigarette?'

'I don't owe you anything. And you know I don't smoke.'

'You keep them for customers,' she challenged.

'Like so many other things, Amy, that's a courtesy I can no longer afford.' He caught a glimpse through the window of Olivia Button's car pulling out on to the main road. He was thankful the two women had not met each other.

Amy glared at him, then suddenly stood up and dashed round to his side of the desk. She pulled out a drawer, opened a silver cigarette-box it, took out a cigarette, slammed the drawer shut and returned to the chair.

His lips tightened. He had remained motionless while she rummaged in his desk, but he was not prepared to tolerate any further invasion.

8

'All right. You've got a cigarette, now go.'

She put the cigarette in her mouth.

'I need a light,' she snapped.

Evan's eyes opened wider. He stuck out a skinny finger and pointed at a chromium cigarette-lighter in the shape of a car on his desk.

She reached out for it and picked it up.

'New, eh? Expensive?' She pulled a face.

Jones shook his head slowly. 'It was an advertising gift from a tyre company!'

She lit the cigarette, examined the lighter again, sniffed and banged it noisily back on the desk.

'Five thousand pounds,' she said staring up at him and blowing a blue cloud across the desk. 'That's about a tenth of what I am due. But I'll settle for that,' she said with a confident nod of the head.

'Don't be so bloody ridiculous! The judge made an award and I have paid it. And that's all you're going to get!'

Her thin lips went even thinner.

'If I hadn't been locked up, I could have got a proper lawyer, instead of that legal aid junior they set on to practise on me. He would have made out a proper case and I would have got a decent settlement out of you!'

'Well, you lost the case. It was all fair and above-board. You got more than you deserved. So forget it, Amy. We're not married now! I'm not responsible for you any more. You mean nothing to me. You've lost me thousands in claims from dissatisfied customers you've swindled.' He wiped saliva off his mouth with a handkerchief. 'You're not getting another penny.'

She stood up, red in the face and looked him up and down. Then she glanced away, took a heavy drag on the cigarette and blew out a big cloud. After a moment, she turned back and switched on a smile like an ad for Steradent.

'I'll tell you what, Evan,' she said quietly. 'I don't want to be unreasonable.'

He sighed and raised his eyes to the ceiling. From experience he knew that that was exactly what she was going to be.

'Oh yes?' he said nodding, causing a lock of silver hair to fall across his temple. He swiftly brushed it back in position with a long, beautifully manicured hand.

She advanced towards him, shaking her bosom and forcing a smile.

'What?' he asked warily.

'I haven't got a car, Evan. I haven't got anything.' She pouted.

'You've had twenty-five grand of mine.'

'Chicken-feed,' she said jerking her hand in the air. 'Tell you what, Evan. There's an old Jag at the front. You've got eight grand on it. I'll have that, and call it quits.'

'No.'

'For old time's sake.'

'No.'

'Now I can't be fairer than that.'

Evan Jones looked her straight in the eye.

'No. Amy. No! You don't understand plain bloody English, do you? The answer is no,' he said, his accent straight from the Valleys.

Amy's jaw tightened. Her eyes shone.

Evan Jones had had enough. He strode determinedly from behind the desk, side-stepped her, made for the front door, pulled it wide open and stood by it, holding the knob.

A passing bus revved loudly to change down a gear to make the hill.

'Get out, Amy,' he bellowed. 'Get out. You are wasting your time. And you're wasting mine. And don't come back here again.'

She sucked in a deep breath. Her mouth contorted with rage. She breathed out noisily and then screamed:

'You — you Welsh bastard!!'

She turned energetically and stormed out through the door.

Evan Jones closed it quickly and breathed out a heavy sigh.

CHAPTER TWO

The following morning, at ten o'clock, Inspector Michael Angel came out of the Chief Constable's office and closed the door. He had wanted to slam it good and hard, but he had managed to restrain himself. He stormed down the steps and along the corridor silently reeling off every expletive he could think of, knowing that he would never ever express most of them out loud.

As he passed the charge-room door, he heard a familiar raucous voice protesting vigorously.

'Take your thieving hands off me. You're hurting! You're hurting,' the squawking voice persisted. 'Leggo! Leggo!!'

Angel stopped in his tracks. His fists tightened. The blood rushed to his face. He turned back and stormed into the room.

'What the hell's going off?' he roared. 'This isn't a cattle market!!'

An untidily dressed little man with the face of a ferret was tussling with a young policeman who was at the counter, taking his fingerprints. The constable was holding the man's finger and rolling it on the ink block. They both looked up in awe as the inspector sailed up to the counter.

'He's hurting me,' the little man squawked.

11

'Be quiet. You'll waken the dead!' Angel boomed, then he pushed between them and glared down at the little man. His eyebrows shot up. 'It's Fishy Smith, isn't it? Yes, it is. Come for your spring break at the country's expense, have you?'

The little man peered up at him and came very close.

'Well, well, well. It's clever-clogs Angel. No I haven't. And I want to express a complaint. This police brutality ought to be stopped. He's exerting too much pressure on my person and using too much violence to take my ruddy fingerprints. Also, this is a wrongful arrest. I ain't done nothin' and I ain't saying nothin'.'

Angel turned to the young policeman.

'What's he charged with? No. Don't tell me. Don't tell me. Let me guess. Mmm. Dipping. He's had his hand in some old lady's shopping-bag and nicked her purse.'

The constable nodded. 'We've found two purses on him. Been working the market, sir. Caught on CCTV.'

'It's a lie.'

'Don't bother, Fishy. Just serve your time and smile, you're on Candid Camera!'

'I didn't do anything,' Fishy Smith shrieked. 'It's not me. It's somebody else.'

'Save it for the magistrate.' Angel shook his head and looked into his watery eyes. 'Don't you think its time you packed it in?'

'I haven't done nothing.'

Angel shook his head and turned to the policeman.

'Do you want any help, lad? Or can you manage the Ripper on your own?'

'I can manage, sir,' the constable said with a wry grin.

'Well, carry on. And do it quietly,' said Angel softly. He turned away.

'Yes sir.'

Then, over his shoulder, Angel said. 'Goodbye, Fishy. See you in court.'

'I'll get even with you one day, Michael Angel,' Fishy Smith spluttered as the door closed.

The inspector buzzed down the corridor to his office. He had just begun to fumble through the morning's post when there was a knock at the door.

'Come in!' he snapped.

It was Cadet Ahmed Ahaz, twenty, slim and always smartly turned-out in a well-pressed dark suit. 'What is it, lad?' Angel said impatiently.

'There's a woman in reception to see you, sir.'

'I'm up to my eyes!' Angel bawled, waving an impatient hand. 'I can't see anybody. Who is it? What's her name?'

'Mrs Buller-Price. She says you know her, sir.'

'Oh,' Angel growled, pulling a face. 'Ay. I do know her.' He hesitated, then made the decision. 'But tell her I'm out.'

'She's been round the back, sir. To see if your car's there,' Ahmed replied with a smile. 'She knows you are in. She says she won't speak to anyone else.'

'Oh,' Angel snapped. He stood up and made for the door. He charged up the green corridor to the security door that led out to reception. He tapped in the code and pulled it open. The reception area was unusually quiet. There was just one enormous body in country clothes, waterproof hat over an abundance of white hair, boots, stockings and breeches. This figure was holding a long stick with a V at the top, a thumb sticking through it like a prize onion, and was reading a wanted poster on the notice-board. At first sight the person's gender was not obvious, but Angel knew from past encounters that it was indeed Mrs Buller-Price. She heard the door and turned round, her mouth open ready to speak.

'Ah! There you are, Inspector,' she began earnestly. She spoke in a deep cultured voice free of any accent. 'How nice to see you. I came in about the train crash. I hoped nobody was hurt or, worse, killed. And to offer my services. It must have been a mighty accident. I am a trained nurse, you know. I was with the Desert Rats in 1943. I was in the Queen Alexandra's. I once dressed a boil on Monty's buttocks, you know. Oh yes. Hmm. He gave me a banana,' she added with a girlish giggle.

'What?'

'Ah. You haven't heard?' She blinked and pursed her lips. 'Early this morning, at two o'clock there was the most dreadful racket. Woke me up. Dickens of a bang. Metal tearing. Men shouting. More racket than VE night. My dogs were bouncing about like jumping crackers. Couldn't settle them down. Then I was up at six. I still have five Jerseys. My milk goes straight to Windsor Castle. The Queen won't have anybody else's. There's no osteoporosis in that family, you know!'

Angel knew exactly where Mrs Buller-Price lived. He had visited her on one occasion during the foot-and-mouth epidemic four years ago. She had a farmhouse two miles northeast of Slogmarrow, and two miles from Tunistone, which was about six miles from the nearest railway track which ran through in the town of Bromersley.

'Whereabouts was this, Mrs Buller-Price?'

'There wasn't a word about it on the radio or the television.'

'But where was the crash?'

'And the phone was on the blink.' Her big blue eyes flashed. 'I don't know, Inspector. That's why I'm here. And don't tell me nothing happened. I heard it. That crashing of metal was unmistakable.'

Angel shook his head. She always tired him out and left him confused.

'If I hear about it and if we need your nursing expertise, I will most certainly be in touch, Mrs Buller-Price,' he said, forcing a smile and edging her to the door.

'Thank you. We must all do what we can, to help one another,' she said sweetly. 'Like you always do,' she added with one of her cherubic smiles.

Angel felt a little guilty at being so impatient with her.

The door opened suddenly and a young, skinny constable came in dragging a large, reluctant, black-backed Alsatian by a short length of clothes-line. The powerful dog hissed

14

and snarled, but didn't bark. Its tail was wrapped tightly down its bottom and between its back legs.

Mrs Buller-Price stared down at the dog, then up at the PC and frowned.

'What you doing with that dog?' she demanded sternly.

The constable looked her up and down as he addressed the inspector.

'Excuse me, sir. The dog was found in an empty house. It's got something wrong with it. It can't move its mouth. I think it's got lockjaw. I'm taking it to the vet's. It'll have to be put down.'

Mrs Buller-Price stared down and pursed her lips. Its paws were the size of a lion's. It hissed and snarled back at her and the hair on its back stood up.

'Careful, missis. He's very vicious,' the constable said, pulling the clothes-line tighter.

'Give me him here,' she said masterfully, and grabbed the makeshift lead. 'Hold that.' She handed her stick to Angel, who took it, blinked and scratched his head.

'What you doing, missis?' the constable said. 'He'll have you!'

Angel watched the old lady struggle down to her knees, pull back the sleeves of her bulky waterproof coat, and boldly take the dog's lower jaw in one hand and the upper jaw in the other. The dog wriggled strenuously and snarled.

Angel sighed.

'Mrs Buller-Price, do be careful!' he insisted.

The dog turned its powerful head from side to side and snarled and hissed as she peered into its mouth, but she hung on regardless.

'Ah. I thought so,' she said with satisfaction. Pursing her lips, she freed the dog. She looked up at the constable. 'Get me a big bowl of fresh, cold water, please.'

The constable gawped at the inspector, inviting his guidance. Angel nodded and the young man disappeared through a side door.

'It looks very dangerous, Mrs Buller-Price,' Angel said.

'Nonsense, Inspector. It'll be all right in a jiffy.'

She pulled up the sleeves of her coat again, heaved the big dog close under her arm, placed a hand round its nose and passed the other hand through the gap of glistening white teeth into its mouth.

Angel saw the dog's eyes flash. He said nothing but he thought plenty. He breathed out slowly, then licked his lips.

A second or two later, she smiled sweetly as she slowly withdrew her hand from the dog's mouth. Securely held between her thumb and forefinger was a grimy tennis-ball. She looked at it, then threw it contemptuously across the floor. The dog coughed twice and sneezed once. Then it barked and bounced and licked Mrs Buller-Price's ample face as she struggled to her feet. It pulled the makeshift lead out of her hand, then ran round her and Angel, barking and beating its big tail intermittently like the branch of a tree against Angel's legs as he put out a hand to assist the old lady.

Eventually, Mrs Buller-Price, red in the face and panting, made the upright position.

Angel smiled and handed her her stick.

'Thank you,' she said, and sighed. Then she looked round impatiently. 'Now then, where's that water?' Her Adam's apple bobbed up and down with every syllable.

The young constable returned through the side door carrying a white basin. The dog saw it, barked and bounded towards him. The constable froze. His jaw dropped and his eyes lit up like Maserati headlamps. He turned back to the door.

Mrs Buller-Price took in the situation.

'He won't hurt you, man!' she roared, her strident voice causing the strip light in the ceiling to rattle. 'He's as soft as Pavarotti's belly-button, now that he's got his self-respect back!'

The constable swiftly placed the basin on the floor by the door; the dog had emptied it by the time he had reached the standing position.

'Right. Now, I'll take him with me,' she pronounced, rolling down her coat-sleeves. 'He wants feeding up.'

'You can't do that ma'am,' the constable said. He looked at Angel who shook his head.

'I'll kennel him for a month free of charge. Then I will adopt him. If the owner turns up, which I doubt, you can send him to me. If he shows that he knows how to look after a dog like this, he can have him back, gladly. I have enough animals to feed. You know my address, Inspector.'

'Yes, Mrs Buller-Price.'

She made her way to the front door. She stopped and turned.

'Hmm, she said, 'I'll have to think of a name for him.'

Angel opened the door.

'You know, I thought at first, I would call him Thatcher,' she said, 'but as he's male, I think I'll call him Schwarzenegger.'

'Sounds as good as anything,' Angel said, smiling.

'Ah yes, Inspector,' she gave a big smile as she pulled on her driving-gloves. 'As usual, it has been very nice seeing you again. You must call in whenever you're passing. I always have a cup of tea and a scone at half past three. You'd be most welcome.'

'Thank you. Thank you very much. Goodbye.'

'Yes. Yes. Must get off. This dog's hungry. Come along, Schwarzenegger.'

Angel watched her pick her way carefully down the station steps to the pavement, closely followed by the Alsatian, its tail high and swaying from side to side. The old Bentley was parked at an angle on double yellow lines, half on the pavement and half off. He watched her unlock the door for Schwarzenegger, and then heave herself laboriously into the driver's seat beside him. She waved up to the inspector and beamed as the car glided away with the dog barking excitedly through the open window.

Angel closed the station door, sighed and was wondering about the mysterious train crash when he heard Ahmed's voice behind him.

'The super wants you, sir. He said it was urgent.'

'Ah. Oh. Right, lad.'

He sped out of the reception area, through the security door, down the green corridor to the furthest office at the end of the line. The door had a white plastic panel with the words DETECTIVE SUPERINTENDENT H. HARKER painted on it. He knocked on the door.

'Come in,' the super bawled.

'I was stuck with Mrs Buller-Price in reception, sir.'

'Ay,' said Harker tonelessly. 'You know that distillery up at Slogmarrow?'

'Imperial Gin?'

'Report's just come in. A triple-nine call from a chap called Fleming. A man's body has been found in a vat of the stuff.'

Angel blinked. 'What?' There are jokes about people drowning in barrels of booze but when it happens for real, it doesn't seem a bit funny; in fact, it seems rather sinister.

'Might only be an accident,' the super went on, 'I've sent scenes of crime, Dr Mac and a couple of uniformed. See if you can wrap it up quickly.'

Angel nodded. 'Right, sir.' He stood up to leave.

'Hang on,' the super said. He reached forward to a pile of papers in front of him. He sorted one out and glanced at it. 'I've had a phone call from a man I met at Hendon years ago: Peregrine Boodle of Special Branch. Done well for himself. He's a commander now. He wants us to look into a whisper he's had about an Evan Jones, car-dealer, Wakefield Road, Bromersley. He says there's a whisper, nothing more, that he might be linked to that big gold robbery two years ago.'

Angel's mouth opened. 'The Bank of Agara job?'

'Ay. He wants someone to sniff around, see what they can find out. I'd like to oblige him. There might be something in it for us.'

'Like what, sir?'

'Brownie points with the commissioner.'

Angel sniffed. 'Oh.' There were plenty of other things he would have preferred. 'Right, sir.'

'One of his men infiltrated a bullion-laundering scam — he didn't say where — posing as a punter with a big load of gold to shift, and came by Jones's name on a list.'

'Jones is a pretty common name.'

'Ay, but the possibility of its being our Jones is increased by the fact that he runs a garage. Ideal as transport manager for a gang of villains. Eh?' He nodded. 'That, and the fact that his ex-wife has just come out of Holloway for fraud.'

Angel's eyebrows lifted. Now there was something to think about. He sped up the corridor to the CID office. DS Crisp was sauntering out of the door reading an email. Angel caught up with him.

'Drop that. There's a car-dealer got a pitch on Wakefield Road. He's called Evan Jones. See what you can find out about him.'

CHAPTER THREE

It was a winding climb up the east side of the Pennines to Tunistone, five miles west of Bromersley. Angel drove through fresh, green woodland showing bluebells and early yellow and white shoots through a light-green carpet. At the brow of the hill, at the sign to Tunistone, the scenery changed to a treeless, windswept terrain of moor interspersed with gorse bushes and areas of budding heather. He turned right, bypassed the village and headed along the old stretch of road towards Manchester. The road was mostly used as access to the few farms, a stone quarry, a water-pumping station, the distillery and the hamlets beyond. It meandered through steep drops here and there, and when he passed eight ft-high snow-markers at the side of the road, he knew he was nearing Slogmarrow. He turned the corner and saw the big enamel sign, black on white, Imperial Gin Plc. He turned off the main road on to a single lane and passed through the open gates. He drove past many stone buildings, and on up to an area where a plain white van, a police car and an ambulance were parked. He pulled up alongside them. He glanced round at the maze of grey stone buildings, chequered with light-grey pointing, with ten regular rows of dark-glass windows surrounded by white frames. It had been a woollen mill many years ago, now it reminded him of photographs he had seen of US prisons. There was no sign of life. He made for the nearest door and pulled it open. The sickly smell of fresh juniper berries hit him in the face.

Angel looked round the big white-painted factory area with the high roof. Immediately in front of him were twenty huge vats, covered with inverted funnel-shaped stainless steel lids, except for the nearest one. Its cover was off and was on the scrubbed brick floor. Above the vats were crane tracks and the crane itself; above those was another level that only partly extended across the ground floor and was reached by an internal stone staircase built against the wall. Lights shone through the upstairs windows, which appeared to be for office accommodation that overlooked the factory area below.

Blue-and-white plastic tape with the words POLICE — DO NOT CROSS, was draped around the vats enclosing most of the floor space. A huge rope net was hanging over the uncovered vat from the hook at the end of a chain suspended from the crane. Dr Mac and two others in white plastic suits, head covers and gloves, were standing on a platform, leaning over the side, fishing about in the contents and tugging at the net.

Standing at the far side of the ground floor, a dozen or so workers in green overalls, hats and waterproof boots, hands in pockets, stared at the forensic team through a space between the vats in shocked silence. A constable with folded arms was standing next to them.

Four small elderly gentlemen in expensive suits were standing near the door. They watched with long faces and sad, eagle eyes the forensic team at work, turning towards each other from time to time to confer.

A uniformed constable held up a hand to stop Angel's entry, then, recognizing him, he smiled and lowered his arm.

'Oh, sorry sir.'

'What's going on, lad?' Angel asked.

'A man has fallen into a tank of gin. Dr Mac is trying to get him out by wrapping him in a net. They plan to hoist him out with the crane.'

The door behind Angel banged. He turned to see a young lad in a blouse and kilt standing in the doorway. The PC had seen him. He stopped him.

'You can't come in here, lad.'

'Oh, officer. Ay. I just need to see Mr Fleming about a wee matter.'

Fleming, hearing his name mentioned, turned round and toddled to the door.

'Ah. What is it, Andrew? Perhaps the constable will permit you to address me if it is only a quick matter.'

The PC nodded. 'That'll be all right, sir.'

'Oh. Ah,' Andrew began. 'I've been to town, Mr Fleming. I've been to the sweetie-shop, you'll remember — for your humbugs.'

'Ay,' the old man said expectantly. He held out his hand.

'The sweetie-shop is closed down, Mr Fleming,' Andrew replied with a long face. 'Been closed six months or so. Old Miss Millington died in October, and the whole street is being demolished.'

'Oh dear,' said Fleming with a sigh. 'Oh dear.'

'Do you want me to try somewhere else?'

'No. No. You'd better give me my eighty-two pence back.'

Andrew handed the money over, then gawped at Dr Mac and the forensic team working at the edge of the gin vat. The old man counted the money and dropped it into his trouser pocket.

'You'd better run along, Andrew. It's not good for you to be here. And the officer has been kind enough to let you in.'

'Yes, Mr Fleming.'

The young man opened the door, went outside and banged it shut. The PC took up his position with his back to the door.

Fleming returned to the little group. He recounted what had happened. They had a few words about it, nodded their heads in turn, then Fleming broke away from the group again. He toddled over to the PC.

'I think you should warn your men that proximity to the fumes from the vat could go to their heids and render them temporarily dizzy,' he whispered.

'Ah, yes. Right sir.'

Angel stepped forward. He had overheard what had been said. He lifted up the blue-and-white tape and crossed to the vat.

'Mac. Watch it! Those fumes can get to you!'

The pathologist in white plastic suit and gloves turned round.

'Oh? Is this your case, Mike?'

'Ay.'

'Not to worry. We've noticed.'

'Well be careful. Don't want you drowning in there.'

Dr Mac didn't reply.

Angel sniffed. 'Well, is it murder or not?' he asked impatiently.

'Oh, it's murder all right,' Mac replied grimly.

'Ay,' Angel replied. He had rather hoped it had been an accident. 'What have you got?'

'Only that it's a man ... and that he's dead.'

'Hmm.' Angel returned to the constable by the door. He nodded towards the group of four elderly men.

'Who are they?' he whispered.

'They are the bosses. The man who was talking to the young lad is the big boss, sir. Mr Fleming. The man in the slippers is the money-man, Mr Finlay. I don't know the names of the other two.'

'Ah.' Angel nodded and moved up to the group. 'Mr Fleming?'

The man turned away from the group. 'Ay?'

'I'm Detective Inspector Angel.' He plunged into his jacket pocket for his ID and badge but it wasn't there. He pushed his hand further into the pocket and fished around. He had intended to produce it instantly, as he had done a million times before, but it wasn't there. It had always been in that pocket. It had been there since his first day in CID, nigh on twenty years ago. Where was it now? He tried the other pockets: his trouser pocket, his hip pocket, even his inside pocket. No. The badge was in a brown leather folder four inches by four, with an ID card showing his photograph, rank, Bromersley police station address, with the ER insignia on one side and his badge on the other. Where could it be? The pocket was good and deep. It couldn't have fallen out. He wondered if he had left it at home. But no. He remembered he had picked it up off the dressing-table that morning as usual. Where the hell was it then? It was a mystery. He must press on … worry about it later. He took his hand out of the pocket.

'It was you reported the man's death, sir?'

'Ay. That's right. It's the chairman of the company. Duncan McFee. The death is tragic news not only for us, inspector, his friends and co-directors, but also the McFee clan, the company and the investors, too.'

'Very sorry.' Angel nodded sympathetically. 'Who might benefit from Mr McFee's death?'

Fleming shook his head. 'Nobody. Nobody. Only our competitors, I suppose. Temporarily.'

'Oh?'

'Well, our share-price will almost certainly drop. The market doesn't like uncertainty.'

'Did you know Mr McFee well?'

'As well as anybody, I suppose. And I knew his father and his grandfather. He was a widower and had no son or daughter.'

'Who would be his next of kin?'

'I don't know. It will require a vote of the directors to install a new chairman. Nobody automatically inherits either position as far as I know?'

'Did he live in Slogmarrow?'

'Only occasionally, ay. There is a flat in the old mill across the way. Most of his time he lived in his Kensington flat, in London.'

'I'll need to see over it.'

'I'll get you the address.'

'Thank you. Who found the body?'

'Angus Leitch, the ageing-room manager. He's over there. If it was murder, then someone must have pushed him in. He would have been on his tasting round. He always did it alone. Ah yes.'

Angel turned to the constable behind him.

'There's a man, Angus Leitch, with those other workers. Get him for me, lad. I'll watch the door.'

The constable nodded and ducked under the blue-and-white tape. Fleming rejoined his three companions who went into a huddle again.

A minute or two later the constable arrived with a man dressed in green overalls, hat and rubber boots.

'Angus Leitch, sir.'

Angel regarded the handsome, athletic-looking young man and judged him to be probably about thirty years old.

'You found the body?'

'Yes,' the man said, shaking his head and looking at his feet. 'Awful. Dreadful.'

'Mmm. Tell me about it.'

'Yes. Well, the last vat was filled yesterday afternoon. I'm responsible for looking after the keeping of the spirit. Making sure the specific gravity is right and the temperature is brought down as quickly as possible after being distilled, and that there is no sediment, it must be perfectly clear and consistent before it goes to bottling. Everything was satisfactory last night when I locked up. This morning I started my checks. I started at the far end and worked up to this vat. I opened the inspection door. I suspended the long-armed glass ladle to draw a spoonful from the centre of the vat and I felt something. The ladle wouldn't go in. I looked down to see why, and that's when I saw the body.'

'Could he have fallen in?'

Angus Leitch shook his head firmly.

'If he had fallen in, the inspection door would still have been open. When I came in this morning, it was closed and latched. And there's no way the latch could have been thrown accidentally.'

Angel's nose turned up. He rubbed his chin with his hand. This was going to be a tricky case. He hoped forensic would uncover something helpful. He leaned over the tape.

'Mac,' he called out, 'have you checked the inspection door for prints yet?'

'Ay. And there aren't any.'

'Hmm.' Angel suddenly turned back to Angus Leitch. ' Your prints should have been on the hatch door, shouldn't they?'

'I have to wear rubber gloves, Inspector,' Leitch said, pulling them out of the front of his overall.

Angel nodded. After a moment he said:

'What was Mr McFee doing in the distillery? Was it common for the distillery to be unlocked after hours?'

'It was locked when I left it at five o'clock yesterday, Inspector. He's the boss. He can come in here whenever he wants. He would be tasting and checking. He always did it. Not a batch was passed without his personal approval. That's why we have such a high reputation.'

'Oh?'

'He was very exacting. It's the great care of distilling and blending that makes it the best and the biggest-selling gin in the world.'

Angel sniffed. 'How often does he do it?'

'Whenever there's a full batch of distilled: when all these vats are full. That was yesterday. About every two weeks or so.'

Angel nodded.

Angus Leitch went on: 'When I arrived this morning, this room was locked as usual with the key. A key like this.' He produced a small bunch of keys from his pocket. He sorted a key for a five-lever lock and held it up between his thumb and forefinger. 'I locked this room up myself last night. The spirit in here is worth over four million pounds. No risk is taken with its security.'

'And who else has a key to this area?'

'There's one in a glass case in the security office, in case of emergency. The directors will have one, and the chairman, of course.'

Angel sighed. There seemed to be enough keys around for anyone who was determined enough to gain access. A mobile phone rang out. It was Angel's.

'Excuse me, sir,' he said. He turned away from Leitch. He dug into his pocket, pulled out the handset and pressed the button. The LCD window showed it was Superintendent Harker. 'Yes, sir?'

'I want you back here smartish. I've got Commander Boodle from Special Branch flying up from the city. He'll want to know what you made of that second-hand-car dealer.'

Angel's eyebrows shot up. 'I'm at the murder scene at the distillery, sir!'

'Oh. Murder, is it?'

'Yes sir.'

'Well leave it. Go and see Jones and then get back here as soon as you can.'

The line went dead. Angel's jaw dropped.

A bubble of anger travelled up from his stomach to his chest. His face went red and his jaw tightened. He stabbed the button and stuffed the phone back in his pocket. The stupidity of Harker never ceased to amaze him. You never desert a murder scene! The superintendent knew that. It was simply that he wanted to impress this Boodle chap. Angel knew he would be a big wheel … well, you have to be something exceptional to be a commander in Special Branch … but this was reprehensible. He sighed and went back up to the man.

'Thank you, sir.'

Andrew Leitch nodded and turned away. Angel leaned over to the constable and pointed to the stone steps.

'Only forensic goes up there. And don't leave this area unattended either. This entire area is a crime scene and is to be treated as such until Dr Mac has OK'd it. I'm sending you some replacements from the next shift. Stay glued until they arrive. Understood?'

'Yes sir.'

'Mac,' he called out irritably. 'Mac, I got to go!'

The pathologist stared at him across the vat. 'We're going to hoist him out now,' he replied urgently.

'Speak to you later.'

Mac continued to stare at him. His eyes were wide open.

'In two minutes!' he yelled.

The door banged. Angel had gone.

*

Twenty minutes later Angel's car pulled on to the forecourt of Evan Jones's second-hand-car site. He parked and strode up to the office. A note on the door read: Back in ten minutes. Angel pulled a face. He looked round. A man in blue overalls was walking swiftly towards him from the building behind the office, wiping his hands on an oily rag.

'Can I help you?'

'You can, lad, if you're Evan Jones.'

'He's gone home. He's got builders in. He'll be back soon.'

'Can't wait, lad. Where's he live?'

'He lives behind Jubilee Park. Orchard House, on Creeford Road. The last big detached house at the end.'

'Ta.'

That was the posh area of Bromersley. Creeford Road was a wide leafy lane built on the edge of Jubilee Park. At the bottom was a long brick wall eight feet high; in the wall were double wrought-iron gates. Angel slowed down and read the sign: ORCHARD HOUSE. Through the gates he could see a car and a small lorry parked on the drive. He stopped his car and walked briskly through the gate up the terracotta-tiled drive. There was a long expanse of apple trees in rich lawns to his left. The house was modern, compact and privately enclosed inside a high wall. He spotted a red burglar alarm-bell box under the eaves. As he approached the front door he heard voices from the direction of the orchard. He made his way in the direction of the chatter and saw two men standing together beneath a tree at the side of the house. A slim, dapper man in a light-grey suit and red bow tie was counting twenty-pound notes into a cap being held by a big man in a boiler suit.

Jones saw Angel approach and looked up angrily. He stopped counting the money.

'Who are you?' he called out challengingly. He pushed the notes in his hand into his pocket. 'What do you want?'

The workman saw Angel, swung the cap with the money inside it on to his head, turned away and picked up an orange-coloured bag of sand.

Angel reckoned he had interrupted a transaction in what politicians describe as the country's grey economy.

'Inspector Angel, Bromersley police. Are you Mr Jones?'

The workman walked unhesitatingly away.

The Welshman hesitated, his eyes slid sideways and then back. He licked his lips, then said:

'Yes.' He switched on a Roger Moore smile, ran his hand over his mouth and added: 'I was just paying this man.' He pointed to a simple brick-built low edifice of two metal grilles three feet from the floor, supported on three sides by a low wall set on stone flags. 'A proper barbecue. Be good in the summer, won't it.'

'Yes, sir,' Angel said. He personally had no time for meals outside that you had to share with insects.

The builder disappeared round the corner of the house with a long bag of builder's tools and the bag of sand.

Angel pulled out his notebook.

'Do you want to go inside?' Jones said, pointing a thumb towards the front of the house. Angel shook his head.

'It won't take long, sir. Word has come down the line that you are in the gold business,' he said heavily.

'The gold business? You mean ... ' Jones looked into the policeman's face, then he shook his head. 'Don't know where you got that from. I'm strictly a dealer in cars, Inspector. I buy them from X, clean them up, make them safe, and sell them to Y. It's a simple application I've got and I'm doing very nicely, thank you. I don't know anything about any gold.'

'That's fine then, sir.'

'It's not illegal to buy gold, is it?'

'Not at all, sir. No. Buying gold is perfectly legal. Have you bought any recently?'

'No,'Jones said unhesitatingly.

Angel looked into his clear blue eyes and sniffed.

'Hmmm. Well, just a friendly piece of advice, sir. Keep your nose clean.'

CHAPTER FOUR

'Come in.'

Angel turned the knob and opened the door.

Superintendent Harker was at his desk as usual, grinding his teeth. He glanced at Angel and then across at a man sitting opposite him, with a sun-tanned face, wearing a camel-hair coat, dazzling white shirt, and silver silk tie.

'This is DI Angel,' Harker mumbled and waved a hand across the desk. 'Commander Boodle. Special Branch.'

Angel closed the door and tried to smile.

'Good morning, sir.'

Boodle barely glanced his way.

'Morning,' he said in a breathy voice, more strained than a jar of Heinz baby food.

Angel took in the situation.

'You wanted to know about Evan Jones, the car dealer, sir,' he said.

Harker pulled out an invisible nail from between teeth at the side of his mouth.

'That's what we are waiting for, lad,' he said drily.

The commander, looking like a patient in a dentist's waiting room who has just heard the drill, slowly turned to look at him.

'Well, there's nothing known, sir,' Angel said.

'Oh?' Boodle sniffed then pulled a disagreeable face. 'Well, what sort of a man is he, this Evan Jones?'

'He's a Welshman, sir. He's — '

'Evan Jones is a Welshman. That's not really a big surprise, laddie!'

Angel's fists tightened.

Then Boodle said rapidly: 'What level would you put on his intelligence? How well do you think he was educated? How quickly does he reply to questions? How well do you think he runs his business? Is his business legitimate?'

Angel looked him straight in the eye and responded with equal pace.

'He is bright-eyed, competent, and I think adequately educated. His replies are prompt. I have no idea how well he runs his business, but he seems efficient and committed to it, sir.'

Boodle smiled like Caligula smiled to the gods.

Angel licked his lips. He was determined not to let this smart-arse from the city get one over on him.

'As to his business ability, there's not been time to get a report from the Inland Revenue.'

Boodle grimaced knowingly and half-closed his eyes.

'Done that. Nothing there,' he said. He shook his head, then went on: 'What else did you find out?'

'He is divorced and lives alone. He's a keep-fit fanatic, likes the ladies, and from all accounts they like him. Recently moved into a detached house he bought for four hundred thousand pounds. He was married to an Amy Jones for ten years. No children. She's served six months for fraud. He divorced her after she went to prison. She was released very recently.'

'Ah. Wife' Boodle's eyebrows lifted. 'Fraud, eh? Now she sounds interesting. Have you interviewed her?'

'We don't know where she is, sir.'

'You could try the probation service,' Boodle said drily. Angel replied, trying to keep his voice even.

'I haven't had the opportunity. I am in the middle of a murder case.'

The super looked up and sniffed.

'Ay. And you'd better get back to it, if the commander has finished with you.' He looked down at Boodle, who nodded and waved a hand to signify his accord.

Angel was glad to leave. He turned and reached for the doorknob.

'Oh, Inspector,' Harker called grandly. 'Organize a car and driver to take us to The Feathers, and bring us back here for 2.30, and then take the commander straight to the airport for the 3.50 shuttle, will you?'

'Right, sir,' Angel said. He could see what the game was. They were going out for a liquid lunch. He hoped it would choke them both. He closed the door and charged up the corridor to the CID office.

A man in blue overalls, a cap and red rubber gloves came backwards out of the gents' toilet carrying a yellow plastic bucket, a squeegee and a plunger. The smell wasn't pleasant. Angel bumped into him.

The man turned round. He had a wet unlit cigarette-end hanging off his bottom lip.

'Here. Steady on,' he grumbled.

'Sorry, lad,' Angel said. 'What you doing anyway?'

'I'm the plumber.'

'What's up?'

'The gents' lav is blocked.'

'Oh? Have you fixed it?'

'I've only just come,' said the plumber indignantly. He turned away and wandered up the corridor, muttering.

Angel reached the CID office and saw Cadet Ahaz at a computer.

'Ahmed, find out who has the duty car, and tell him to report to the super's office. Then ring up the probation office in King's Cross. Get the address of Amy Jones. She was released from Holloway about a week ago. And then find DS Gawber and DS Crisp pronto. I want them both, urgently.'

'Right, sir.'

Angel went into his office and slumped down in the swivel-chair. He gazed up at the ceiling and closed his eyes. It must have been twenty years since Bromersley nick was invaded by Special Branch; they weren't often here, but when they did come, they were always full of their own importance. He remembered that they had been looking into the chief players and background to the miners' strike to see if there was any foreign political involvement. Angel remembered the arrival of the commander of that team. He had been an ex chief constable who headed a team of two very young DIs and half a dozen DSs, who swanned around, running their investigation in secrecy, making use of the local force without any briefing, behaving as if the station was a pub and treating senior officers, including himself, no better than waiters. The super had always expected him to kowtow to them and offer the visitors the very best courtesy and hospitality. He suspected that the super privately thought he had the chance of being awarded the police medal or even an MBE. He shook his head and smiled as he recalled it all.

There was a knock at the door.

The smile died. He opened his eyes and pressed the chair downwards.

'Come in.'

It was DS Gawber.

'You wanted me, sir?'

'Yes, Ron. I want you to get in touch with Bow Street and get them to put a security ring around Duncan McFee's flat in Kensington until Mac and his team can get there. Ahmed's got the address.'

'Right, sir.'

'And I want you to go to the distillery at Slogmarrow, sus it out and organize shifts round the clock to secure the crime scene, the office in that building and any other area Duncan McFee visited in the last twenty-four hours of his life. Speak to a man called Peter Fleming. He's the boss there.

Then get a good night's kip and I'll see you back there first thing in the morning. All right?'

'Right.'

'And have you seen Crisp?'

'I'm here, sir,' the sergeant said, coming through the open door, breathing heavily.

'Ah. Right. And I want you to put a personal dawn 'til dusk watch on Evan Jones. Better take Scrivens with you.'

'Yes sir. For how long?'

'Till I tell you to knock off!' Angel barked.

*

Angel had had enough of Tuesday. He didn't leave the station until seven o'clock, and even when he was sitting at home in his sitting-room, in his shirt-sleeves with a can of German lager in his hand, awaiting the call from the kitchen from his patient wife, Mary, that his dinner was ready, his mind was still at Bromersley nick. He was gawping at the television screen, but he didn't see or hear the skinny girl with the lisp and the hairdo like a pineapple, reading the news. He had the murder in the distillery at Slogmarrow on his mind. There weren't any obvious clues, suspects or motives. It was looking decidedly tricky. And he'd hardly started the investigation, when he had been abruptly summoned from the scene to act as skivvy to Special Branch. He sniffed. He didn't care for that man, Boodle. He had sat in the superintendent's office like an orangutang with toothache. Angel was pleased his visit had been only brief, and he hoped he might find enough evidence to keep him at bay. He wanted to get to that murder. Tomorrow, he must whip Gawber and Crisp into line. Gawber was always dependable, but Crisp was hard work. The lad simply hadn't the drive to work unsupervised, to sniff out evidence, find a suspect, pin-point a criminal and get him put away. He was far more interested in trying to get WPC Leisha Baverstock into a dark corner in the locker room. If his father had been gunned down by a thug while chasing him over the roof of a warehouse in Leeds, and he'd then seen him deteriorate in hospital and eventually die from a gunshot wound to his aorta, as Angel had experienced ten years ago, his attitude might be very different. 'Did you hear that, Michael?'

Angel came out of his reverie and looked round at Mary. She was standing at the door with a big spoon in her hand and staring at the TV.

'Michael!' she said urgently.

'What's that, love?'

She nodded knowingly. 'I thought so. You were asleep. You weren't taking a scrap of notice of it, were you?'

'What?' he said irritably.

She smiled. 'You were nodding.'

'No. What is it?' he replied looking back at the screen.

'A plane crashed in heavy rain during the night. Three men, two passengers and the pilot, died.'

He nodded knowingly. 'It's happening all the time.'

'Listen,' Mary said persistently. 'She said it was on a moor on the Yorkshire Pennines, two miles north of Tunistone.' Angel leaned forward, open-mouthed and stared at the screen. The newsreader had moved on to an item about the Dow Jones.

'That's only seven miles from here,' he said. His face changed. 'Oh. That's very close to Mrs Buller-Price's farm!'

'And your dinner's on your plate.'

'Ah,' he said, trying to sound interested.

*

Next morning Angel went straight to the Imperial distillery at Slogmarrow to the ageing-room entrance. After some protracted knocking the outside door was opened and a uniformed constable peered out.

'What's up, lad? Have I woken you up?'

The PC grinned. 'Oh it's you, sir. Good morning.'

'Quiet night?'

'Yes sir.'

'Dr Mac arrived yet?'

'No sir'

'Has he finished upstairs, do you know?'

'He finished up there last night, sir.'

The door opened behind him. It was DS Gawber. 'Morning, sir.'

'Oh. There you are, Ron. Let's have a look upstairs.'

They climbed the stone steps in single file, and passed through a door into a long narrow room that was obviously used as an office and storeroom. There was a desk and chair by the middle window, with the usual potpourri of office furniture and effects. On a wall and a bench at the back were various tools of the trade: copper ladles, filters, thermometers, funnels and various lengths of stainless-steel tubing, taps and spanners. Angel looked down and observed that the internal windows all along one side gave a bird's eye view of the cone-covered ageing-vats and the track, chain, hook and heavy motor of the overhead crane which traversed and operated across the entire ground-floor area. In the days when the building had been used as a mill, the supervisor would have overseen the workers at the looms from those windows.

It was then that Angel noticed an unusual smell. He sniffed. 'Hey, Ron. Come here.'

Gawber came to the window. 'What?'

'Can you smell anything?'

'Juniper berries, isn't it?'

'No. Just here.'

Gawber screwed up his nose. 'Yes. Mint. Mint, sir?'

'Ay. That's what I can smell. You wouldn't expect to smell mint in a distillery, now would you?' Angel released a window catch and pushed open the frame.

'No.'

Angel put his head out through the window. 'I couldn't smell it when I was downstairs.'

'No. Nor could I. Just that sickly sweet pong.'

Angel closed the window and wrinkled his nose.

'That smell is in here, in this office. Somewhere round this desk. Have a look.'

Gawber pulled open drawers and his fingers scrambled quickly through papers, letters and files, while Angel sauntered over to the bench and glanced at a thermometer surrounded with cork to float in liquid, copper ladles and stainless-steel piping and taps on the floor. He poked behind a filing cabinet, then, finding nothing, he came back to the desk, and fished through a waste-paper basket under the kneehole. Neither man found anything to explain the smell. The office door opened behind them. Angel turned. It was Dr Mac.

'There you are, Mike. Where did you disappear to yesterday? Just as we were heaving the man out of the tank; it was the highlight of the day.'

DS Gawber took the opportunity of the intrusion to write up his notes. He stood by the wall with his notebook in his hand.

Angel pulled a face. 'Ah. The super wanted me.' He turned to the desk. 'Can you smell mint?'

'No,' said the doctor.

'Come over here. By this desk. Now, can you smell it?'

Dr Mac looked surprised. 'Yes. Yes I can.'

'We've been trying to find where it comes from. There's nothing in the desk.'

Mac shrugged. 'It's not important, is it? Ask that Angus Leitch chap. It's his office. He probably chews gum.'

'Ay. I will. I thought you would know.'

'I'm a pathologist, not a herbalist,' the little man said with a grin and turned to leave. Angel stopped him.

'Ay. Well, what did McFee die of, then?'

'Well, I haven't done the PM yet,' Mac said patiently, 'but he has a mighty fracture to the back of the head, which has made a hole in his skull I can put my fingers through.'

'I thought he had drowned.'

'I'll know tomorrow.'

'Anything else?'

'Ay. There's a spanner downstairs you might be interested in.' 'Ah. The murder weapon?'

'It's not heavy enough. It's from up here.'

Angel raised his eyebrows. 'Oh?'

Angus Leitch came through the door; his jaw dropped when he saw the three men in his office. He eyed all three, one after the other, as he slowly took off his coat. Mac nodded towards the newcomer.

'Mr Leitch will show you where the spanner came from, won't you, sir.'

Angel said: 'Has it been dusted?'

'Nothing on it.'

'Photographed?'

'Ay. I'm going to carry on,' Mac said, then he went out and closed the door.

Leitch looked round uncertainly as he hung his coat behind the door.

Angel pointed to the desk.

'What's this smell over here, sir?' he asked.

Leitch crossed to his desk. He sniffed a couple of times. 'Mmm. I don't know. Ay. It's sort of the smell of humbugs. I've no idea.'

'Humbugs? Is anything that smells like that used in the course of distilling and bottling gin?'

'Certainly not, Inspector.'

Angel sniffed. 'Why is that smell just here?' Leitch shook his head and pulled open the middle drawer of the desk.

'Hey, look at this, Inspector.'

'What?'

'This handle's not right. It wasn't like this. It's been strained or pulled or something.'

Angel looked at the handle. 'I can't see anything.'

'It always swung loose. Now it's tight. Somebody's given it a thump or something.'

Angel rubbed his chin. 'Looks all right to me.'

'It is all right, but something's happened to it. It's not like it was. I know it isn't. I sit at this desk every day. Somebody's been messing around.'

'Look in the drawer. What do you keep there?'

'Just stock-sheets and records of the batches.'

'See what's missing.'

Angus Leitch riffled quickly through the papers.

'It looks OK.'

'Well, if you find anything missing, let me know.'

'I will. I will.'

'Right, well, what's this spanner Dr Mac was talking about?' 'Oh yes. It's down the stairs. On the shop-floor, Inspector.' Leitch made for the door. Angel followed, then he turned to Gawber who was still writing up his notes.

'We're going downstairs, Ron.'

'Right, sir.'

Leitch led the two policemen down the steps, round the back of the vat in which McFee had been found, which was directly under the middle window of the office above, and pointed to a spanner on the brick floor inside a blue-chalked circle.

'That was on the bench upstairs with the other tools,' he said.

Angel stared down at it. There was nothing else near the spanner; it was between the white-painted wall on the one side and the vat on the other.

He leaned over it to note exactly how it was positioned and then picked it up. It was a steel, one-ended ring spanner ten inches long, and would fit a three-quarter-inch nut. He gripped it tightly. It certainly would have made a sort of weapon. He loosened his grip and shook it loosely in his hand.

He supposed it weighed about twelve ounces. He certainly wouldn't have wanted to confront a man intent on belting him with it, but Mac said it was not heavy enough to have been used as the weapon that killed Duncan McFee, and in his experience Mac was never wrong. He turned to

Gawber and handed him the spanner. The sergeant turned it over and went through the same routine.

'What do think?' Angel said.

'Dunno.' Gawber held it up to his eyes and read the moulding. It simply said: SUPERIOR SHEFFIELD STEEL, 3/4 INS. He passed it back to Angel. The inspector turned to Leitch.

'What does this spanner fit?'

'I never use it. I believe it fits the brackets holding the radiators to the wall. But the radiators are not in use. We never have any heating on in here. It makes the spirit evaporate. Even one degree could amount to thousands of pounds. The spirit arrives direct from a still by those overhead pipes, and it is still tepid. It's my job to get it cool, as soon as possible. I've never had to use that spanner.'

Angel nodded. He could understand that.

'Does it fit anything else?'

'Not in here.'

Angel turned to Gawber. 'See if any of the radiators have been touched.'

The sergeant pocketed the notebook and began a tour round the perimeter of the shop-floor. There were twenty big cast iron radiators located against the walls.

Angel looked down at the place where the spanner had been.

'Wonder how it got there?' he murmured. He looked up at the office window and then back down at the floor again. If it had been thrown or dropped out of the window, it might have chipped the brick floor. He leaned over the floor area where the spanner had been found. There were no fresh chips. He scrutinized the spanner. There were no bright scratches on that either. So it didn't appear to have been thrown. He stood up and rubbed his chin. His lips tightened. He wished he hadn't been called away by the super: the crime scene was cold.

Gawber arrived back from checking the radiators.

'None of them is loose, sir, and all the bolts are still covered in old paint.'

Angel nodded. He turned to Leitch.

'Are you sure it doesn't fit anything else on this floor or in your office?'

'It doesn't fit anything else, I'm positive.'

'We need to find out what else it fitted.' Angel tossed the spanner to Gawber. 'Bag it,' he said. 'Label it.' Then he walked up to the vat that had so recently held the dead body. The cone-shaped cover was still resting on the floor. He climbed up on to the narrow ledge round the vat.

'How do you get this cover on, Mr Leitch?'

'You want it on now, Inspector?'

Angel came down off the platform.

'Ay.' He was interested to see the crane at work.

Leitch turned back and went to the wall by the door. There were three simple control levers, in a frame; each lever had three positions. Leitch manoeuvred the heavy chain and hook over the centre of the cover, then, winching down, he lifted the cover from the floor. Then he moved the crane track over the vat and lowered the cover into position. He let the hook come down a little too far, so that the hook dropped below the loop, released itself and then he winched the hook and chain up out of the way. The entire operation took less than a minute.

Angel leaped back up on to the platform round the edge of the vat, leaned forward to the latch on the inspection door. He noticed the dusting of aluminium powder left by SOCO. He unfastened the latch and pulled open the door. The hinges allowed the door to swing open a full 180 degrees, so he pulled it open all the way and let it rest against the outer side of the cone. The door was about five feet high by three feet wide, easily big enough for a person to fall through. Angel turned to Gawber.

'Look at this, Ron.'

The sergeant climbed up to the platform and peered into the vat.

'If you belted me at the back of the head, hard enough, and I was in this position and wasn't expecting it, do you think I'd fall in there easily?'

Gawber nodded sombrely. 'I reckon you would.'

'I reckon I would too. What would you hit me with?'

'Mmm?' Gawber looked round. 'Maybe a hammer, sir?'

'You'd have to be up here to use a hammer. Do you reckon you'd get enough of a swing without me seeing you?'

'P'raps not.'

Angel pursed his lips. 'No. It would have to be a weapon with a longer handle to it ... like a shovel.'

'Wouldn't be heavy enough, sir. A spade maybe?'

Angel turned back to DS Gawber. 'Or a golf-club?' he suggested.

'Yes,' Gawber replied thoughtfully. 'A golf-club. Is a golf-club heavy enough?'

'Those big heavy ones, in the hands of somebody really athletic, could be,' Angel said as he stepped down from the platform. 'But you'd have to swing it from down here, to get plenty of power behind it. If the weapon is not here, the murderer would have had to bring it with him and then take it away. Now that would have been an inconvenience.' He turned to Angus Leitch. 'Is anything in your office missing?' 'No.'

A mobile phone rang. It was Angel's. He dipped into his pocket, pulled it out, glanced at the LCD. DS Crisp was calling him. He was supposed to be watching Jones. It was only twelve noon. What did he want?

'What is it, lad? And where are you?' he growled.

'I'm with DC Scrivens in Blackpool, sir.'

'Blackpool?' shrieked Angel. 'On your holidays?'

'We've followed Evan Jones here, sir. He's bought a plane ticket to Douglas. That's in the Isle of Man.'

'Ay. I know where Douglas is.'

'Do you want us to follow him?'

Angel was surprised that Jones was doing anything other than attending to the business of buying and selling cars at his pitch on Wakefield Road on that quiet spring morning. This surveillance was getting out of hand. He had only decided to have the man watched so as to stay one jump ahead of Special Branch. He couldn't have Commander Boodle outsmarting him on his own patch! Crisp was still holding on. Angel had to make a quick decision.

'Has he booked a return ticket or a single?'

'A return, sir. Thing is, the plane is due off any time.'

'Has he any luggage?'

'He's only carrying a laptop case.'

'Right. What's he wearing?'

'Light-fawn macintosh, blue shirt, brown shoes. No hat.'

'Right, lad. You two stay there. I'll get back to you.'

He ended the call and made his way through the factory door to the outside. He wouldn't be overheard in the carpark. He phoned the station and got the Isle of Man constabulary number, then he phoned the superintendent there and arranged to have Jones followed from the plane while he was in Douglas. Then he phoned Crisp and Scrivens to instruct them to stay in Blackpool and resume their role on the mainland when the Welshman returned, he would hope later that day. He sighed, dropped the phone back into his pocket and came back into the ageing-room.

Gawber was updating his notebook and Leitch was running water into the vat that had so recently held the body of Duncan McFee.

'I can't do much more here, Ron.'

'Right, sir.'

'Mr Leitch,' Angel called.

The young man wiped his hands on a sponge as he came across to him.

'Yes, Inspector?'

'Are you sure you can't think of any reason why Mr McFee has been murdered. I mean, there must have been somebody who didn't like him.'

Leitch shook his head. 'Well, I liked him. I didn't know him well, but he was always pleasant. Always a cheery word. Never a moan. Although he was the chairman, I think everybody liked him.'

'Ay,' Angel said with a sniff. He rubbed a hand across his mouth. He would rather have heard that someone didn't get on with Duncan McFee. At least it would have provided him with a suspect. He turned to Gawber.

'Well, you finish off here, Ron. I'll see you at the station in an hour or so. I'm off. I've something very important I must see to.'

CHAPTER FIVE

Angel drove through the distillery gates and turned left towards town. He motored slowly along the road for three-quarters of a mile, looking for a narrow, unmarked track on the left. He remembered it was after a sharp curve, near a boulder and just before the Tunistone boundary sign. He spotted it and turned up a steep, unmarked private lane. It was a tedious drive in low gear with blind bends; he was hopeful that he would not meet any traffic coming down the hill or he would have to employ his best reversing skills to the bottom, as there were no passing-places. About half-way up, he passed an open timber gate to a field, with a sign swinging in the wind with the words BULLER-PRICE Farm neatly painted white on black. The sign was suspended from a post sticking out of the ground at a jaunty angle of forty-five degrees; it appeared to have suffered some recent knock, probably from a Bentley car bumper. A hundred yards beyond the gate, at the end of a track through the field, round a sharp curve and out of sight was the farmhouse, barn and outbuildings snuggled in a dip in the hillside which provided some well-needed protection from the elements.

Angel pressed on further up the rise. At length he reached the summit. There was a white-painted tower, like a lighthouse, 600 feet high with windows at the top. It was a television, radio and telephone aerial booster station with an asphalt carpark big enough for three cars. He pulled on to it, switched off the ignition and got out of the car. A gust of wind almost blew the car door out of his hand. He recovered his grip on it and closed it firmly. He brushed his hair out of his eyes and turned up his coat collar. The wind wailed across his ears making a sound like an Aeolian harp.

He gazed across the purple-and-green patchwork moors below. He was looking for a crashed helicopter. There was nothing. He moved round to the other side of the tower and there it was: 200 yards away, a pile of silver and yellow metal and a black propeller blade skewered into the heather at an unhappy angle; parked nearby were two police Land Rovers and an unmarked car. He stepped out eagerly towards the crash site. As he got nearer he could see two men in the familiar forensic white suits and headwear, sorting through the debris. He had to pick his way carefully around a clump of gorse, and when he next looked up a uniformed police constable in a cape, struggling against the wind, was advancing towards him. He was holding a hand up. He stopped about twenty yards away from Angel.

'Sorry sir. You can't come any closer.'

He didn't recognize the man. Angel smiled.

'That's all right, lad,' he said. 'I'm a DI from Bromersley. Angel is my name. Who's in charge?' He reached to his pocket for his badge and stopped. Of course, it wasn't there.

'Oh yes, sir?' said the constable, patiently.

The PC was no doubt thinking that if Angel really was a DI he would have instantly produced his identification badge and pass. It was standard practice. Angel wiped his mouth with his hand.

'Ah. I misplaced my badge and ID yesterday, lad. I haven't had an opportunity to replace it. I am investigating a murder at the Imperial distillery. I was just passing, and I may be able to assist you with your enquiries. Who is in charge?'

'If you have any information about the accident, I should be pleased to hear it. Otherwise, I am instructed to keep everybody away. You can't come here, sir, whoever you are.'

'I have an unmarked police car and an RT tuned to Bromersley nick parked under the tower. You can radio my super at Bromersley' said Angel, hopefully.

'I am sorry sir. I can't leave my post here. You will have to leave,' said the constable. 'Now,' he added firmly.

Angel sighed. Underneath he was fuming, but it was not with the constable. The man was behaving impeccably, as per textbook.

'Very well, lad. What force are you with?'

'Elmersfield, sir.'

Angel nodded. That was the town immediately north-west of, and sharing a border with, Bromersley.

'Now move along, sir, pleased

'Right lad. Right lad. I'm going,' said Angel gruffly. He turned away, and began to pick his way back up to the car. Being ejected from a site by a PC didn't quite suit his temperament. The trip had been an embarrassment and he had learned nothing. He would have to find his badge and ID card as a matter of urgency. The loss was highly embarrassing, and what was worse, he would have to endure further humiliation when he reported the matter to the superintendent.

He arrived back at the car and dropped angrily into the driving-seat. He reversed away from the tower, engaged a low gear and made his way down the hillside. He was halfway down when he saw a big figure hanging on to the upright of the gate of the field that lead to the Buller-Price farm. It was the proprietor herself, wrapped up against the weather like a barrage balloon. She stood there with her long stick, surrounded by five dogs of different shapes, colours and sizes. When she saw him approaching, she stepped confidently into the lane and held up a hand like a traffic policeman. The dogs followed and were all around her, barking and bouncing around.

Angel recognized the big black Alsatian nearest to her as Schwarzenegger. When the car came to rest, she pushed forward through the wind to the driver's window. He wound the window down.

'Ah! Hello there, Inspector. Looking for me?' she bawled against the wind. 'I saw your car go up the lane and I thought it was you.'

'Good afternoon, Mrs Buller-Price.'

'Ah. Good afternoon, Inspector,' she replied, giving him one of her angelic smiles.

The dogs continued the rumpus, all the more now that her attention had been taken away from them. She suddenly became aware of the commotion. Her face changed. Her eyes flashed.

'Excuse me,' she said and turned round angrily. She glared down at the dogs. 'Quiet!' she bawled. 'And sit!' They all obeyed her instantly except for one small indistinguishable mixture of terrier, bulldog and ferret, who stuck to his ground and continued yapping.

She pursed her lips stubbornly and turned back round to him.

'Quiet, Bogey. Quiet!' The dog gave four more yaps then stopped and stared up at her, indignant and defiant. She turned back to Angel, panting and put her hand on the car door to steady herself. 'Just a minute, Inspector. Let me get my breath.' She swallowed, shook her head, causing her chins to wobble, then she blew out a sigh, looked downwards and said, tentatively: 'Somebody's come along and claimed Schwarzenegger, haven't they.'

Angel smiled. 'No. No, Mrs Buller-Price. No. I've heard nothing.'

Her face immediately brightened. 'Oh! Good. Good. Ah. I'm glad you happened along, Inspector. Come along in. Have a cup of tea, and I have some home-made digestives that I'm sure you would enjoy.'

'It sounds very tempting, Mrs Buller-Price, but I have to get on.'

'Oh,' she said, pouting. 'Have you? They are really most special, although I say it as shouldn't. And I have baked them

49

in the shape of a bone. They are the same recipe I gave to Delia Smith. The dogs adore them.'

'Hadn't you better go inside, out of this wind?'

'No. No, Inspector. It doesn't bother me. I am used to it. Ho! You wouldn't believe that they shot some of the exteriors of The Sound Of Music here, would you. Of course, the weather was a lot better then.'

Angel's eyebrows shot up. He stared at her.

'Oh yes. The entire unit was here for a week. Julie Andrews used to change out of her nun's outfit in my sitting-room. There's many a time after a day's shooting she would nip in for a mug of tea, and I would go through her lines with her. And while she relaxed, I'd starch her wimple and have it dry for the next shot; had to keep it bright and white. She was very nice. And if she was really tense, I'd relax her by playing my banjo. Hmmm. She was very fond of items from the Black and White Minstrel Show, which was *verboten* in America. All rather revolutionary you know. That show has became rather apolitical. Mmmm. Her husband directed the thing. No. Not The Black and White Minstrel Show. No. That was George Best, wasn't it? No, I mean the film.'

'Erm, Mrs Buller-Price … '

'In fact, Julie popped in about a month ago. She was passing through. Called in for a chat and a quart of milk.'

'I really have to get back to the office.'

'Would you like some milk, Inspector?'

'No thank you.'

'I have plenty. There's a churn just been collected for Windsor Castle.' She pursed her lips. 'Very well. Ah. Now. Yes. Before you go, I have something very important to tell you.'

'Oh.'

'That train crash I told you about yesterday.'

'Yes.'

'Well, it wasn't a train crash.'

'Oh?'

'No. No. Of course not. The nearest line is at Bromersley. Eight miles away. How could it have been? I thought you would have realized that.'

Angel's face was blank, but he was pleased to hear that she had worked it out for herself.

'No,' she went on. 'No. It was a rocket ship that had crashed somewhere round here. It must have been off-course. That explains all the noise and the lights. Now it wasn't long since the Allies sent an exploratory one to Mars, you know. Looking for water, they said. What they want to be looking for water there for, I have really no idea. We have plenty of water here. We have five oceans full of it! And it always seems to be raining! Maybe this one has been sent back from there to have a look at *us*.'

Angel smiled at her. 'I don't think it was a rocket ship, Mrs Buller-Price. I think it was a helicopter,' he said reassuringly.

Her eyes closed briefly in thought.

'Really?' She shook her head. 'No. It was from outer space all right. Must have been. Yes. I saw one of the spacemen this morning. Running over my top field. And he looked nothing like ET. Ridiculous conception. Don't know where Steven Spielberg got his idea from. Ridiculous. Of course, I realize that that was fiction. Now this was the real thing. It was a big black creature, like a gorilla but with fabric-type wings. And with a big black head with a shiny knob on the top. I think that must be its eye. I was looking at it through my binoculars from the bathroom window. Ugly-looking creature.'

Angel bit his lip thoughtfully. He didn't know whether he should try to explain or let it go.

'Don't you think you should arrest it, or something? Can't have strange monsters running up and down the country, Inspector.'

Angel sighed. 'Ah. Don't you think it could have been a man?' he said persuasively. 'In a cape?'

She shook her chins at him again.

51

'No. No. If it were a man, why would he dress up like that? It doesn't make sense. I hope they're not planning crop-circles in my hayfield!'

Angel decided he must go, but he didn't want to leave the old lady troubled.

'You're not afraid of the — er — spaceman, are you, Mrs Buller-Price?'

'Bah! Certainly not. I have my faith, my shotgun, and Schwarzenegger. I am as safe as houses. And if it's something I cannot handle, I can always telephone you, can't I,' she said, looking closely at him and smiling.

'You most certainly can,' he said earnestly.

'Thank you, Inspector.'

'It's a pleasure. Well, I must go. Goodbye, Mrs Buller-Price.'

'Goodbye, Inspector. Call any time. Any time at all. Wednesday is a good day. We have sausages on a Wednesday,' she said, her chins wobbling.

She let go of the car door and made for the gate.

Angel smiled as he turned the key in the ignition.

She stopped at the gate and turned back. She put a hand sideways to her mouth.

'I make them myself,' she hollered. 'With my own meat-filling. Ann Widdecombe says they're the best she's tasted. The secret is to use proper pig intestine, none of this synthetic rubbish. Keeps the bowel collagen free!' she added triumphantly.

Angel blinked and nodded.

'Come along children,' she said, flourishing the stick. The dogs began barking excitedly again and gathered round her back at the gatepost. She waved briefly at the inspector as he wound up the window and released the handbrake. The car glided smoothly down the hill.

*

Twenty minutes later, he arrived at the station and charged into his office. There was the usual daily pile of letters, reports and paperwork on his desk. He pushed it to one side and picked up the phone.

'Tell DS Gawber and Cadet Ahaz I want to see them.'

He took off his coat and hung it on the hook behind the door. He glared at the pile of post again, pulled a face, dragged the pile back to the middle of the desk and began fingering through it.

There was a knock at the door.

'Come in.'

It was Ahmed waving a piece of paper.

'Hello, sir. Yes?'

'Where's DS Gawber?'

'Haven't seen him, sir.'

Angel looked up from the desk.

'What's that paper you're fumbling with, lad? Is it your resignation?'

Ahmed grinned. 'No sir. It's that address you wanted. That woman. Amy Jones.'

Angel held out his hand. 'Oh yes. Well, let's have a look at it, then, or is it top secret?' he said testily.

Ahmed passed it over. 'She isn't there, sir,' he said.

Angel began to read it. It was an address in Hackney.

'The King's Cross probation office said she had not registered since she was released,' Ahmed read out. 'An officer has been to the flat but he drew a blank. They've no idea where she is.'

Angel sniffed and pulled a face. 'Right. Hmm. She'll turn up. Somewhere,' he said, sombrely. Then a second later, he added: 'Maybe?' Then he suddenly said: 'Find out if Fishy Smith has been to court yet, and what's happened to him. And find out who his escort was, and tell him I want to see him, now! Do it on the phone. Look sharp.'

'Right, sir.' Ahmed disappeared and closed the door.

Angel returned to the pile of post. His mind was elsewhere.

He fingered the envelopes, speculating on what was inside without actually pulling out the contents. He was becoming interested in an attractively hand addressed envelope when there was a knock at the door.

'Come in.'

It was DS Gawber.

'Ah! Ron,' said Angel enthusiastically. He pushed the pile of post to one side. 'Come in. Take a pew. I don't get this. Nobody has anything helpful to say to us. Everybody is running away. I set Crisp and Scrivens to watch Jones. I thought it would be a simple, local job. They followed him to Blackpool. Blackpool Last I heard, Jones has flown to the Isle of Man! I hope he hasn't done a bunk!'

Gawber gave a slight shrug. 'Why would he do that?'

'Well, I saw him yesterday and gave him an unofficial warning; he might have got scared. We might have lost him to somewhere exotic!'

There was another knock at the door.

'Come in.'

It was Ahmed.

'Yes lad?'

'Fishy Smith, sir.'

'Yes lad. What about him?'

'He got twenty-eight days suspended sentence and was released immediately.'

Angel and Gawber looked at each other. Their jaws dropped.

'I don't know why we bother!' Angel growled. 'Who was the escort?'

'Todd, sir. He's on his way down to see you.'

'Right, lad. Now hop off and make me a cup of tea.' Ahmed left and closed the door. Gawber stood up.

'Hang on a minute, Ron. I've got a little job for you. And it's urgent. Very urgent. I want you to search Fishy Smith's cell. I want you to give it a thorough going over.'

'Do you want me to look for anything in particular?'

'No,' Angel lied. 'No. Just see if you can turn anything up. Take a screwdriver. Undo the fittings. Look behind the radiators. Try behind the little mirror over the hand-basin.

Check the plaster between the bricks. See if any of the parquet floor has been disturbed. He's a crafty little devil.'

'Right, sir.'

Gawber opened the door. A constable was hovering there. It was PC Todd. Angel saw him.

'Come on in, lad.'

Todd removed his flat hat, tucked it under his arm and strode smartly into the room. Gawber went out and closed the door.

'You wanted me, sir?' Todd said cautiously.

'Relax, lad. Nothing to worry about.' Angel pointed to a chair. 'Sit down.' He blew out a sigh. 'You escorted Fishy Smith to court this morning?'

'Yes, sir.'

'Did you search him in his cell before you left?'

'Yes, sir.'

'Thoroughly?'

'Yes. Emptied his pockets and padded him down.'

'Mmm. And you found nothing?'

'Nothing.'

'I suppose you went with him in the van direct to the court, into the cell there, and up into the dock. Then, after he was discharged, you brought him back here, returned the contents of his pockets and pushed him out by the back door?'

'Yes, sir.'

'Hmmm. Just like that?'

Todd nodded. 'Yes sir. Just like that.'

'And you were with him every inch of the way? All the time?'

'Yes sir. There was nothing wrong with that, was there?'

'No. No. Did he have the opportunity to mix with any of the other defendants in the cells, or in the court house?'

'No sir. It was a quiet morning. He was the only one from the station.'

'Did he speak to anybody on his way there and back, apart from when he was actually in court?'

'No sir.'

Angel blew out a loud sigh, then nodded. 'Right lad. Thank you.'

Todd hesitated. 'Is that it, sir?'

'Aye, lad. That's it. Go back to what you were doing.'

The young policeman frowned and shook his head; he hesitated, then stood up. There was a knock at the door.

'See who that is, will you?'

Todd opened the door. It was Ahmed.

'Excuse me, sir.' The cadet pushed in urgently as Todd went out.

'Where's my tea?' Angel said abruptly.

'Sorry, sir. There's no water,' replied Ahmed, still holding the door. 'The plumber has turned it off. But he said it'll be back on soon.'

Angel's jaw dropped. 'Is he still working on that gents' loo?'

'He says it's a big job. Something about lack of gravity.'

Angel shook his head and growled. 'He'd tell you owt.'

'Sir,' Ahmed said tentatively. 'I thought you'd want to know, I've just heard that a patrol car has been called out to Orchard House on Creeford Road. That's where that man with the car sales pitch, Evan Jones, lives, isn't it? The man DS Crisp is following?'

Angel felt his pulse quicken. His eyes narrowed. He looked up.

'What's that, lad?' he said urgently.

'A triple-nine call, sir.'

'Ay!' Angel said, his eyes shining. He reached over to the phone and stabbed in a two-digit number.

A woman's voice said: 'Communications room.'

'Have you just had a triple-nine about Orchard House, Creeford Road?'

'Yes sir. A passer-by, wouldn't give his name, saw two men coming down a rope ladder through a bedroom window. He thought it suspicious.'

'Did he hear a burglar alarm?'

'He didn't say.'

'What time was this?'

'Three minutes ago. I've sent Bravo Foxtrot One.'

'Thank you.' He slammed down the handset and turned to Ahmed.

'Get DS Gawber for me, Ahmed, pronto. He'll be down the cells.'

'Yes sir.' Ahmed dashed out of the room.

Angel leaned back in his chair and rubbed his chin. It was strange for burglars to break into a drum like that in broad daylight. It was a large house in a posh district, which would look well worth turning over. He remembered he had seen a red alarm-box on the front elevation of the house, immediately above the front door. The bold and unusual MO suggested the thieves were professionals. Did they know Jones was away?

Ron Gawber rushed in through the open door.

'You wanted me, sir?'

'Ay,' Angel said quickly. 'Just had a triple nine call. Intruders at Evan Jones's home on Creeford Road. Find out what's happening. Bravo Foxtrot One has been sent. Keep me posted.'

'Right, sir,' said Gawber, and dashed off. Ahmed came in.

'Well done, lad,' Angel said. The cadet beamed and saw his opportunity.

'Is it a convenient moment, sir, to talk about my holidays?'

'Holidays?' roared Angel. 'Holidays? No. What about my tea?'

Ahmed's face straightened. 'I'll see if there's any water now, sir.' He left the room and closed the door.

Angel smiled. He picked up the phone and dialled a number. A few rings out and it was answered.

'Mac here.'

'Mac. There you are. Have you got anything for me yet? Fingerprints, footprints? Anything? I haven't even got a straw to clutch at.'

'Oh. Well, Mike, there are no fresh fingerprints on the critical places in the ageing-room or the office above it. The ageing-vat had been wiped clean, as had the door and window-handles upstairs in the office. I had another sus at that humbug smell you mentioned by the window. I could smell it; I thought it was mint, but there was nothing I could pick up. There were, however some rare fibres — quite minuscule but unusual — near that spanner on the deck by the ageing-vat, also on the carpet in the upstairs office place. I've identified them, but I don't yet know what they're from.'

Angel liked the words 'rare' and 'unusual'. They could mean that the clue would be significant and easy to identify. 'Ay, Mac. What are they, then?'

'From the plant, agava sisalana: it's mainly grown in Central America.'

'What?' roared Angel. 'Never heard of it. Is it poison?'

'No. I don't think so.'

'What then?'

'Could be from deck-shoes. Those easy, summer shoes with rope soles, you know the sort of thing.'

'Who the hell would be prancing round a rock hard brick floor in a distillery in deck-shoes?'

'Dunno. Just telling you what I have found.'

'Hmm. Anything else?'

'No. I should be finished here tonight. If so, I'll do the PM tomorrow. There might be something there.'

'I hope so. Thanks, Mac. Thanks very much.'

He put the phone down and it rang back immediately. He picked it up.

'Angel?'

'It's Crisp, sir.'

'Yes, lad. Where are you?'

'We are on the M55, the Preston road out of Blackpool, sir. Jones flew back to Squires Gate from Douglas a few minutes ago and got into his car. We are behind him, on the Preston road. He's presumably heading for Bromersley. Should be home in about two hours.'

'Ay. Well, stick to him. What did he bring with him in the way of luggage?'

'Just the laptop case, sir. The same one he took with him.' 'Oh. Right. Now, see if he goes straight home. If he does, stand down and I'll speak to you in the morning.'

'Right sir.'

Angel was relieved that Jones appeared to be returning. He kept his hand on the phone and dialled a number. It was soon answered.

'The police station, Douglas.'

'Inspector Mulvaney, please.'

'Who's calling?'

'Inspector Angel, Bromersley.'

'Right, sir. You're through.'

'Mike Angel here.'

'You'll be wanting to know about the suspect we've had under observation?'

'Yes, please.'

'Well, we picked him up. It was easy enough from your description. He took a taxi straight to Englebert Investments, where he bought a bar of gold for eighty thousand, five hundred and forty pounds cash; then he took it across the road, to the overseas branch of the Northern Bank, deposited it there and got a receipt for it. After that, he walked to a public house, the Manxman, had a prawn sandwich and a tomato juice at five pounds twenty-five. He then called a taxi to Ronaldsway and caught the fourteen thirty flight to Squires Gate.'

'Thanks very much. I'll do the same for you sometime.'

'You are welcome.'

Angel replaced the phone, sighed and leaned back in the chair. Why would Jones want to buy gold? If he'd a stockpile of it somewhere, he'd be more likely to want to sell it. It didn't make sense.

CHAPTER SIX

The following morning Angel arrived at the station early and was dashing down the corridor, eager to get to his office. He had a lot on his mind. He wanted to solve the Duncan McFee murder with whatever clues there were available and before the evidence and witnesses' memories became hazy. As he reached the gendemen's loos, the powerful smell of disinfectant invaded his nostrils. The door was propped open by a plastic bucket full of green water. He peered into the room and saw the back of the plumber's blue-boiler suit sticking out of a cubicle. The man was apparently jiggling an instrument with a long handle into a water closet. Angel pulled a face, withdrew and pressed on down the passage. When he turned the comer he saw Ahmed hovering by his office door. The young man looked relieved when he saw him and rushed forward.

'What is it, lad? Joan Collins after you ... looking for a new husband?'

'No, sir,' Ahmed said earnestly. 'The super wants to see you as soon as you arrive.'

'Oh?' Angel sniffed and looked at his watch. It wasn't yet 8.30. He hoped he wasn't being clocked in. He hadn't left the station until seven o'clock the previous night. And he didn't want delaying by some nit-picking disciplinary routine.

'Right, lad.' He took off his raincoat, threw it at the cadet and continued down the corridor to the very last office. He knocked on the door.

'Come in.'

Angel opened the door. 'You wanted me, sir?'

'Ay,' the superintendent growled from behind his desk.

Angel saw Boodle sitting as spruce as a bridegroom. He closed the door. The super pointed to the nearest chair.

'Sit down. You know Commander Boodle,' he said and reverted to grinding his teeth and shuffling papers round the desk.

Boodle had his eyes lowered, but opened them wide when he heard his name. He looked up at Angel with eyes like Monday's fish at a Friday market.

Angel pulled up a chair and nodded to the commander. 'Morning, sir.'

Boodle nodded. He looked his usual miserable self, as if he hadn't had a bowel movement since Boxing Day.

Angel wondered what was on the agenda. Must be something pretty important that brought him back to Bromersley again, and so early in the day. He must have spent the night at the Feathers or caught a very early flight. He suddenly had an uncomfortable thought. Had his ID and badge turned up, having been used in some monstrous crime? He had not reported them missing yet. He was ever hopeful of their turning up; it was a serious offence not to report them lost.

Boodle looked across at him again.

Angel thought he might have detected the beginnings of a smile. He wondered. Perhaps he wanted to throw up.

The super picked off an invisible drawing-pin from his bottom lip, rubbed it between his forefinger and thumb until it disappeared and then said:

'The commander wants to — er — discuss something with you.'

Angel considered the phrase, discuss something with you. That in itself was a laugh. In this business, the usual language was to give you an order.

The super stood up. He looked down at Boodle.

'And I have some things to see to, Perry. I'll be about ten minutes,' he said, and without looking back he left the room.

There was never anything casual about anything Superintendent Harker did; his exit had obviously been arranged between the two of them. Angel glanced at the closing door.

Boodle promptly moved across to the swivel-chair at the desk the super had just vacated, put his elbows on the desk, rubbed his elegant manicured brown hands briskly, leaned forward and peered closely into Angel's eyes. The inspector knew he would have to pay close attention and watch his step; something unusual was in the offing.

'Now then, Michael, I've got a job for you,' said Boodle, in that strained public-school voice which sounded incongruous in the super's office. 'Very important,' he added. 'I've cleared it with the chief and the super.'

Angel sighed silently. He wasn't canvassing for more work. He thought he had enough on his plate. Progress in the McFee case was practically non-existent. He had no suspect and no motive, and up to now, information from forensic had been very thin on the ground. Also, he didn't feel kindly enough disposed to tell the commander that he was having Jones followed. After all, it might simply be a waste of time.

'I have an unusual mission for you, Michael.'

Angel pursed his lips. Oh yes? Well, what was it then? Shark hunting on the back of a crocodile? He was all ears.

'You remember that big gold robbery from the security van outside the Agara Bank in the city in April 2003? A guard was shot.'

'Yes, sir.'

'The robbers got away with sixty-six million pounds in gold. It was a colossal haul. I was assigned to the case. It was an inside job, of course. I got the inside man, the security manager,

Taylor. He got ten years. And, after a right old chase, I caught the gang-leader, a man called Morris Yardley. I arrested them both myself. Now you knew Yardley, didn't you?'

'Morris Yardley? No sir,' Angel said after a second's thought. 'No. I may have read about him in the papers at the time, but I don't know him. I have never met him. I've never even seen him ... in the flesh, so to speak.'

Boodle's jaw dropped. 'Oh? He says he knows you? he said slowly, running his snakelike tongue over his thin lips. 'Curious. Ah well,' he continued, 'I'll come back to that. Now he got twenty years for the manslaughter of the security guard and eighteen years for the robbery, the sentences to run concurrently. Which appears to be a pretty good result. However, we have not recovered any of the gold. Yardley has served only one year. His legal team has already tried twice to get an appeal hearing without success. Anyway, it would be a waste of time.'

Boodle stopped abruptly and stared at him. Angel knew what he was doing. He was watching his reaction. Angel did the same thing when he was interviewing.

Then the commander said: 'Anyway, for the last six months, at least, Yardley has been asking to set you.'

Angel stared hard back at the man. This was very strange. He couldn't understand why Yardley would want to see him. He had never knowingly met him. He suddenly had a thought.

'Have you a photograph of him, sir?'

Boodle produced a pack of a dozen police pics from a file on the desk with the dexterity of a card-sharp. He slapped them down in front of Angel, then began to read off the copy of a prison admission sheet:

'Morris Yardley, last known address, fifty-five Broad Street, Birmingham, age fifty, six feet two inches, fourteen stone four pounds, eye-colour, grey blue, blah blah, blah blah.'

Angel riffled through the photographs, obviously taken in prison. Morris Yardley had a square head with a very close hair-cut, podgy, lined face, big Roman nose and bags under his eyes. Angel scrutinized them carefully. He didn't want to make a mistake. After a few seconds, he spoke.

'No. No. I don't know him, sir. I've never seen him before, and I certainly haven't met him. I would have remembered,' he said firmly. He handed the bundle of photographs back.

Boodle shook his head. He was clearly thrown.

'He specified you. He knew your name, your rank and that you were at this station. He knew your age. How old are you?'

'Forty-eight.'

'Yes. He's fifty. He said you were about his age.'

'He's not from round here, sir. I don't know him,' Angel said evenly.

'No. He's from Birmingham way, but still ... '

Boodle slowly leaned back in the swivel-chair. The tiny tongue shot out again and ran over his lips several times. He looked up at the ceiling, drummed 'Colonel Bogey' with his fingertips on the desk and then said, 'You must be the one. We'll go ahead. He's anxious to see you. And we do need to recover the gold. Now I expect he wants to propose a deal of some sort. So I have arranged for you to see him on your own, wearing a wire, of course, with plenipotentiary powers to make the best deal you can. OK? He's in Welham gaol. So I want you up there tomorrow at ten o'clock.'

Angel's pulse rate increased. He realized he was in big trouble. His secret was out. He'd never get access to HMP Welham without his ID.

'I can't do it, sir,' he said quietly.

Boodle's eyes lit up like searchlights. He was used to getting his own way.

'What?' he said, his voice rising an octave.

Angel knew that when you have to make a fool of yourself, it's best to do it quickly.

'I am without a badge and ID card, sir.'

'What?' Boodle shrieked again. 'How the hell did you manage that?'

Angel licked his lips quickly. 'In the course of interviewing a prisoner, who turned out to be a pickpocket, he stole my badge and ID card. And before I had discovered the loss, he had been to court and been released.'

'You idiot! When was this?'

'Day before yesterday.'

'Have you reported it to the super?'

'Not yet, sir.'

'Have you informed the Police Gazette?'

'No.'

'Well, you'd better get on to it right away. Have you another recent ID photograph of yourself?'

'Yes sir.'

'Let me have it. I'll speak to the super myself and get that organized. I'll have them both ready for you to pick up from here at 5 p.m. Right?'

'Right, sir. There's something else.'

Boodle's mouth tightened. 'What now?'

'You want me to get this man's trust, don't you, sir?'

'Of course.'

'He sounds a tough nut.'

'He is a tough nut!'

Angel pursed his lips. 'Well sir, if I do this, I do it without a wire.'

Boodle blinked. 'He has assaulted three officers,' he yelled. 'One of them nearly lost the sight of one eye. He has a violent temper: a bad record. I cannot take the risk of you going into his company alone without a wire.'

Angel shook his head. 'It won't work. I won't do it then, sir.'

'You bloody well will!'

*

It was five minutes to ten on the following morning when Angel arrived outside Welham prison. He parked his car with fifty or more others, walked through the carpark and across

65

the road to the grimy stone entrance. The fresh-painted sign, white on black, said, SIDE ENTRANCE. RING BELL. He pressed the big porcelain button set in the brass fitting on the wall. There was a short delay, then, with a clang of metal there was a whirring sound and the iron door slowly opened. He went through the gloomy, stone entrance-arch into a covered area cluttered with signs:

'All traffic 5 mph. All visitors must sign the book. Visitors without passes not admitted. All passes to be shown. HMP Welham Prison Category A (Male only). Rules and regulations for visitors. No mobile phones. No radios. Visitors this way.'

As he was reading them, the whirring noise of the door mechanism stopped and the door clanged shut behind him. He moved along the arched area to a window with a sign over the top that read: ENQUIRIES. He could just make out the movement of a shadowy figure through slits in a steel grille. A distorted voice from a speaker above him said: 'Can I see your pass?'

Angel pushed the cream-coloured paper through the slot. It disappeared.

After a few seconds the voice said, 'Have you got your ID, inspector?'

'Yes.'

'You're here to see two nine seven Yardley?'

'Yes,' Angel said and offered his brand-new ID card to the machine.

'Hmm. Yes. Commander Boodle has just gone through.' The pass and ID card came back through the slot.

'Thank you.'

'If you wait there, I'll get someone to take you up.'

'Right. Thank you.'

A few minutes later, a uniformed prison officer escorted Angel silently across the stone-surfaced courtyard, into the main building, up two flights of black-painted iron steps, along a corridor, to a door with the words, 'Reception No 11', stencilled on it. The escort unlocked the door, which opened into a small room in which two prison officers were seated behind a trestle-table. There was a small, low cupboard at the side with a telephone and a wire in-tray on the top. There was another door behind them.

'Visitor for two nine seven Yardley,' the escort called.

'Right,' said one of the men.

Angel felt pressure on his elbow.

'In there, please.'

He went into the room. The door closed. He heard the click of the lock and the rattle of keys behind him.

One of the uniformed men took off his hat and placed it on the table.

'Can I see your pass, please? And your ID,' he said.

Angel handed them across. The officer glanced at them and then went out through the door behind him. The other man pulled the in-tray on to the table.

'Empty the contents of your pockets into this.'

Angel said nothing. He licked his lips.

'Also your watch and any jewellery. Do you wear belt or braces?'

'Neither.'

Angel tugged his expandable watch wristlet over the back of his hand, then began on his pockets: his wallet, his notebook, pen, keys, handkerchief, a few coins and his car key. He didn't wear any jewellery.

The man turned away to the cupboard and came out with a contraption that looked like a small vacuum-sweeper, with earphones. He put on the headset and plugged the flex into an electric socket.

'Face the wall, spread your legs and put your hands in the air.'

Angel turned round.

The prison officer deftly waved the head of the metal detector down his arms, across his back and down both legs.

'Turn round, please.'

Angel turned to face him. The man repeated the business.

'Right,' he said. He dragged off the earphones, pulled out the plug and began to roll up the flex.

The door banged and Commander Boodle, another much younger man in plain clothes carrying a small case, and the first prison officer came in.

'Ah. There you are, Michael,' Boodle said, his voice even higher than usual. 'Found the place all right? Good. Like a cup of tea?'

'Thank you, sir,' Angel said.

'There's one coming. No sugar. I hope that's right.'

'That's fine, sir.'

'This is Inspector Oscar Quadrille. He's in my team. He's a computer wizard and a crack scientist. He'll be monitoring you throughout the exercise.'

Angel and Quadrille nodded and shook hands.

Boodle looked at him. 'Fit him up, Oscar,' he said.

'Will you take your coat and shirt off,' Quadrille said, opening the case on the table and taking out a length of black wire about three feet long. It had a miniaturized microphone at its head and two AA batteries at its tail.

Angel undid his coat and began to take it off.

There was a knock at the door. It opened and a little bald man, wearing a red armband over rumpled grey shirt, jeans and trainers, stood there holding a tin tray with five beakers of tea on it. He looked across at the men and blinked.

Everybody looked back at him.

The senior of the two prison officers stared at him severely. 'Enderby!' he bellowed like an RSM addressing a battalion.

The little man froze. Some of the tea spilled out of the beakers on to the tray.

'Wait there, Enderby!' The officer stretched up to his full height, reached out for his hat, which he placed very precisely on his head, and said. 'I didn't give you permission to enter, did I, Enderby?' he bellowed.

'Er — er — no, Mr Jubb,' the little man muttered and looked down at his trainers.

'Well go out, close the door, wait there and I will have the tray collected from you when we are ready,' bawled the officer.

The little man stepped back. The door closed.

Boodle shook his head and glared at Jubb. The commander was not pleased. He sniffed noisily.

Angel noticed his face; he looked as if he had just caught a whiff of the prison stew.

'Sorry about that, sir,' Jubb said.

'Yardley is isolated, isn't he?'

'Yes sir. He's ready in room fourteen, across the corridor. With an officer.'

'Has he been thoroughly searched?'

'Thoroughly, sir. I was present throughout.'

The commander nodded.

'It won't happen again, sir.'

Boodle sighed, shook his head and turned back to Angel.

Jubb caught the eye of the other prison officer and directed him with a finger to nip out and collect the tray from the trusty.

Angel had removed his shirt and was watching Quadrille fasten the wire at his waist and across his chest on to his vest with flesh-coloured adhesive tape. When he pressed on the last piece of tape and was satisfied that all was secure and in the correct position, he stepped back, looked at his handiwork and nodded.

'Right,' he said. 'That should be OK, Michael.' He turned back to the table and tossed the reel of tape into a box.

The tea arrived and Jubb handed round the beakers.

'Ta,' Angel said. He took a sip, put it down on the table and pushed a fist into a sleeve of the shirt and pulled it on. As he was buttoning up the front, Boodle, rubbing his chin, stepped up close up to him.

'Something I forgot to mention, Mike,' he said softly only eight inches from his ear. 'Yardley has a long-time girl-friend, Enchantra Davison. Lives in Birmingham. Bit of a tart. Blonde, long legs, a lot up front. She's probably closer to him than anybody. She is his only visitor. She has visited him every visiting-day since his arrest; never missed once. Now she might know where the gold is.'

Angel nodded and pulled up his tie.

'Right, sir.'

Boodle turned away, looked round the room and rubbed his chin again. Angel noticed that his hand was shaking.

'Are we ready,' Boodle suddenly called out irritably.

Quadrille held up Angel's coat, and Jubb crossed to him, holding out the in-tray. Angel reached out for his belongings and put them back into his pockets. Lastly, Jubb returned his ID and pass, which Angel dropped into his inside pocket.

The young man returned to the open case on the table. He took out a coil of wire and a pair of headphones and flicked a switch. He draped the wire over the table and plugged it into a socket on the outside of the case. Boodle's small eyes darted in every direction.

'Are we all set?' he snapped.

Angel looked over Quadrille's shoulder into the case. He could see a green light on a control panel, and reel-to-reel tape running slowly.

'Almost,' Quadrille said reaching out for the headphones. 'Will you say something, Mike?'

'Yes. Like what?'

'That's enough. That's great.'

Boodle sidled up to him. 'One last thing, Mike,' he whispered in his ear. 'It's taken six months to set this up. It's imperative you find out where the gold is. We can't wait twenty years until he is released, in the hope that we might recover it. Furthermore, the Bank of Agara, whose gold this is, is wholly owned by the king and his brother, the crown prince. Number Ten is under tremendous pressure from them. Apart from trade implications, the brothers are threatening to withdraw NATO flight-path agreements across the Mitsoshopi Desert. If there was another war in the Middle East — er, well … ' He put his hand on Angel's arm and squeezed it. Through gritted teeth, he said, 'Promise him anything, but find out where he's hidden it.'

Angel blew out a long silent sigh. 'Yes sir.'

Boodle moved away. He was biting his lower lip and wiping his forehead with a moist handkerchief at the same time. He ran his hand down his neck and rubbed it hard. He glared across at Quadrille in the headphones and raised his eyebrows, his eyes glowing like fire-opals.

Quadrille read the signal and stuck up both thumbs.

Boodle turned instantly, put up a finger and called out: 'Mr Jubb.'

The prison officer straightened up.

'Sir!' He looked at Angel. 'This way, sir,' he said. He unlocked the door.

Angel reached out for the beaker of tea, which he had hardly touched, and followed him out of the door, carrying it. Jubb marched down the corridor for twenty yards. His polished boots clomped loudly on the tiled floor, the echo resonating round the bare green walls. Angel ambled behind him, stopping half-way along to take a sip. Jubb arrived at reception room fourteen and pulled out a bunch of keys. By the time the door was opened, Angel had caught up. He eyed Morris Yardley sitting at the table, his mouth slightly open, his jaw set like the Rock of Gibraltar. He had his arms folded and a cigarette smouldering between his fingers. He was staring back at Angel with an unreadable face.

Jubb peered round the door at a uniformed officer standing inside with his back to the wall.

'Everything all right, son?'

'Yes, Mr Jubb.'

'Right. Off for your tea-break, then.'

The young officer went out.

Jubb looked at the prisoner, then back at Angel.

'There you are, sir,' he bawled. 'Yardley two nine seven.'

Angel, still holding the beaker, stepped into the room. Its layout, size, cupboard, table and chairs were the same as those in No. eleven.

Jubb went out. The door closed. The key turned in the lock. The two men were alone.

Angel looked down at the bulky man. He looked bigger than the photographs suggested. His thick arms pulled at the seams of the shirt-sleeves. Angel could well believe that it would take three men to hold him down in a punch-up. He noticed the nicotine stains on his fingers and the fingernails like bath-plugs, as he took a big draw from the cigarette then jerkily dabbed a length of ash into the Nescafe jar lid standing on the table. There was a half-drunk beaker of tea in his right hand.

Angel stepped forward. 'I'm DI Angel.'

'I know,' Yardley said wryly, in a broad Birmingham accent. He stared up at Angel as he put down the mug of tea. Angel dipped into his inside pocket and pulled out his ID. He tossed the card on to the table. Yardley barely glanced at it. Angel leaned forward, turned the card round the right way and pushed it towards him. The man peered at it, nodded and sucked silently on the cigarette.

Angel then, with deliberation, unbuttoned his coat, took it off, put it round the back of the chair, loosened his tie and unbuttoned his shirt.

Yardley stared at him.

Angel reached into his shirt, found the microphone and began to peel the wire from his vest.

Yardley's eyebrows went up a little when he saw what he was doing.

Angel jerked at the wire until the entire unit came free and he pulled it out of the front of his shirt like a dead snake. He then dropped the microphone end into his beaker of tea.

Yardley closed his mouth and sniffed.

'That's great, that,' he said. 'What do you do for an encore?'

Angel didn't reply. He buttoned up his shirt, straightened his tie, put on his coat and sat down at the table. He couldn't help but wonder what pandemonium there would be in reception room 11.

'You wanted to speak to me?' he said evenly. 'I thought we should start on an even keel.'

'It's a good job you did that, you know,' Yardley said, pointing his finger at Angel's chest.

Angel looked through a wisp of smoke into the hard, steel-blue eyes. Their faces were only eighteen inches apart.

Yardley continued: 'Yes. I wouldn't even have opened my mouth to you, if you hadn't taken that mike off.' Another pause. 'I knew you was wired up,' he said cockily. 'I was tipped off.'

'Who by?' asked Angel.

'A nonce called Enderby,' said Yardley. He stubbed the cigarette out in the Nescafe lid. 'And that's going to cost me half an ounce of snout,' he added grudgingly. Then he grinned and stuck his chest out. 'There's not a lot going on in this nick I don't know about.'

Angel shook his head. There were no internal windows in the room. The only window was barred; it was two floors above ground-level, and looked out on to fields. The door was locked. How could he have been tipped off? This chap was too smart by half.

'You've had a guard in here all the time, haven't you?'

'Yes,' Yardley said and smiled.

'How did he manage it then?'

There was a pause. Yardley slowly leaned backwards in the chair, then he smiled, gave a slight nod, reached his hand out and deliberately rotated his beaker of tea through 180 degrees.

'I'm giving away trade secrets' he said. He pointed to the drink. 'Pick it up' he said. 'Pretend you was going to sup it.'

Angel reached out for the beaker and brought it up to his face. As he tilted it, and the level of the tea at the further side of the pot lowered, he saw, scrawled on the inside, in red crayon, the words: *Yor visitor wired.*

Angel put the cup down. He allowed himself the tiniest of smiles; so much for Jubb's security.

Yardley confidently ran his tongue round the inside of his mouth.

'I think we're even-stevens, Michael, don't you?'

Angel looked at him. There was a pause as each man tried to weigh up the other.

Angel eventually said: 'You wanted to see me. I understand you asked for me. You said you knew me.'

'No. I jus' knows of you.'

'From where?'

'Let's jus' say — mutual friends.'

Angel couldn't think of anybody he knew, who also knew Yardley.

The man lit another cigarette quickly.

'I'm on my own, you know,' he said. 'Yes. I was brought up in an orphanage in Brum. My mother deposited me there fifty years ago. Don't know who the 'ell my father was. The boss there, we called him Himmler, had me sent to technical college. I was learnt to be a builder. Yes. I was a brickie for thirty-three years. Every bloody day — slapping one brick on top of another. Outside. All weathers. Even in six foot of snow. Yes. I reckon, single-handed, I built the equivalent of the NEC and the M1 put together. I was a damn good builder. Still am. Got all my certificates. Yes. And I earned a good screw. Some weeks I earned half a grand. Last full week I worked, I brought three hundred quid home. Mindst you, I had to grind. No dallying about.'

'I'm sure you did, but you're not a saint, Morris.'

'No. No. I know I'm bloody not,' he replied quickly.

'You killed a man.'

'It was an accident,' Yardley retorted. 'He wanted to be a hero. He was coming for me. I didn't shoot at him. I shot at his legs. It was an accident. The bullet hit a steel grate, ricocheted off and entered his chest. It was all explained at the trial. I didn't aim to kill him. I didn't want to kill him. If he hadn't charged at me, I wouldn't even have pulled the trigger.' 'The jury were unanimous.'

'My barrister was a clown.'

There was another pause.

'So you're hoping to make a new life with Enchantra?' Yardley's eyes slid to the left, then to the right and then settled dead centre. He stared at Angel closely.

'Huh. Boodle been talking to you, has he?'

The inspector didn't reply.

'Is he your boss?'

'Sort of. I've been seconded to him temporarily because you asked to see me.'

'What exactly is his job?'

'He's a commander in Special Branch. Chases blokes like you. Big operators.'

Yardley grinned. 'So I warrant a commander from Special Branch, do I?' He thought about it for a while. 'Mmm?' Suddenly the flippant mood left him. His jaw stiffened. 'He thinks he's smart. He isn't. All he wants is my gold.'

Angel thought he could be right, but he wanted to open him up ... find out what made him tick.

'You were telling me about Enchantra.'

'I wasn't. But I will. Enchantra. I dream about her, you know. Yeah. I'm a good ten years older than her. I've been in here over a year, now. A year and twenty days. And there's one thing certain. She'll not wait twenty years for me, I can tell you that. And you could hardly blame her. She's a beautiful woman. Look at me. I'm sweating. I get all in a lather thinking about losing her. All I ever think about is Enchantra ... and getting out of here.'

'And the gold.'

'Yeah. The gold and Enchantra ... and here I am like a bloody monkey in a cage.'

'Looks like she's prepared to wait for you ... and the gold? Does she know where it is?'

'Nobody knows where it is,' Yardley snarled dangerously. 'Only me. It's my ticket out of this hole.' He glowered at Angel. His eyes were moist. His bottom lip quivered. He paused, took a big drag at the cigarette, then wiped his mouth roughly. 'I'll get straight to the bloody point. Over the past two years, I've had a lot of runaround from the police. Before I was charged, after I was charged and since I've been in here. They interviewed me without any conscience at all. They say anything. They told me lies jus' to get information out of me. Well, I've had enough of that. I'm not taking any more from anybody.

After all, I'm in a strong negotiating position. I've got enough gold to buy anything I want in this world. I could buy my own Mediterranean island if I wanted to. And the longer I am in here, the more desperate the bank and the police will be to get it back. And they, the police, the courts can't do nothing more to me. I'm locked up. Got the maximum sentence. I'm fifty years of age. If I serve the full term, I'll be seventy! My life will be virtually over. Even if I murdered somebody, my life couldn't be made any worse than it is now. Hanging is out. This is a category A prison. I have no privileges worth talking about. I'll just fade away: I'll bloody die. So I have to get out. Now I am ready to negotiate my ticket. And I need an honest intermediary to act on my behalf. I am told reliably that you are an honest man, even though you are a copper. And I believe it. Now, Michael, if you are honest, you are the best chance I've got. If you are dishonest, and you trick me, I will have you killed. I have now got the connections. I can do that from in here. I can do it any time. I can do it from anywhere in the world. And I'll have your bloody entrails draped all the way round the Bull Ring. Do you understand that?'

Angel didn't like being threatened, but it wasn't new. He'd been threatened a million times before.

'What's the deal?' he said evenly

Suddenly Yardley changed. He leaned back and switched on the smile again.

'Didn't you bring me any ciggies?' he asked brightly.

'No.'

'You mean bastard,' he said, with a grin. 'Boodle always brings me a couple of packs.'

Angel looked across the table at him; he sensed the crux of the deal was imminent. Outwardly he tried to remain calm and expressionless, inside, the Flying Scotsman was pounding relentlessly down to King's Cross.

Yardley thoughtfully took a drag on the cigarette and leaned forward.

'The deal. Yes. I've given this a lot of thought, Michael. Three hundred and eighty-five days' worth of thought. It's simple enough. I want a full pardon with no strings, no catches, no conditions, no tricks, with an early release-date and I will hand over half of the gold. That's thirty-three million quids' worth at the last count.'

Angel pursed his lips. He ran his hand over his chin. 'Where is it?'

Yardley stared at him. A wry smile appeared on his face.

Angel added: 'I mean, is it in the UK or ... abroad?'

'It's safe enough. *I* put it there. *I* know where it is. I can get it, easily enough.'

'Is it all there?'

'It's all there. All eight hundred and twenty bars,' snapped Yardley.

'In one place?'

'Yes!' Yardley roared.

Angel leaned back in his chair. 'Hmmm.'

'Well? What do you say?' Yardley bawled. 'Is it a deal or isn't it?'

There was a pause. Angel rubbed his chin.

'Does anybody else know where it's hidden?' he asked.

'No,' snapped Yardley. 'Well, what do you think? Is it a deal or isn't it? What do you say?'

Angel massaged the lobe of one ear between finger and thumb.

Suddenly Yardley's eyes flashed. He stood up. The chair went over with a clatter. He threw his hands in the air.

'No. Never mind what you bloody say,' he shouted angrily. 'Look. Put it to Boodle. No. No! Put it to the Home Secretary. No, the Prime Minister. See what he says. He can only say 'yes.' If he doesn't, I'll tell you this, that gold will never see daylight again. It'll take a damned sight more finding than his flaming Weapons of Mass Destruction!'

CHAPTER SEVEN

Angel arrived back at the station at four o'clock. He stormed into his office and threw his coat at a chair. It had been one hell of a day. And it wasn't over yet. He'd had the early morning drive up to Welham, the interview with Yardley, the de-briefing, the threats, the cursing and the general dressing-down from Boodle, and the tedious drive south on the very busy A1. He didn't feel like any more trouble.

He lowered himself into the swivel-chair and gave out a long sigh.

There was a knock at the door.

'Come in,' he bawled.

It was Ahmed.

'Oh. It's you lad,' he said crisply. 'How are things in Glockamora?'

The cadet's mouth opened. 'What's that, sir?'

'What do you want?' snapped Angel.

'Saw you come in, sir. Can I talk to you now about my holidays?'

Angel screwed up his face. 'Your holidays. What about them, lad?'

'Ah.' Ahmed's eyes brightened. 'Well, sir, you know that all the regular bank holidays are on Mondays?'

'It's not one of those quiz questions is it? I really haven't time for it, lad.'

'It's not a quiz, sir.'

'Well, I'll tell you what. Is the water on now?'

'Er — yes, sir. Do you want a cup of tea?'

'That'd be great,' Angel said slowly. 'That would be really great. Is Ron Gawber in?'

'Don't know, sir. He was down the cells looking for something, I think.'

'Find him, send him in.'

'Right, sir.'

The door closed.

Angel leaned back in the chair and gazed up at the ceiling at the circle of dust above the light-fitting. He blew out a long, noisy sigh and yawned. He ran his hand across his mouth. What a rotten day … He didn't much like being a shuttlecock between Boodle and Yardley, and he didn't enjoy all the mouth he had had to put up with at the debriefing. Thank goodness it was Friday. This had been one of those days he would rather forget. He'd be glad to get home. Out of this place for a couple of days. It could only be good. He had always thought he wanted to be an inspector. It had been an ambition of his after seeing his father come home one day in a crisp, new uniform with one silver pip up. Ever since he could remember, he had thought inspector was the best rank of all: it wasn't so high that you carried all the cans, nor so low that you had all the repetitive and dirty jobs to do yourself. Things were changing. Maybe it was middle age creeping up on him. He was beginning to think he would have to revise his ideas. It was beginning to look as if commander was the best rank. Yes. Especially in Special Branch. It was looking as if Peregrine Boodle had the best job of all!

There was a knock at the door. Angel brought down the chair.

'Come in.'

It was DS Gawber. 'Ah. I thought you'd go straight home, sir.'

'I wish I had. This place is about as much fun as a crematorium.'

Gawber shook his head.

'Did you find anything, then?'

'What were you looking for?'

'To tell the truth, Ron, he nicked my badge and ID.'

Gawber pulled a face. 'Wow. Didn't find that. Didn't find anything.'

'Huh. It will be in the Gazette on Monday, and then every copper in the country will know that I let a known pick-pocket fillet me!' He pointed to the chair. Gawber sat down. 'What happened at Evan Jones's place? Did they take much?'

'There's nothing missing.'

Angel frowned. 'Nothing?'

'That's what he said. Two men, silenced the alarm with quick setting foam. Made the upstairs windows with grappling-irons. Left no fingerprints and no handprints. They were spotted making their getaway down a rope ladder. And no transport was seen in the vicinity. Sophisticated villains, eh?'

Angel nodded. 'Any damage?'

'A smashed window-pane upstairs, that's all.'

'Unbelievable.'

'Perfect, eh?'

'Like Richard and Judy.'

'What?'

'Who was the informant?'

'Never found out. Anonymous. Not on the scene when the squad car arrived.'

'Neighbours see anything?'

'It's all very quiet up there, sir.'

'Was it worth turning over?'

'There were a few silver pieces, two paintings and a fifteen-carat gold Edwardian pocket watch on a stand I wouldn't have minded.'

'Mmm. What were they looking for then?'

'Gold?' Gawber suggested pointedly.

Angel thought about it. After a few seconds he nodded. 'How did Jones take it?' he said.

'Surprised. Angry. Said he'd no idea who might have done it.'

'Ay. No forensic at all?'

'Nothing sir.'

There was a knock on the door.

'Come in.'

It was Ahmed carrying a tin tray with a cup of tea on it. Angel beamed. He turned back to Gawber. 'Anything else?'

'No, sir,' said Gawber, getting to his feet.

'Right then, carry on.'

Gawber made for the door.

Angel called after him. 'Oh, Ron. If you see anything of Fishy Smith on your travels, bring him in. I haven't finished with that little ferret yet!'

Gawber nodded and went out.

Ahmed put the tea on a beer mat purloined from the Feathers.

'Thank you, lad. You've saved the day.'

Ahmed beamed.

Angel stirred in the sugar and looked up.

'Hey, Ahmed. Do you remember on Valentine's day, you got me a box of continental chocolates from Millington's sweet-shop.'

'Yes sir. But that was February last year, sir. This year you bought Mrs Angel roses. I remember because you said how expensive they were.'

'You're right, lad. Ay. Those flowers were daylight robbery. Well, she right liked those foreign chocolates.' He reached into his pocket. 'Will you get me the same again?'

'Can't sir. It's closed down. The old lady in there died.'

Angel's jaw dropped in surprise. 'When was this?'

'Oh, erm, it must have been before Christmas. Yes. Round about October.'

'And I never heard. Dear Miss Millington. And she was a lovely lady. Been there years. Open all hours that God sent.

Used to be open until eight o'clock of an evening to catch the people going to the Odeon and the Theatre Royal. She used to keep a big pot of pepper on the counter in case she was attacked. Mmmm. There was a young thug, I remember, got his hands in the till once. She fought bravely but he was too strong for her. But I caught him. I brought him in. I had him put away myself. He got four years. I was sergeant at the time. It was a quaint little shop. Had a very low roof and I remember it was the only shop I ever went into where you had to step down to get into it. The shop floor was lower than pavement-level. In fact, after a heavy rainstorm, it used to flood and she still used to be seen in Wellington boots, splashing round weighing out sweets and bringing them to the door. Lovely stuff she sold too. A really nice woman. I have known her all my life. She was a dear. Sorry about that.' He shook his head. 'Another old bit of Bromersley gone.'

'Sorry, sir,' Ahmed said sympathetically. He turned towards the door and then came back. 'Can I talk to you now about my holidays, sir?'

'No.'

Ahmed went out and closed the door. Angel sipped the tea. Then he picked up the phone and dialled a number.

'Crisp? What's happening there, lad?'

'It's all quiet, sir. We are in the car across the street from Jones's pitch. We can see Jones in his office. Nothing's happening.'

'Right. Pack in the obo at five, and I'll see you in my office eight-thirty Monday morning.'

Crisp sounded pleased. 'Right, sir.'

'Oh. Yes,' Angel added irritably. 'And if you see anything of Fishy Smith on your travels, bring him in.'

'Right, sir.'

Angel replaced the phone and finished off the tea. It was on his mind that the announcement that his badge and ID had been stolen would appear in Monday's issue of the Police Gazette. An announcement about their prompt recovery might help him to recoup some lost pride.

The phone rang. He glanced at the clock. It was 4.45 pm. He frowned and reached out for the handset.

It was the superintendent. 'Come in here,' he growled.

'Right, sir.' Angel pulled a face as he replaced the receiver. He knew he was in trouble. He made his way down to the super's office and knocked on the door.

'Sit down,' Harker growled.

Angel took the chair.

The superintendent looked more sour than usual.

'The commander's not very pleased with you,' he began. 'You're not the little Lord Fauntleroy he thought you were. You ripped out the wire, you didn't find out where Yardley's hidden the gold; and you didn't even close a deal even though he handed it to you on a plate.'

'I told him everything Yardley told me.'

'Ay. That he wanted an unconditional pardon and an instant release, in exchange for half the gold.'

'That's right.'

' You should have agreed to it.'

'I couldn't agree to that. I don't suppose even the Home Secretary would have agreed to that sort of a deal.'

'Of course he wouldn't, but you're not the Home Secretary! We would have recovered half the gold for starters, wouldn't we? Thirty-three million quids worth! And we would have picked up the rest in due course!'

Angel's mouth dropped open. He said nothing.

Harker arched his bushy eyebrows and slowly nodded his head.

'Oh? Have we suddenly gone all ethical? I see. Oh. Since when has a crook's word been worth anything? It isn't his gold. He stole it in the first place!'

Angel swallowed. 'I couldn't be party to a trick like that. He'd asked for me because he trusted me.'

'Whose gold is it?'

Angel looked defiantly into the super's bloodshot eyes. He didn't reply.

'Well, whose gold is it?!' bawled Harker, his eyes flashing.

'Not his,' Angel eventually muttered.

'Exactly. Have you gone doolally?'

'No.'

'I think you have. Well, look, it's Friday. Go home. And this weekend, you had better take some time to consider your position. You'll have to make up your mind whether you want to serve the community as a disciplined police officer in a sophisticated team of crime-busters, or whether you want the short-term luxury of being a high principled renegade copper who is about to start looking for a job as a night-watchman!'

*

Angel couldn't get home fast enough. He drove quickly. His heart was thumping his hands were sweating. He swung off the main road, round the corner, along the street to his bungalow. He drove straight into the garage, pulled down the door, locked it, closed the gates and strode down the path to the back door. He was looking forward to a bit of peace and quiet.

He put his hand on the handle, and it was pulled open strongly by his wife from the inside, unexpectedly catching him off balance.

'Steady lass. Steady,' he said sharply as he entered the kitchen. 'What's going off?'

She closed the door smartly and turned the key.

He looked round at her curiously. He could tell by her face she was not a happy bunny.

'What are you doing?' he said evenly.

Mary stared at him fiercely. 'I've been waiting for you.'

'Well I'm not late, am I? It's not Yorkshire puddings is it?'

She launched into the attack. 'Why didn't you tell me you were thinking of having gas installed? I would have thought you would have consulted me about it!'

Angel undid his coat as he walked away to the hall.

'What are you talking about? We don't want gas. I know they say it's better for cooking, but all that muck and expense … '

'I don't want gas now. I've managed without it since we came to live here, I can manage without it a bit longer. It'll ruin our decorations, and we've only just finished the hall.'

'Ay,' he said closing the lobby door. 'What's for tea?'

'You haven't answered my question.'

'What?'

'It's not a secret now. The cat's out of the bag.'

'Oh yes,' he said vaguely and ambled to the fridge; took out a can of German beer, found a glass in the cupboard and pulled the ring off the can. He glanced towards the oven. 'Are we having salmon and new potatoes?'

'Are you going to explain?' she snapped.

'Explain what?' he said as he poured the beer into the glass. 'Have you, or have you not, asked the gas board to quote us for installing gas central heating?'

'No. I haven't. I have told you. I don't want to bother. Any post? Why?'

'On the sideboard. Because two men from the gas board came this morning to measure the place up for a quote!'

He put the glass down on the worktop and looked at her curiously.

'Why didn't you send them on their way?'

'They said you'd asked them to call.'

'Well I didn't.'

Mary looked worried.

Angel thought for a moment. Then he shook his head slowly. The truth came to him and he didn't like it.

'Oh no! I suppose they were two men in their thirties. Rather smart. Wearing sunglasses.'

'Yes. And they were wearing gas-board badges and hats.'

'Ay. Carrying clipboards with official-looking gas board papers on them, I expect?'

'Yes.'

'And they needed to see all over the house? Even the pantry and broom-cupboard?'

'Well, yes.'

'And one of them had a metal thing on a long handle.'

'Yes.'

'And he told you it was a gas detector?'

'Yes.'

'And the man wore earphones. And one of them kept you talking down here, while the other went round the other rooms with his machine. And they both wore gloves.'

'Yes. Yes. Yes. Who were they?'

'I didn't ask them to call. I don't know where they were from. What about their van?'

'I didn't see a van. I looked outside when they left.'

'They weren't from the gas board! Why didn't you ring me on my mobile?'

'I did! Who were they then? It was switched off!'

Angel's eyes half-closed as the whole picture became clear to him. 'Ah. I bet they came at ten o'clock.'

Mary's eyes glowed in amazement. 'That's right. That's right. How did you know that?'

*

Angel was never late. He liked to get to the station promptly by eight thirty. This Monday morning was no exception. He had a lot on his mind.

He turned the car into Church Street and saw a white van parked outside the front entrance. As he passed it, he noticed four traffic cones around a pile of fresh earth, and the head of the plumber in blue overalls bobbing up and down, out of a hole in the road.

He drove round the back, parked in the yard and entered by the back door, went past the cells, and arrived at his office at the same time as Ron Gawber, who had made his way up from the sergeant's locker-room.

'Have a good weekend, sir?'

'Ay. I suppose,' said Angel, taking off his coat. 'Come on in, Ron. Sit down.'

There was a knock at the door.

'Come in,' he called.

It was Ahmed, smiling and waving a sheet of paper.

'Good morning, sir. Morning, Sarge. You'll be interested in this, sir.'

'Is it a cheque from Camelot? How much have I won?'

'No sir.' Ahmed said earnestly. 'No. It's a round robin from Special Branch to all forty-three forces.'

'Special Branch?' Angel's eyebrows shot up.

'It's about that helicopter crash near the Tunistone television mast on the Elmersfield patch, last Monday.'

'Oh ay? Well, what's it say?' Angel reached out and took the paper. 'Let's have a shufti.' He read:

Mark Shadwell Penn, aged 26, of Queen's Street, Birmingham, and Harrison 'Tinker' Bell, 40, of Tennyson Close, Wolverhampton. Wanted in connection with armed robbery of gold from security van outside Bank of Agara, City Road, London, 17 April 2003. Request all stations report info urgently to Commander Boodle ref: 11257.'

Angel lowered the paper. 'Mmm. Never heard of either of them. Are they on our books? They must have previous.' Suddenly, he ran his hand thoughtfully across his mouth. He shook his head and blew out a short sigh. What a coincidence! Yardley had no known connections with this part of the world, yet for months, apparently, he had been asking to see Angel. And now two of his gang had died in a helicopter crash only ten miles up the road.

Angel didn't believe in coincidence. He turned to Gawber, 'Find out the name of the inside man in this gold robbery. He's in prison somewhere. Find out where. It might move us on a pace.'

Gawber nodded and dashed off. Angel watched the door close and then turned to Ahmed. 'Now, lad. Look up those two dead men, they must have previous. They wouldn't cut their teeth on a bank robbery.'

'Yes sir.' Ahmed turned towards the door.

'Hang on, lad. Another job for you and that computer. I want you to find the address of Enchantra Davison. She's Yardley's girlfriend. I don't know where she lives now, but she was living with him at fifty-five Broad Street, Birmingham, when he was arrested.'

'Won't Commander Boodle know it, sir?'

'Ay,' Angel sniffed. 'But I don't want you to bother him.'

'I could ring the prison. She'd be on his list of visitors. All visitors have to give their name and — '

'Yes. I know that, lad,' Angel said patiently. 'I know that.' 'The arresting officer would know, sir.'

'Yes, lad. Yes. But I want it done surreptitiously.'

'Oh?' the cadet said uncertainly.

'Listen, lad.' Angel leaned forward and spoke quietly and slowly. 'I'm prepared to spend a bit of time finding it out, secretly. I know it's a slow way, uneconomical, old-fashioned even, and that it will therefore cost the force and the taxpayer a copper or two more, but there are good reasons. Almost everything costs something.'

Ahmed looked blank, but nodded. 'Right, sir.'

Angel smiled. 'One day, lad, you'll learn that the only cheese that's free is in a mouse-trap!'

CHAPTER EIGHT

Angel tramped down the hospital corridor and knocked on the door marked MORTUARY. A man in green overalls let him in. He picked his way through the white-walled theatre, stepping over tiled channels of running, multicoloured liquid of unmentionable origin that flowed to a gurgling drain. He passed three operating-tables and a bank of twenty-four buzzing refrigerated drawers, until he came to a tiny office at the end. The door was ajar.

'Come in, Mike!' the familiar Glaswegian voice called out. The doctor was at his desk, puffing a pipe and perusing a file of papers.

Angel wrinkled his nose. 'This place pongs!' He closed the door.

'Only ammonia.' Mac said. 'Sit down.'

The corners of Angel's mouth turned down as he eased himself into the chair.

'That's not ammonia.'

Mac smiled.

Angel added: 'I'll tell you what, I'd sooner spend a fortnight in Scarborough than an afternoon in here.'

The pathologist turned, flicked a switch and an extractor fan in the wall above hummed into life.

'You're always complaining.' He took another puff at the pipe and said: 'Now, I've finished going over his clothes. Nothing remarkable there. Simply everything of the best Savile Row tailors, I wish I could afford them. Nothing off the peg; hand-made silk shirts. And so on. Immaculate. No damage to them. No missing buttons. No signs of a struggle or anything like that.' He leaned down to the floor, lifted up a polythene bag and put it on the table. 'Contents of the pockets. I've finished with them. You can have them. Nothing remarkable there, either.'

'Let's have a look.' Before Mac could say anything, Angel had opened the bag and tipped them on to his desk.

The doctor wasn't pleased, and moved a file and some papers out of the way.

Angel rummaged quickly through the items: a handker-chief, a few coins, a wallet containing credit-card, driving-li-cence, £200 in cash, and a photograph of a young woman.

Angel looked closely at the face.

'That's his late wife. Photographs of her all over his flat.'

Angel nodded. 'Nice looking.' He put it back in the wallet and shoved all the stuff into the polythene bag. 'Is that all?'

'Yes.'

'Nothing fell out, into the vat, anywhere?'

'No.'

Angel rubbed his chin.

'What's the matter?'

'Something missing.'

'What?'

Angel didn't reply. He pushed the bag into his raincoat pocket.

Mac picked up the file. 'Now, where do you want me to start?'

Angel shrugged. 'Wherever you like.'

'Let's start with the cause of death. He died from a heavy blow to the back of the head with something blunt, curved and very heavy. Then I assume he fell into the vat of gin. I can't begin to imagine what sort of a weapon was used, or how the murderer had the strength to hold it up to use it; it equates to a direct hit to the skull by a car travelling fast, say at least fifty miles an hour.'

'Did he die there, or was he moved?'

'He died in situ. His residual blood shows it. He died instantly. He was dead before his nose hit the surface of the liquid. He had imbibed a small amount a short time before, but I don't think it was enough to affect his senses.'

'Just one blow?'

'Yes.'

Angel rubbed his chin and rearranged his position in the chair.

'Are you telling me he died from one hefty clout to the back of the head with a ten-ton scud missile with a curved nose-cone?'

'Something like that,' Mac said and shoved the pipe back into his mouth.

Angel sniffed.

Mac pulled hard on the pipe. Wisps of smoke wafted upwards to the fan.

'What time was this?'

Mac fingered the notes. 'My calculations make it between six and nine on Monday evening.'

'Any signs of a struggle? Marks on the body? Skin under the fingernails? Scuff-marks on the steps or on or around the vat? Anything?'

'No.'

Angel blew out a long sigh. 'What else have you got?'

Mac lifted the bunch of A4 sheets out of the file.

'It's all here.'

'Come on, Mac. Save my time. Give me the meat. You've seen over his flat and his private rooms at Slogmarrow. Was there anything there?'

'No. Nice, well-furnished London pad for a man on his own. Expensive. Luxurious even. Overlooks the river. Nothing unusual or illegal. No drugs, firearms, ammo, cash, gold, pornography. The same in his rooms at the distillery.

It's all in here,' he added, tapping the file. 'Nothing worth mentioning, but everything of the very best.'

'Women?'

'No signs anywhere. A few photographs, looked like antecedents. Nobody apparently contemporary except his late wife. He had a daily in London. She kept it spotless, but hardly ever saw him.'

'Men?'

'No,' he said firmly. 'I don't think there's anything like that about the man.'

'And the scene of the crime. You were telling me about that plant, native to South America.'

'Yes. Fibres round that spanner, and in the office upstairs, on the carpet by the desk.' He fingered through the sheets in the file, found a page and read from it: 'Agave sisalana. Or sisal, from which matting, rugs, textiles, footwear, millinery, cordage, twines and brushes are made.' He looked up from his notes. 'The examples found were not dyed or bleached. They were perfectly natural. So we can probably eliminate rugs, textiles, and millinery.'

'Which then?'

'Don't know.'

Angel pulled a face. This forensic wasn't much help. He went down a mental list of queries. He began with the mysterious smell in Angus Leitch's office.

'And what did you make of the pong of humbugs?'

Mac blew out a short sigh. 'I couldn't make anything of it. I could smell it, but I couldn't bottle it, and I can't put odours under a microscope. I'm afraid it won't make forensic.'

Angel nodded glumly.

'I thought it was more the smell of a sweetie to soothe a cough, menthol or similar,' Mac added.

'Menthol?' Angel said rubbing his chin.

'Ay. It's an elderly person's sort of thing, isn't it?'

Angel blew out a sigh. 'Those old chaps ... Imperial's four senior directors ... '

'Ay?'

'I don't suppose ... Would they have the strength, jointly or severally, to cause McFee's death by belting him on the back of the head with an implement ... say, a golf club?'

'No. No chance, Michael. It would have required a lot more muscle than they could muster to crack McFee's skull with one blow ... and from a standing position. The injury required great weight and/or great speed, or both.'

'Hmm. What about a young man in his thirties ... in good physical shape?'

'You're thinking of Angus Leitch?'

Angel nodded.

'It's possible. I go no further.'

*

Peter Fleming shuffled along the corridor.

'Please follow me, Inspector, we can talk in here.'

'Thank you, sir.'

Angel stepped into the boardroom. A fire roared noisily up the back of the big fireplace. He looked round and took in the grandness of the room.

The old man switched on the chandelier. He indicated the long table surrounded by twelve chairs in the middle of the room.

'Please sit down.'

Angel waited for the man to hobble across the tartan carpet to the chair at the head of the table, and then sat down next to him.

'I understand you're the chief executive officer, you'll be the next chairman, won't you?'

'No. No, Inspector. There's certainly a vacancy for the chair of Imperial Gin plc. I would have relished the position years ago but — ah well, I am retiring. I am eighty, you know, I have already resigned. I simply want to get the best person possible installed as CEO, and then I am off to Florida. Yes. Hmm. To be near my son and his family. And I tell you, I can't wait to get out there. I doubt I would survive another English winter.'

Angel nodded sympathetically.

'Duncan McFee doesn't seem to have any close relations.'

'That's right. His wife died four years ago. He never quite recovered from it, and they didn't have any children.'

'Ah. And I suppose he was well off.'

Fleming flashed his new BUPA teeth.

'He was very well off. He was in the top two hundred in the rich list, you know.'

'No, I didn't know. Hmmm. Interesting. And who will benefit under his will?'

'I will, for one, and my executive co-directors, Mr Menzies, Mr Reid and Mr Finlay. His entire estate was left in equal parts to the four of us.'

Angel rubbed his chin. At last, a possible motive? The lack of one had been very frustrating.

'Hmmm. And where were you last Monday evening, between five and ten o'clock?'

'Oh. Am I a suspect, Inspector?' Fleming shook his head. 'Tut tut.'

'It's a question I have to ask.'

'Yes, of course. Well, I would be doing what I have been doing every night for the past two years. After a day's work in the office, I am too weary to do much at all. I would leave at five o'clock, arrive home about ten past. I did have a house-keeper, but she has very recently left. They never stay long. I find something easy to cook or prepare. I eat it or throw it in the bin. Then I watch television or read the paper until around eight o'clock when I would have made myself a glass of tea and taken it to bed.'

'You didn't go out?'

'No. No. I am on my own. Where would I go?'

'Hmmm. Can you think of anyone who would have wanted Hector McFee dead?'

'Not a soul. He was a kind man. Everybody liked him. After his wife died, I believe he contracted his interests. His social life, like mine, dissolved. From conversations with him, he seemed to have been mainly concerned with strengthening the position of Imperial on the world scene and consolidating his personal financial interests.'

'What were they?'

'Oh, investment opportunities. He had a big portfolio of stocks and shares.'

Angel rubbed his hand across his mouth.

'Right. Thank you. That's all for now. I'd like to see your other executive co-directors: Mr Menzies, Mr Reid and Mr Finlay.'

'Ah. Yes. Well, please feel free to use this room, Inspector,' Fleming muttered as he pushed the chair away from the table.

'Thank you.'

Fleming pulled a face of pain as he straightened his back and shuffled to the door. 'I'll ask them to come along and see you, shall I? Who would you like to see first?'

Angel interviewed Reid, and then Menzies.

The men were cousins and good friends and both expressed views about the laird that were similar to those of Fleming. Also, Angel learned that both of them, and Finlay, who were all in their seventies, had sought the approval of the main board to retire and intended to do so in the near future.

Regarding their alibis, Angel was told that on the evening of the murder, Menzies walked to Reid's house in Slogmarrow, enjoyed a meal with Reid cooked for them by Mrs Reid, then the two men had retired to the billiard room at the far end of the house, where they played snooker until after nine o'clock. Then Menzies walked back to his house 200 yards away.

The last of the four directors shuffled in.

'My name is Finlay. You wanted to see me? I am the financial director here.'

The little man was wearing a suit as sharp as a steak knife, a crisp white shirt and a dark tie. Angel's eyes caught sight of his footwear: he was wearing light-coloured straw slippers.

'I'm Inspector Angel. Please sit down. I have just two questions, Mr Finlay.'

'Anything I can do to help,' the little bald man said, taking out a neatly folded white handkerchief and shaking it out to wipe a very red nose.

A gentle whiff of menthol drifted through the air.

Menthol! Angel's heart began to thump. His mind raced back to Leitch's office. He tried to breathe evenly and keep composed. It was exactly the same smell he had noticed lingering in that office the morning after the murder. He said nothing. He licked his lips thoughtfully and stared at the wizened little man. He seemed no taller than a vinegar bottle and weighed less than a Barnsley chop. Surely he could not have belted the life out of a big Scotsman?

'Can you tell me anyone who would want to see the death of Duncan McFee ... anyone who would benefit from his death?' he asked.

'I am a substantial beneficiary of his death, Inspector, but I would rather have him here alive today than have one penny of his money. After all, I am well enough off in my own right. I don't need any funds. I have worked for Imperial since leaving school. I have been an executive director for twenty-two years. I knew his father and his grandfather. His loss is a great one, especially to the company at this time. I am seventy years of age and well past conventional retirement age. I have already advised my co-directors of my wish to retire and they have accepted my resignation. The idea that Mr McFee has been murdered for pecuniary advantage is preposterous.'

'Nevertheless, Mr Finlay, he was murdered.'

Finlay nodded. 'You say so.'

'He was murdered on Monday evening last. Where were you?'

'Well, I usually spend my evenings at home quietly with my wife, here in Slogmarrow. That evening it was rather cool, so unusually, I went into Bromersley town to the pictures. There was a particular film I wanted to see at the

Ritz. My wife wasn't interested, so for a change, I went on my own.'

'Did you see anybody you knew there?'

'No, Inspector.'

'It would have been helpful if you had met someone who might have remembered seeing you there.'

'I don't think I saw anybody I knew.'

'That's unfortunate,' Angel said. He couldn't think of any question he could pursue. He couldn't hold Finlay on suspicion because he smelled of menthol. That simply wasn't enough. He pursed his lips. He certainly intended watching him very carefully. 'Ah well, thank you sir. That's all for now.' Finlay rose to leave. He pushed the chair back from the table and made for the door.

Angel remembered the light coloured straw slippers. He stood up.

'Excuse me, sir.'

The man turned.

'Unusual footwear?' he said pointing to the floor.

'Ah yes, Inspector,' Finlay said, making a sad face. 'I have to wear soft shoes. I have the most painful bunions. I wear these in the office and at home. They are not appropriate for the office, but they are far more comfortable than leather. I have promised myself that when I retire the first thing I shall do is have the operation.'

'I understand. May I see one of them, sir?' Angel said, holding out a hand.

Finlay looked both mystified and displeased.

'I suppose so.' Using the back of the chair for support, he lifted his foot, slipped one of the slippers off and held it out.

Angel looked at the soft soled-slipper with the raffia-like flower motif on the upper. 'Ah, native-made shoes. Are they from South America?'

'Not quite,' Finlay said smiling. 'They were a present from a friend who holidayed in Bali last year. They have proved unexpectedly welcome.'

Angel crossed to the window. With his back to the man, he held the slipper to the light.

'Yes. Very nice.' Then he returned and handed the slipper back. 'Thank you. Thank you very much.'

Finlay nodded and slipped it back on his foot. 'Is that all?'

'Yes. That's all, for now, Mr Finlay. Thank you.'

The old man went out. Angel watched the door close, then swiftly felt in his inside pocket for a transparent envelope. He opened it, inserted the pinch of fibres he had managed to pull from the slipper, sealed it and put it back in his pocket, patting it with a satisfied beam. It was the first time he had smiled for a week.

He left the boardroom and made his way down to the car. He drove through the distillery gates on to the main road to Tunistone. He wanted to get the fibres into Mac's hands as soon as possible. If they matched, they could form the backbone of a case. The smell from Finlay's handkerchief was identical to that isolated by Leitch's office window, but he would never be able to use it as evidence. There would be nothing to show in court. You couldn't bottle it; you couldn't photograph it, and anyway, it had probably dispersed by now. He wanted to know exactly what it was and what it was doing in Leitch's office. That unusual smell must fit into the case, but he didn't yet know how.

The story about Finlay going to the cinema on his own and meeting and seeing nobody was highly unsatisfactory; if he had gone somebody must have seen him.

As Angel drove past the town boundary sign into Bromersley, he reckoned the other three hadn't got watertight alibis either. As Fleming lived by himself, he could easily have made his way back to the ageing-room at any time during the evening. The two cousins, Menzies and Reid could be providing each other with alibis, or they could have committed the murder jointly. Also, Menzies had had ample opportunity to call in at the ageing-room both before he arrived at Reid's and on his way home. None of them had really watertight alibis. Furthermore, he thought it was highly surprising that all four key executives chose to resign their directorships at the same time. They were all well past the usual retirement dates and would no doubt receive handsome golden handshakes from a company as big and reputable as Imperial. Now that McFee had gone, they could, no doubt, vote each other thousands!

He arrived in the town centre and turned the car into Church Street. He was surprised to see that the plumber's van and traffic cones were still cluttering up the front of the station. He drove round to the yard and entered through the rear door. As he charged up the corridor, he saw Ahmed hovering by his office door. The young man's face lit up, and he eagerly stepped forward waving a piece of paper.

'What's that you've got there, lad? Your P45?' Angel asked as he pushed open the office door.

'No sir. It's the address of Enchantra Davison.'

Angel grabbed the paper, glanced at it and slapped it on the desk.

'That's great, lad,' he said smiling. 'Great.'

'But I wasn't able to find any record of any previous for either of those two wanteds, sir, who died in that helicopter crash, not on the NPC, nor in our own records.'

Angel's smile disappeared. He frowned as he thoughtfully unbuttoned his coat. In a second, he was as downcast as a bank-holiday weather forecast. He shook his head.

'No previous?' he said ponderously. 'No previous?' He rubbed his chin. They surely didn't cut their teeth on a job that size? Somebody must have deleted it. There aren't many people who would have had the audacity and the authority! It must have been Boodle. After a moment, he made a decision. 'We're running short on time, lad. We'll have to cut some corners. You can't catch a rat when it's in a pipe.'

Ahmed blinked. 'No sir.'

'You've got to smoke it out,' he said waving his hand in a flourish. He picked up the phone and dialled a number.

A local young woman, assuming a posh accent, answered.

'Bromersley Chronicle. News desk.'

'Here's something for you,' he said, feigning enthusiasm.

'Who is calling?'

'That doesn't matter. It's about the murder of the big boss, Duncan McFee, up at the Imperial distillery. I can tell you the police know who the murderer is, but they can't prove it. They are privately calling it the 'menthol murder', because the crime scene reeks of the stuff. Also, the police can't find the victim's bunch of keys!'

He replaced the phone gently and smiled.

Ahmed's jaw dropped. 'Do you really know who killed the man, sir?'

Angel sniffed. 'There were five suspects originally, Ahmed. I've got it down to two,' he said confidently. He reached into his jacket pocket, took out the transparent envelope and tossed it on the desk. 'Now hop off, and get that to Dr Mac, pronto.'

Ahmed eagerly reached out for the envelope and held it up to the light. His eyes lit up.

'Fibre, sir,' he said excitedly. 'Is it a clue?'

'No,' Angel grunted without looking up. 'It's evidence.'

CHAPTER NINE

There was a knock at the door.

'Come in.'

It was Gawber.

'Yes, lad?' Angel said,

'The name of that prisoner is Martin Taylor, sir. He was manager of security at the London branch of the Bank of Agara.'

Angel's face brightened.

'And he is currently residing in HMP Hallas End.'

'Ah! Even better. That's not far. This side of Lincoln. I'll go and see him first thing in the morning.'

There was a knock at the door.

'Come in.'

It was Constable Scrivens.

'What is it, lad?'

Scrivens's face and voice showed signs of embarrassment and exasperation.

'Sorry to bother you, sir. There's a man in reception kicking up a fuss about a missing German shepherd dog.'

'That's 'Lost Property' isn't it, lad?' Angel bawled. 'What you bothering me for?'

'Yes sir, but the constable I'm on with says that you were in the station when it was brought in last Tuesday. That you dealt with it. It isn't in the book, and this chap won't go away, and I don't know what to say to him.'

'Arrr,' Angel snarled and jumped to his feet. 'Right lad, I'll come.' He looked back at Gawber. 'I won't be a minute, Ron.' He darted out of the office, up to the top of the corridor and through the security door into reception. Scrivens came running behind.

A red-faced, skinny man in a flat cap, mustard-coloured corduroy suit and wearing a red scarf eyed the inspector as soon as he came through the door. Waving a bony hand displaying on the fingers a collection of sovereign rings in gold mounts, he advanced towards Angel, his small eyes staring piercingly. Licking his thin blue lips, he fumed:

'Are you this Inspector Angel?'

'Yes, sir,' Angel said evenly, easing back from the spray of saliva. 'What can I do for you?'

'I have just come back from a few days in Majorca to find that my German Shepherd dog has been stolen. What's more, a neighbour of mine saw a policeman in uniform putting it into a police van, so I know it was brought here. Some lad said you knew all about it. And this lad here says there's no record of it. What sort of jiggery-pokery's going on, that's what I'd like to know! You will know which dog it was, because there was something wrong with its jaw. It must have recovered by now, and I want it back. It's a valuable animal.'

'Yes sir. Of course you do,' Angel said slowly and quietly. 'You can certainly have your dog back, sir. No man should be parted from man's best friend, should he. I can tell you that he is being very well looked after in police-approved kennels at the moment. But I will arrange to have the dog brought here for you to collect on receipt of the recovery fee of thirty-six pounds, the veterinary fee of four hundred pounds for the operation on his throat, and the kennelling at six pounds a day for six days.'

'What?' exploded the red-faced man.

'Also, you will realize, sir, that we have been looking for you. We weren't to know that you were abroad on holiday.

The dog had no collar, identification disc or microchip. Now that is an offence. The standard fine is one hundred pounds. Then there is the court case to answer, which will be brought by the RSPCA, supported by us, for neglect. That will result in an additional fine.'

The man suddenly turned and made a swift dash for the station door. It banged noisily behind him.

Scrivens's eyebrows went upwards. His mouth dropped open. He turned to Angel.

'Do you want me to fetch him back, sir?'

'No. That case is now closed, lad,' Angel said as he made for the internal security door.

Scrivens's face slowly turned to a smile. 'Oh yes, sir. I see, sir.'

Angel returned to his office and closed the door.

'Now then Ron, where were we?'

'Did you want me to go to Hallas End?'

'No,' Angel said quickly. He wanted that doubtful pleasure ... any excuse to be away from the station and thereby avoid further contact with Boodle. The phone rang.

'What's this?' He reached out for it. 'Angel.'

It was the super.

'I want you down here. Now!'

'Right sir.'

It didn't sound good. Angel pulled a face. He dropped the phone into its cradle.

'I have to go.'

They both stood up. Angel made for the door, then he turned back.

'I'll tell you what I want you to do, Ron.'

'What, sir?'

'Find out all you can about menthol.'

Gawber screwed up his face. 'Menthol?'

'Ay. Menthol,' said Angel. Then he belted down the corridor to the super's office and knocked on the door.

'Come in. Sit down.' Harker bawled without even looking up.

103

Angel knew that was a bad sign. He settled in the chair by the desk.

The super peeled a piece of loose skin off his nose, spat out a nail and then muttered:

'Ay. Well, I haven't had chance to speak to you since Friday.'

Angel nodded. He wondered what was coming next; he knew it wasn't a coconut!

The super sat forward in the chair and held on to its arms like a rocket about to take off.

'I had a long chat with Perry Boodle this morning. You've left him in somewhat of a dilemma. You broke all the rules. You found nothing out. You didn't close a deal. He wonders whether if you did happen to extract any useful nugget of information out of Yardley, you might just be keeping it to yourself.'

Angel sniffed. He thought that last comment a bit rich! The superintendent was certainly making his position sound very precarious. He didn't reply.

'The question is, where do I go from here? Do I dismiss you … my best investigating officer … for deliberate disobedience, obstruction and wilful damage to police property … or what?'

There was another pause.

Angel stared at old alligator head, chewing a nail and rubbing his chin.

'Well, sir … ' Angel began.

'That was my first inclination,' the superintendent continued, ignoring the interjection. 'Then the commander pointed out to me that you are the only person Yardley is willing to talk to, and that you have us, therefore, well and truly "by the short and curlies".'

Angel released a silent sigh.

'What is also putting him out is that he says you have persistently refused to tell him how you came to know Yardley … and where and when you actually met.'

There was another pause. The super ground his teeth again for an encore. Eventually he said: 'Well?'

'I don't know where to start, sir.'

The super groaned impatiently.

Angel began: 'I didn't refuse to tell the commander how Yardley knows about me or says he knows me. We have never met, as far as I know.'

'Hmmm.' Harker sounded unconvinced.

'Also, sir, the commander did not tell me that he had any agenda other than recovering the gold. I was briefed to listen to any proposition from Yardley and make a deal that would lead to its recovery.'

The superintendent's face went scarlet; he turned his cinder-like eyes on to Angel.

'Yes, but you didn't do that!' he roared.

Angel's pulse banged in his ears.

'Well, I thought the proposition of handing over half the haul for his immediate release would not be acceptable.'

'Of course it's not bloody acceptable!' Harker bellowed. 'It's outrageous, but you should still have agreed to it.'

Angel's mouth dropped open.

'I find it difficult giving my word on something that I know could not be honoured.'

'The man's a crook. What he's offering isn't his to offer. It isn't his gold. And there are national security implications in all this. The commander told you, didn't he?'

'Yes.'

'Well, what's the matter with you, Michael? Have you gone soft in the head? Yardley killed a man!'

'It seems to have been an accident.'

Harker's eyes shot out like balls on elastic.

'Well he would say that, wouldn't he.' There was another pause, then he gave a long sniff and pushed himself back in his chair. He looked across at Angel. 'Well, the commander wants you to see Yardley again — tomorrow. But this time, he wants you wired up, and he wants you to do as you are told. He wants that gold returned to Agara so that the PM can get back authority for the RAF to get an unimpeded flight path across the Mitsoshopi Desert any time it likes. These are not tourist routes for fun. They are to help police the Middle East and keep the world safe from terrorists! Now if this is a problem for you, Michael, you'd better pack the job in!'

*

'Ah, Michael, there you are,' Boodle said, showing a big smile and holding out a sweaty hand. 'Come on in. Hope you had a pleasant journey We're all ready for you.'

Angel had expected the meeting with the commander to be very sticky after last Friday's fiasco, but Boodle was over him like treacle on a ginger pudding.

'You remember Oscar, of course?'

DI Quadrille in the smart dark suit looked up from his suitcase of switches, wires and flashing lights. He forced a smile across the table.

Angel shook his hand and nodded.

Boodle put his arm on Angel's shoulder and edged him towards a corner of the room. He rubbed his chin. His fingers were shaking.

'I'm glad you agreed to go through with this again, Michael, and wear a wire,' he said. 'I can tell you that Yardley is quite desperate to see you, so I think that this time we may very well be able to pull it off.'

The door at the far side opened noisily and a man in uniform strode through balancing a tray of tea. It was Senior Prison Officer Jubb. He turned back to the door and with a big flourish of the keys locked it.

'Ah, Mr Jubb,' said Boodle. 'Is everything all set up down there?'

'Everything's ready, sir. Same room as before.' Jubb looked at Angel and gave a knowing chuckle. 'Oooh. Good morning, sir.'

'Morning, Mr Jubb,' Angel said, evenly.

Boodle steered Angel away from Jubb to a quiet corner of the room.

'The thing is,' Boodle continued in a hoarse whisper, 'The commissioner has had a flag from the Joint Chief of Staff of an upcoming insurgence of the Bhajis. Now we have five hundred and forty men on standby at Lyneham, and he still hasn't clearance for a flight path across the Mitsoshopi Desert. So we simply have to get on the right side of the king and return his gold. Keep the old dear sweet, you understand?' Angel was not much into this political intrigue. He thought he'd better try and say something intelligent.

'So this is a bit of an emergency?'

'Absolutely. It's a national crisis. The security of the UK is at stake. We don't want a nine eleven here, do we.'

'And so you want me to agree to anything, anything at all, that will lead us to recovering the gold.'

'We are on our backs, Michael. On our backs. Her Majesty's government offers all its facilities: men of every skill, weapons of any kind, unbounded technology, unlimited budget, all at our disposal. We can do anything, and I mean absolutely anything, to recover the gold, but we need to know exactly where it is!'

'But we won't be able to keep our side of any deal I make?' Boodle demurred. His left eye twitched.

'We take the gold first and then see how things are.' Angel's face dropped.

Boodle jumped back quickly. He put up a hand.

'Well, we might. We might. It would depend on what he wants, Michael. Look, don't corner me on this.'

'He wants his freedom and half the gold.'

'Maybe. No. I don't know,' Boodle said, his eye twitching again. 'Just find out where it is,' he said impatiently, and then, gently, he added: 'Leave the consequences to providence, old chap. As I said, it would depend upon all the circumstances at the time … must remain flexible.'

He turned away quickly and moved to the window. He wanted to dodge any further questions on that tack.

Jubb came forward with a mug of tea and chuckled knowingly as Angel took it.

'One sugar.'

'Thank you.'

Boodle came back up to Angel. 'By the way, have you remembered where you met him ... Yardley?'

'No, sir.'

'Hmmm.' Boodle shook his head and crossed to the table. He looked at Quadrille and said: 'You'd better get him wired, Oscar.'

Angel quickly turned to the table and took off his jacket, tie and shirt.

Quadrille dug into his case, and pulled out the wire connecting the microphone, transmitter and batteries.

Angel noticed that Boodle's hand was still shaking as he reached out for his tea; he watched him as he meandered over to the window and looked out through the bars. Jubb faffed around, neatly rolling down the top of the sugar-bag and wiping the spoon on the piece of kitchen-roll on the tea tray. Quadrille busied himself cutting strips of pink sticky tape and fitting the wire across Angel's chest.

Angel was feeling quite chipper in himself. He had the occasional fluttering in the belly and, in quiet moments, heard his pulse drumming in his ears. The pressure was on him, but he felt tolerably calm about it all. His conscience was almost squared; as it was a matter of national security, he could live with betraying a crook like Yardley, for the security of the lives of British troops. All he had to do was agree any deal that would of necessity reveal where the gold was hidden and let Boodle do the rest. Put like that, he could live with it.

'There we are, Michael,' Quadrille said, pressing home the tape nearest the microphone head. 'I think that'll be fine.' He returned to the table and put on the headphones.

Angel pushed his fist into the shirt-sleeve. Boodle came over to him.

'Oh yes, now, Michael, if he discovers the wire, or it goes faulty or we can't hear you for any reason, we'll come in and pull you out ... for your own safety, you understand?'

Angel smiled to himself. He didn't understand anything of the sort, but he nodded and continued buttoning up the shirt.

Boodle sighed and looked at Quadrille.

'Is everything OK?'

'Yes.'

'Is Yardley ready, Mr Jubb?'

'He's in reception room fourteen, sir. Under guard. He's been searched. And he's ready and waiting, sir.'

'Good. Good. Ready when you are, Michael. There's no rush.'

Angel smiled to himself. There certainly was a rush. He pulled up his tie, and Jubb helped him on with his jacket. 'Thank you.'

'Follow me, sir.'

'When you get in there, speak up and stay close to him,' Boodle called.

Angel nodded.

'Good luck.'

Jubb rattled the keys and unlocked the door. He marched the ten yards down the corridor to reception room fourteen as if he was on the square at Aldershot. Angel walked quietly behind.

He unlocked the door, peered in, and bawled at the guard.

'Right, lad. Off you go.'

The guard came out and Angel went in. The door closed. There was a rattle of keys. There were just the two of them.

Yardley was sitting at the table smoking, just as Angel had seen him four days earlier.

Angel took the chair opposite.

Yardley looked up at him, and nodded slightly. He was the first to speak. He pointed to Angel's chest.

'Well, are you going to take it off?'

Angel felt his pulse race. He managed a smile.

'I'm not wired,' he lied. He went to undo his shirt buttons. 'Do you want to see?'

'Nah.'

Angel resumed even breathing again. He took in the thickness of those tattooed arms. He would rather have Yardley for a friend than an enemy. Lying to him wasn't as difficult as he had expected, but he wasn't anxious to get found out. He dug in his pocket and produced two packs of Player's full strength and put them on the table.

Yardley's eyebrows lifted slightly. Angel forced a smile.

'If you think these might compromise our relationship, I can always chuck them out of the window.'

Yardley smirked. 'That's better, Michael.' He reached out for them and stuffed them into the pocket of his jeans. 'I can see I'm getting you trained right.'

Angel thought everything was looking good. He went straight for it.

'I'm sure you'll be pleased, Morris, to know that I have the authority to agree a deal with you on the basis we discussed last Friday.'

'Oh?' Yardley sniffed. 'That's what you said last time, but you didn't, did you. You had to go snivelling back to Boodle for his say-so.'

'I didn't have the authority last time. And I didn't say I had,' Angel said, looking Yardley right in the eye. 'Today, I have that authority. But I'm not a pushover, Morris. I want top money for what I've got!'

'That's tough talk, Michael. You're in no position to bargain. I'm the one with the gold.'

Angel leaned back in the chair, forced a smile and ran his tongue round his mouth.

'When I leave here today, Morris, whatever the outcome, I'll be going home to my little bungalow. And tonight, I'll be sleeping in my little bed ... with my little wife. You'll be returning to your little cell, and tonight, you'll be cuddling up under a scratchy blanket with an old copy of The Sun and forty Player's full strength!'

Yardley pulled a sour face. His lips tightened. He scowled at Angel, then suddenly he smiled and said:

'Let's get down to business.'

Nothing would suit Angel more. He nodded.

'The deal is that you set me free with an irrevocable pardon from a high court judge, effective immediately and I take Boodle to the gold and give him half of it.'

'No,' Angel said bluntly.

Yardley's eyes flashed. 'What?' he snarled through tight lips.

Angel became aware of a frog inside his ribcage.

'You get your pardon on receipt of the gold,' he managed to say confidently. He even fooled himself.

There was a pause.

'All right,' Yardley said. 'And there'll be no guns, no arms, no wires, no bugs, no tracers, no telephones, no tricks, or it's off.'

'OK.'

Yardley leaned back in the chair, sniffed loudly and breathed out a long sigh.

Angel noticed the sudden change in him; he looked brighter and more relaxed.

'Right. Now there are some things I want,' Yardley said boldly. 'I've made a list in my head. I couldn't get any paper. Write it down; I want it just like this.'

Angel pulled out his leather-bound notebook and clicked his pen.

'Yes.'

'I want a three ton white van, filled with petrol and without any bloody tracing bleepers on it.'

'Yes,' Angel said, writing.

'I want fifty thousand pounds in unmarked used notes, twenties and tens.'

Angel frowned. 'That's a lot of money. I don't know about that.'

Yardley pulled a face. 'Take an extra gold bar out of my half. Each bar is worth about eighty-one thou. There are eight hundred and twenty. I take four hundred and nine. Boodle gets four hundred and eleven.'

'All right. Is that it?'

'Is it hell. I want a posh Savile Row suit, made to measure, dark grey or black, with a charcoal-grey stripe about every about half inch. I shall want to choose from a pattern book. And I want three white silk shirts with my initials, MY, embroidered in maroon on the pocket. A tie, maybe a paisley pattern. A pair of eighteen-carat gold cuff-links engraved with my initials, a pair of broad-fitting black all-leather Gucci shoes size nine, a pair of silk pyjamas, leather slippers, and a dressing-gown, all to fit me … not a bloody dwarf! And I want a proper light-fawn trench-coat, and a pair of black leather driving-gloves. Have you got that? And you can put that lot in a nice real leather suitcase.'

Angel was writing as fast as he could. He shook his head. 'Anything else?'

'Yeah. Two hundred Capstan full strength and a bottle of Imperial gin.'

'Is that it?'

'No. But it'll start me off. The rest I can get on the road.' Yardley took a satisfied drag from the cigarette. 'Yes, there is something else. My ruddy pardon!'

Angel looked at the list, added the last bit, crossed a few 't's and shook his head.

'It's a fair list.'

'It's peanuts! Now, when you've got that lot together — I reckon it'll take you about a week — put it in the van and bring it here. I'll check it over. If it's OK, I will drive Boodle straight to the gold, take my half, less one bar, and drive off.'

'Is that it?'

Yardley blew out a long sigh. 'I think so,' he said. And then, after a few seconds, very positively, he said: 'Yes.'

'All right,' Angel said quietly. 'You're on.'

Yardley beamed, stretched out his arms, stood up, then punched the air with a fist and yelled: 'Geronimo!'

Angel sat there, watched him, felt a little sad and felt fifty frogs jigging around his stomach.

*

Angel walked sadly up the corridor, followed by Jubb. Boodle was waiting in the doorway of reception room 11, wearing a smile wider than the M25. As Angel reached the door, the commander took hold of his right hand, squeezed it and pulled him into the room.

'Well done, Michael,' he said in an excited whisper. 'Well done. I couldn't have done it better myself.'

Quadrille whipped off the headphones and dashed across from his box of tricks. He shook his hand warmly.

'That was great, Michael.'

Jubb followed Angel into the room and locked the door.

'Congratulations are in order, I see, sir,' he beamed.

Angel didn't say anything. He smiled weakly. There was a distinct buzz in the air. It was electric. His pulse rate must have been over a hundred. He loosened his tie and began undoing his shirt-buttons.

'Let's get that wire off, Michael,' Quadrille said eagerly, putting Angel's hands on his collar from behind to assist him to remove the jacket.

Boodle moved across to the window. He clasped his hands behind his back, and strode quickly up and down the room, his head bent forward.

'Oscar, I want you to get a copy of that tape off to Doctor Dubrovski. Yes. Today. She's one of the top psychologists in the country, Michael. She'll be able to tell us what Yardley is thinking today, what he thought last year and what he'll be thinking tomorrow. She's so damned smart! She doesn't only work on what people say, but what they don't say, and their choice of words, their vocabulary, the priority and structure of their sentences, the emphasis, intonation, the length of pauses between phrases, and between question and answer. She'll read him like a book. Fantastic, isn't it?'

Angel said, 'Yes,' but he thought no.

He peeled off the wire and handed it to Quadrille.

'Dubrovski will need his personal and career details, Oscar. She'll want a transcript of the trial, details of his behaviour and conduct while in custody and the police psychologist's report at the time of his conviction. Got that?'

'Yes, Perry.'

Boodle went on, 'And Oscar, I want a twenty-four-hour surveillance put on Enchantra Davison. I want to know every move she makes out of that flat, on foot or in a car. I want to know about every phone call — both in and out, every letter vetted and x-rayed, and I want a personal verbal report direct to me. Put Willy Simcox on to it. And I want that twice daily until we've got the gold and Yardley's safely back in a cage. Got that?'

'Right.'

'I don't want any surprises.'

'No, Perry.'

'And Oscar, contact CPS and get them to dummy up some release papers, a pardon. Make it look good. And get them to spell his name right, for God's sake.'

CHAPTER TEN

Angel was glad to get back to Bromersley, into his own office, doing his own thing. The next two days were spent trying to get back to grips with the murder that had been at the forefront of his mind before Boodle had appeared and this mad hunt for gold had started. He made further enquiries into the possible reason why fibres of sisal and the smell of menthol should have been found in Leitch's office, but no positive progress was made. It was later that week, on Friday afternoon, when Gawber knocked on Angel's door. 'Come in.'

Gawber closed the door.

'Don't know if you've heard the news, sir. The four executive directors at Imperial have just announced their intention to resign as soon as replacements for their jobs could be found. It was on the radio.'

'They would be those four little old men Fleming, Menzies, Reid and Finlay. They did tell me they were retiring. I'm not really surprised, considering their ages. I would have gone years ago, wouldn't you? They must be rolling in it.'

'Something else, sir.'

'What's that?'

'About menthol.'

'Ay?'

'I looked it up, sir. It's from a Japanese flower. It's sometimes called peppermint camphor. It has a strong, minty, cooling smell. Used in flavourings, cigarettes and cosmetics.'

'I know all that,' Angel said impatiently. 'It's used in cough-sweets and to dab on your hanky for a cold. You can get it in crystals from the chemists to put with boiling water to inhale. Old man Finlay reeks of it.'

Gawber looked glum. 'Oh.'

Angel threw down his pen.

'What I don't get is why Leitch's office smells of it. They don't use it in the process of making gin! It's a smell that's out of context. It was there the morning after the murder. Leitch can't offer any explanation. He says that that smell has not been in his office before. There has to be some explanation.'

The phone rang. He reached out for the handset. 'Angel.'

It was Dr Mac. 'Michael. Those fibres you sent across to me from one of the suspects, Finlay's slippers.'

'Ay —'

'Well they're not the same. It's sisal all right, but it's been bleached. The fibres we found in the ageing room were not bleached.'

'Oh. Thanks, Mac. Goodbye.'

He replaced the handset and turned to Gawber. He told him the result of the doctor's tests.

'That rules Finlay out then, sir.'

'I'm not surprised. He wouldn't have had the physical strength, and he hasn't any known motive. Hmm. If we were to believe the facts, we'd be looking for the world's strongest man, who has a use for sisal, hides keys and has a menthol fetish.'

The phone rang. He reached out for it.

'Angel.'

It was the super. 'The commander's just been on the phone. I have arranged for him to brief his lads here on Monday at — nine hundred hours. He wants you and Gawber there, and he wants the services of you both for the operation on Tuesday.'

The corners of Angel's mouth turned down.

'Right, sir.'

'Tell Gawber to get his suit pressed and his hair cut, and you could do with bit of smartening up, yourself.'

*

The weekend came and the papers were full of the news of the resignations of the four men from Imperial Gin plc. It was forecast by the financial tipsters that when the stockmarket opened on Monday morning, the share price would be marked down by between 30% and 50%. There were old photographs of the retiring directors, many column-inches devoted to the long careers of each of them, the perceived state of the company and the young blood that might replace them; predictably, one of the candidates coming to the fore was Angus Leitch.

Angel read all about it but spent most of the weekend gardening with Mary. On Monday morning, he gave his shoes an extra shine, grabbed a clean handkerchief from the drawer and was bright and early out of the house. At 8.28 a.m, he drove into the police carpark. His usual parking spot was occupied by an unfamiliar red sports car. He growled and angrily banged the steering wheel. The area was bursting with cars, mostly unknown to him, and mostly unmarked. He looked round for an alternative space, eventually found a tight spot by the gate and reversed into it. He locked the car door, crossed the Tarmac, tapped the code in the rear-door lock of the station and went inside. When he reached the main corridor, he found it awash with bronzed, slim young men talking animatedly as they sauntered down from reception in groups of twos and threes. They were mostly dressed in dark suits and white shirts; some jackets bulged where they concealed handgun holsters. Cadet Ahmed Ahaz was shepherding the visitors between the large washroom, the coffee machine in the locker room and the CID briefing room, whilst deftly steering them round the backside of the plumber and the plastic pipe trailing out of the gents' loo.

Angel overtook some of them and made his way directly to the briefing room, past the notice on the door that read: OPERATION MIDAS 0900 hrs. He nodded to Ron Gawber, who was standing on his own by the door, drinking coffee. The sergeant responded with a wry smile.

To one side of the room were two chairs and a table in front of them; Oscar Quadrille was standing over the table, sorting A4 printed sheets into cream-coloured folders.

'Ah. Morning, Michael.' he said over the hubbub.

'Everything all right?'

'I think I've got everything.' He pushed a cream folder into Angel's hand. 'That's yours.' He placed the other two neatly into positions on the table in front of the chairs.

Angel glanced at the file cover and frowned.

'What's this? It's your party. I won't want this, will I?'

'The commander wants you along.'

Angel grunted. 'Oh?' He opened the folder, looked at the first page, then closed it. 'What for?'

'In case it's sticky with Yardley ... when he takes over the van.'

Angel's eyebrows shot up.

'Oh?' He pulled a face. That meant a trip up to Welham again.

Quadrille smiled and nodded.

'It'll be all right, I expect. He's worried about it, but then, he always is.'

Angel shrugged, forced a smile and dropped the folder on to the end of the table. His inside felt as if he had swallowed a pair of frogs who were intent on making enough tadpoles to fill every jamjar in the UK.

An outburst of noise caught his attention as more Special Branch men congregated at the far end of the room, holding plastic cups of coffee, talking noisily and occasionally laughing far too loudly — Angel thought — to reflect genuine light-heartedness. Something was happening by the door. He turned.

The commander and the super had arrived. Boodle looked very smart in a navy-blue blazer and light-grey trousers; the super looked his usual dour self in an ill-fitting dark suit.

The chattering declined. Some of the men found chairs and settled into them; others leaned against the tables and walls.

Boodle nodded to Angel then looked at Quadrille.

'Shall I sit here, Oscar?'

'There, sir,' said Quadrille pointing to a chair behind the table. 'And Super, will you sit here?'

The super flopped into the other chair like a sack of potatoes and began grinding his teeth.

Boodle opened the cream folder, glanced at a few pages and then closed it. He looked at his watch, then up at Quadrille.

'Is everybody here?'

The room fell silent. Quadrille did a quick count of heads.

'Twenty-eight. Yes sir.'

Angel stood at the front next to Quadrille with his back to a blackboard upon which were pinned blown-up photographs of Morris Yardley.

Boodle rose to his feet and, with a hand in his blazer pocket, cleared his throat. 'Ah, now,' he said. 'Good morning, gentlemen. Let me first introduce Superintendent Harker, DI Michael Angel, and DS Ron Gawber, who are our hosts, and we are grateful for their assistance in this operation.'

'A pleasure,' the superintendent lied. He tried to smile, but he looked as if the smell from the gents loo had wafted in from the corridor.

Boodle continued: 'Now, what this jaunt is about — is the retrieval of sixty-six millions pounds' worth of gold, that's eight hundred and twenty gold bars, stolen from the Bank of Agara two years ago. The ringleader of the gang is Morris Yardley, who is at present serving twenty years in Welham prison for robbery and manslaughter. He is the only person alive, to our knowledge, who knows the whereabouts of the gold. And the gold has to be returned to the King of Agara damned quick to secure the continuation of flying rights over the Mitsoshopi desert for the RAF, which is absolutely vital at this time. As you know, things are very dicey out there at the moment. Now Yardley thinks that for the return of half of his haul of gold, thirty-three million quid's worth, the judiciary will release him and cancel the rest of his sentence.'

The commander paused. Most of the men tittered, some guffawed loudly; Angel looked up in surprise. Boodle smiled appreciatively and carried on:

'In actual fact, we are going to recover all eight hundred and twenty gold bars and return him to his cell in Welham prison by tomorrow night.'

There were mutters of approval. Angel's eyebrows rose.

Boodle continued: 'Now part of the terms of the deal with Yardley is for us to supply a van, fifty thousand pounds in cash and certain specified items of clothing and personal effects in a suitcase. Oscar Quadrille has organized a tracer in the heel of a shoe, which is in the suitcase, and a radio beacon, which is in the suitcase handle. I doubt if Yardley will take — or have — the opportunity to wear the shoes before his recapture; anyway he'll surely not in any circumstances discard the case, as I am judging that he will want something in which to carry the money, his expensive custom-made clothes and his other personal items. Should either signal fail, then there's the backup of the other. Also, there will be six of you with Kalashnikovs in the chopper, code-named for this operation, 'Flying Doctor', which, I am told, has just come back from refit, and now has even better heat-seeking rays, powerful enough to find a flea in a bride's nightie.'

There were several sniggers from the attentive audience. Boodle beamed appreciatively.

'And there are four ARV teams, here, code named Doctor 1, Doctor 2, Doctor 3 and Doctor 4. You all know who you are. Oscar will give each driver and the pilot the map references of your starting positions in North Yorkshire, at the end of this briefing. You are to make your own way there, and not in convoy. We want an absolute minimum profile. And note, all of you, you need to be in your positions by nine forty-five hours tomorrow. Now the van is ready at a local rental depot for collection, and Ron Gawber will drive it with the suitcase and contents aboard, up to Welham prison tomorrow morning, to arrive at nine forty-five hours. He will then join the control car as driver. I will be travelling up there with Oscar and Michael Angel. Michael and I will meet Yardley, surrender the van, the money, the clothes, including the shoes, and the suitcase, and his release papers.'

There were more sniggers and guffaws. Angel shook his head slightly.

'Assuming all is satisfactory,' Boodle went on, 'Michael will then rejoin the control car, and Yardley and I will leave the prison together in the van. Now, I expect that to be about ten hundred hours. Yardley has undertaken to drive the van straight to the hiding-place of the gold. Now you must all keep your heads down. There will be no marked police cars in the area; North Yorkshire police have agreed to keep out of sight until thirteen hundred hours. I don't want Yardley nervous. All right? Now this is very important. Once the van has left the prison, no approach is to be made to it under any circumstances, not until I have actually seen the gold and phoned Oscar on his mobile. Has everybody got that?'

There was lots of nodding and a few mutters of: 'Yes, sir.'

Boodle stopped and looked across at the men as if he wanted to expand on it, but he didn't. There was a short pause.

'I will have to make the call via the nearest line I can get to, because Yardley may ask to search me at the prison, and Michael has agreed that I shall not have a phone or a wire on my person. Through Oscar, I will advise the location and he will instruct Flying Doctor, and Doctors One, Two, Three and Four where to rendezvous to collect the gold and rearrest Yardley. I will then make ad hoc arrangements to return him to Welham Prison, and ship the gold back to the Bank of Agara. Any questions?'

'Yes sir,' a voice from the back spoke up. 'Do we know if Yardley has any contacts outside the prison with any members of the gang or anybody else who might support him in the event of an escape attempt?'

'Good point,' Boodle replied. 'Of course, we have checked, and he has received no letters at all since he went to prison, and he hasn't sent any. The only visits … '

A voice from the back muttered something. Angel didn't quite catch it. The commander's eyebrows shot up. He had heard it.

'Very well,' Boodle said, 'He could have smuggled a letter out, Alan, but we have no knowledge of it. And, as far as we know, the only member of the gang that robbed the Bank of Agara who is still living, is safely in prison in Hallas End. OK?'

'Yes sir.'

'I was saying, the only visitor he has had during the time of his imprisonment has been his long time girlfriend, an Enchantra Davison. And she has been under close surveillance for the past six days and nights, by members of the team, and there is nothing untoward to report. As a matter of fact, I had a phone call just before I came in here, and Willy Simcox reported that she was in bed in her flat as safe as houses. And her car, which during the early hours of this morning was disabled by Willy personally, without her knowledge, stands parked up in his team's vision, under her flat window. She's not going anywhere. Anybody anything else?'

Another voice from the back called out.

'Yes sir. What is there to stop Yardley, once you get out of the prison gates, ditching you and the van and effecting his escape?'

'Nothing,' replied Boodle. 'But I think he would have a devil of a job surviving and staying out of our clutches when we have a chopper and four ARVs and a control car already in position, observing him. Also, if he takes the fifty thousand pounds, and I would be amazed if he didn't, as he would certainly need it, all we have to do is follow the signal from the suitcase. OK?'

'Yes sir.'

'Anything else?'

Some shook their heads, others fidgeted with their coffee-cups.

'No? Right. Now, Oscar has arranged for accommodation for everybody. You have the rest of the day to sort yourselves out. Check over your weapons, and your vehicles. Make yourselves familiar with the map round HMP Welham and North Yorkshire. Take it steady this evening. Give the local talent a miss. Get a good night's kip, and the next time I see you, we will be knee-deep in gold bars.'

Some of the men cheered quietly. Boodle turned to Quadrille.

'Have I missed anything, Oscar?'

'Don't think so, sir,' Oscar replied with a big grin.

Angel looked on, and said nothing.

*

It was 0935 hours the following day, Tuesday, 19 April, when Oscar Quadrille drove the Mercedes on to the carpark opposite Welham prison gates. His two passengers, Boodle and Angel, got out into the bright spring sunshine and strode purposefully on to the Tarmac, and across the cobbled street to the prison gate, where they were promptly admitted and directed through the archway to the quadrangle in the prisoners' recreation area. They looked up at the six rows of poky windows overlooking all sides of the square as they made their way along to the new, white, three-ton Transit van parked in the middle. Ron Gawber climbed out of the cab to greet them. Angel nodded to him.

'Everything all right, Ron?'

'Yes sir.'

'Suitcase in the back?' Boodle asked.

'Yes sir.'

Boodle looked at the van and then at Angel.

'I don't think we need him here any more, Michael.'

Angel agreed. 'Thanks, Ron. DI Quadrille is on the car-park opposite the main gate in a black Mercedes.'

'Right, sir,' Gawber said and walked briskly off to the archway.

'Better lay out the spoils,' said Boodle.

Angel opened the rear van door. Inside was a light-brown leather suitcase with a broad leather strap round the middle. He reached in, dragged it to the rear of the van and began to unfasten it.

Suddenly, there was the clang of iron on iron. It came from the main cell-block entrance: a warder had pushed open the gate. Into the quadrangle bounced a big, smiling, Morris Yardley in a baseball cap, blue shirt, jeans and trainers, carrying two bulging Tesco plastic shopping bags. He held up a hand with one of the bags in it to shield his eyes from the bright sun as he looked up and round at the cell windows.

Unexpectedly, the sound of voices, at first a few, and then quickly many more, echoed round the quadrangle. The prisoners were cheering; the cheering was augmented with the clatter of metal hitting metal, as cutlery and shoes were being banged enthusiastically against iron bars.

Angel and Boodle looked up at the rows of small, barred windows. It was the same scene on all four sides. Faces appeared and clothes and objects were being waved. The rumpus increased, like a crowd at Wembley.

Yardley grinned and waved the plastic bags enthusiastically as he approached the waiting van.

Senior Officer Jubb was not pleased; his lips tightened and his jaw set firm as a rock as soon as he heard the uproar begin.

He barely glanced at the windows as he strode out across the Tarmac; he was familiar with the changing mood of the prisoners and this boisterous outburst was potentially dangerous.

He could have anticipated that the news of Yardley's release would have spread through the prison, but this reaction was unexpected. Most of the inmates seemed to be happy for him; they must have thought how cleverly he had negotiated his freedom and made clowns out of the judiciary. As the two men came further into view the volume increased and amid the cheering, cries of: 'Scab', 'Boo' and worse, could also be distinguished. A few hard nuts would be envious and enraged at how a comparative new boy had worked his ticket after only twelve months of a twenty-year stretch. Jubb knew that the outward show of solidarity was the formula for a riot, a fire, the taking of a hostage or an escape attempt, and he and his officers would have to be very careful through the next twenty-four hours or so.

Yardley arrived at the van. He smiled, nodded at it favourably and turned to the cell windows, seeking their endorsement. By the racket, it seemed that the majority wholeheartedly approved. He looked at Boodle and Angel, then back at the van and sniffed. 'Yeah.'

Jubb wrinkled his nose.

'Morning gentlemen.'

'Morning, Mr Jubb.'

Boodle nodded. 'Has he been searched?'

Jubb nodded, 'Thoroughly, sir. I did it myself.'

'What's in the bags?'

'His own clothes, sir. Nothing else.'

'Have you been through them?'

'Oh yes, sir. Most rigorously.'

Angel was the first to speak to Yardley. He nodded towards the van.

'Now then, Morris, does this fill the bill?' he asked.

'Yes,' said Yardley. He dumped the bulging Tesco bags in the back next to the suitcase.

The barracking suddenly eased and then stopped. There were still many interested faces peering through the windows, but they watched in silence.

'Well, let's have everything checked off and get on our way, shall we?' Boodle said.

'Can't be too soon for me. Is everything like what I said?'

'Yes.'

'Where's the money?'

Angel opened up the suitcase. In bank wrappers was the £50,000 in twenties and tens just as Yardley had requested.

Yardley pulled out a wrapper of tenners and zipped through it like a pack of cards. He nodded approvingly.

'Yeah. Yeah. Great.'

Boodle and Angel exchanged glances.

'Is everything there?'

'Yes,' Boodle replied. 'I've checked it. Everything is there. Eighteen-carat gold cuff-links with your initials on. Gucci shoes. Cigarettes. Everything.'

Yardley scrambled further down the case. He pulled things out and then pushed them back in again, like a child going through a stocking on Christmas morning.

'Has Yardley been discharged, Mr Jubb?' asked Boodle.

'Yes sir. All the formalities have been dealt with. He's free to go at any time. The van will be given a superficial search at the gate, and you will need to show his release papers,' he said with the slightest knowing blink of the eye. 'That's all.'

Boodle nodded and turned to Yardley, 'Well, are you satisfied?'

Yardley looked from one to the other and then back to Boodle. 'No,' he said coldly. 'No. I'm not bloody satisfied.'

The response surprised everybody. This wasn't the time for anything to go wrong. Angel and Jubb stared at him.

The fingers on Boodle's left hand shook. He plunged it instantly into his blazer pocket presumably to hide it.

'No?' Boodle enquired, licking his lips.

Yardley advanced slowly on him.

'How do I know that when we get to the gold, you won't pull a shooter on me and call in your troops before I can get my share?' he said.

Boodle didn't reply. With a face like thunder, and his jaw set firm, he stared into Yardley's deep-blue watery eyes, took off his jacket and threw it at him. Then he put his hands in his trouser pockets, withdrew the contents, keys, coins and a handkerchief, slapped them on the van floor, pulled out the pocket-linings and left them hanging out.

There was uproar from the cell windows, there were more yells of approval and encouragement, more clattering on the bars, and on this occasion, there were no sounds of disapproval at all.

Jubb shuffled uneasily.

Yardley didn't seem to hear the racket. He patted the coat lightly.

'I suppose you're wired,' he said.

Boodle's red face went redder. He reached up to his shirt, unfastened the front buttons and yanked it open. He held the shirt in position.

'Satisfied?' he asked.

The barracking grew louder.

The corners of Yardley's mouth turned up slightly. He didn't say anything. He was enjoying the moment.

Jubb's eyes flashed. He stepped forward.

'Come along, lad. That's quite enough.'

Yardley licked his lips, nodded and tossed the jacket back to Boodle who caught it, glared at him, and held it under his arm as he fastened the shirt-buttons.

'Where's my pardon?' said Yardley.

'In my pocket,' Boodle snapped, his eyes glowing like red hot cinders. 'You'll get that when we get the gold. Not before.'

Angel wanted to take the heat away from Boodle. He pointed towards the driver's door.

'Have a look in the cab, Morris.' he said.

Yardley hesitated, then followed him round the side of the van. His face turned grim again.

'I suppose it's fitted with a bleeper.'

'No it isn't,' Boodle called from the back of the van. 'There are no bleepers,' he lied convincingly.

Yardley didn't reply. He jumped in the driver's seat and began to look over the controls.

The racket from the cells died down when Yardley was out of view.

Jubb sighed quietly as he closed and fastened the van doors.

Boodle came up to the cab and stood next to Angel. His hands were shaking as he struggled to fasten the jacket-buttons.

Yardley pushed the gear stick into different positions, depressed the clutch pedal, pulled the steering wheel a little in both directions, bounced up and down on the seat several times and adjusted the driving-mirror.

Angel watched him and licked his lips.

After a few moments, Yardley said: 'OK.' He grinned. 'OK. OK. I'm ready. Let's roll.'

Those were the words Boodle had been waiting to hear.

Angel sighed silently.

CHAPTER ELEVEN

Angel ran out through the prison gates, across the cobbled street to the carpark where Quadrille and Gawber were waiting in the Mercedes. He jumped into the back seat.

Quadrille looked up from the illuminated screen resting on his knees.

'Everything go all right, Michael?' he asked urgently.

'Yeah,' Angel said breathing heavily. 'They'll be coming out of the gate any second.'

Quadrille nodded and adjusted the microphone fitted under his chin.

'Signals coming through all right?' Angel asked.

'Like a dream,' Quadrille said, his eyes shining.

'The chopper and the ARVs all set?'

'The chopper's hovering ten miles due south, and the ARVs are located approximately one mile away at the four compass points.'

Angel nodded. He leaned forward and tapped Gawber on the shoulder.

'Are you all right, Ron? Can you handle this bus?'

Gawber looked back and grinned. He was pleased to have the opportunity of driving the luxury car.

Angel pushed back into the well-cushioned upholstery. 'Looks like I'm surplus to requirements.'

Quadrille pulled out a large book of maps open at a page.

'I hope you are good at map-reading, Michael,' he said with a smile.

Angel grunted and took the book. Quadrille pointed to a place.

'We are here,' he said.

'Yes. Right,' Angel said and stuck his head into it.

A mobile phone rang.

It was Quadrille's. He quickly pulled it out of his pocket and pressed the button.

'Yes? ... Thank you Mr Jubb.' He shoved the phone back into his pocket. 'They're coming out now.' He looked at his screen. 'Hmm. Yes. I can see it's moving. Both signals working.' He spoke into the microphone: 'Stand by. All doctors stand by. The ambulance is on the move.'

Angel, Gawber and Quadrille stared through the parked cars across the road at the front of the prison. Seconds later, the big steel-clad doors opened inwards and the white van eased forward. They could just make out the big face of Yardley at the wheel and the smaller head of Boodle in the passenger seat.

Gawber's hand went up to the Mercedes' ignition key.

'Not yet Ron,' Angel said. 'Give them a good minute's start.'

'Right, sir.'

The white van pulled forward and then turned left out of the gate.

Quadrille gripped the edges of his screen and spoke into a mike.

'Ambulance is leaving the hospital now. Turned northwards towards the castle. I've just had an eyeball of patient and surgeon. Everything looks OK.'

The three men watched the white van filter into the traffic, behind a lorry and in front of a cream-coloured coach.

Cars closed in as the van progressed along the busy road. It was intermittently in view, and then, ten seconds later, it went round a bend in the road out of sight.

Both Angel and Quadrille sighed.

They waited.

Gawber drew his teeth over his lower lip and looked back over his shoulder.

'Now, sir?

Quadrille said: 'Yes.'

Gawber turned the key in the ignition. The powerful engine purred into life. He nervously let in the clutch and pointed the car in the direction the van had taken.

'He's going on Neville Road,' Quadrille said.

'It's a one-way street,' Angel added.

After a minute, Gawber found himself boxed in with traffic and only moving forward in spurts. He brought the Mercedes to a stop again.

Quadrille and Angel looked up. Gawber sensed they were watching him.

'Can't get through,' he said agitatedly.

'That's all right,' Angel said. 'Let him move on a bit. Keep straight on.'

'Stay in the left lane,' Quadrille added.

Four minutes later and the van had left the busy town traffic and was out in the countryside.

Quadrille spoke suddenly.

'Ah! He's turned left again. Down a small road. It's not numbered on my map. It's smaller than a B road. It's slowed him down.'

'I've got it,' Angel said. 'Leads to a hamlet called Dalling Fields.'

'He's stopped.'

'Are you sure?'

'Yes.'

Angel touched Gawber on the shoulder.

'Pull up, Ron. We'll wait.'

Quadrille switched on the mike.

'Control to all doctors. Ambulance has stopped at map reference H for hotel, 8. Keep back. Don't overrun your positions. Out.' He switched off the mike.

'What's up?' Angel said. 'Hope the van's OK. Could have had a puncture.'

'It's a new van.'

'He might have got lost.'

'Maybe the gold's down there.'

'In the middle of nowhere?'

Angel looked out of the window at the passing traffic. He pressed a button and the window slid down. It was a beautiful day for snoozing on a beach. He looked at his watch. There was nothing to be done. Even if Yardley and Boodle had reached the gold, they were still under orders to sit tight.

Five minutes passed, then Quadrille suddenly spoke. 'They're off again. They must have turned round. They're coming back this way, eastwards. Must have taken a wrong turning … now he's turned left, on to the ring road.'

'There's a big roundabout there,' Angel said. Quadrille switched on the mike.

'Calling all doctors. Ambulance is on the move again and is two miles north of Welham moving in a westerly direction. Doctor 4, make your way ahead of it, doctors 1 and 3 you'll have to come north, then west. Doctor 2, it should be passing you soon. Keep your head down.'

A voice through the car speaker said: 'Doctor 4 here, Roger Control.' Another voice said, 'Doctor 2 calling Control. Ambulance has just gone past. I estimate it was doing sixty miles an hour.'

Quadrille said, 'Roger doctor 2. Follow on, after a minute.'

'Roger, Control.'

'He's on the A1 travelling south. Out,' Quadrille said and switched off the mike.

Angel was pleased the entourage was travelling in the general direction of Bromersley, although it made him wonder where the end of the trail might be. There was seemingly no requirement for map-reading, so he pushed back into the upholstery and looked out of the window, checking off the road signs and mileages for Quadrille who was tracking the van on the computer screen.

Gawber drove the car smoothly down the motorway. Ahead, the van was travelling a regular course at speeds varying between sixty and seventy miles an hour. It was not easy to hold back the powerful car to avoid visual contact. The Mercedes could easily have eaten up the mile between them in seconds.

Quadrille concentrated on the flashing yellow dot on the screen, anxious for them not to overrun. He maintained contact with the chopper and the ARVs, to inform them to adjust their formation, and he occasionally called out to Gawber to hold back. Doctor 2 was ahead of the van by about two miles, and doctors 3 and 4 were spaced at one-mile intervals behind the Mercedes. The chopper, flying doctor, was down in a field near Doncaster, ticking over. They had been travelling in a straight line due south for more than an hour, when Quadrille's screen indicated that the van had peeled off the A1, and was travelling westwards.

'He's turned right! That's towards Bromersley.'

Angel raised his eyebrows.

Quadrille responded promptly; he had quickly to change the direction and formation of the team, and for the succeeding few minutes he was busy on the RT.

Gawber steered the car on to the slip road, turned under the motorway and on to the road to Bromersley.

'We're gaining on him, Ron. Drop down to twenty,' Quadrille said. Gawber nodded.

Angel watched bemused as they glided through the hamlets and villages familiar to him. They reached Bromersley and were slowed down by the traffic in the town centre. The trail led them on to the main Manchester Road towards Slogmarrow. They were soon out of the town and travelling through the countryside, where there was very little traffic and they gathered up speed again. They reached the unfenced moorland; the gorse bushes at the side of the road were beginning to show their yellow blossom. The van had slowed as it had started its climb up the Pennines. After a few minutes, Quadrille gave a heavy sigh and turned to Angel. 'Where is he going to, Michael?' he asked. 'This is your stomping ground, isn't it?'

Angel shook his head. 'Dunno,' he replied. Where had Yardley hidden the gold? Manchester? Slogmarrow? The distillery?

'He's coming to a place called Tunistone. Do you know it?'

'Pretty well,' Angel said. 'A small market town.'

'He's not turning into it. He's going straight past.'

They drove slowly for another mile or so, then Quadrille suddenly yelled:

'I've lost him! I've lost him!'

'What?'

'He's gone off the road! He must be going up a hillside!' Gawber slammed his feet on the brakes.

Angel reached for the map.

'Where? Where?' he yelled.

Quadrille pointed to it on his screen.

'There isn't a road there. Look! He must be driving through a field or into a cave or something. He's stopped dead! I think. Yes, he's stopped.'

Angel looked up from the map, realization on his face.

'I know where he's gone. He's gone up the lane to Mrs Buller-Price's farm!'

Quadrille stared at him. 'What's that? What do we do now?'

Angel licked his lips. He spotted a lay-by, a hundred yards ahead, where the road, which was cut into a mountain, widened.

'Pull in there, Ron.'

Gawber let in the clutch, drove the Mercedes into a parking area marked off for three cars, and switched off the engine. Everything suddenly became quiet except for the wind whistling through the radio aerial.

Angel's thoughts were everywhere as he looked out of the window at the steep drop below. Why would Yardley drive up there? Was the gold at the farmhouse? Boodle would be cock-a-hoop! This was some coincidence! He hoped Mrs Buller-Price was safe.

Quadrille switched on the mike.

'Control to all doctors. The ambulance has stopped at a farmhouse, map reference Victor 2. We are five hundred yards away from it on the highway. Flying doctor and doctors 1, 3 and 4 hold your positions. Doctor 2, overtake us, and proceed west on Manchester Road and take up a position at Victor 1. Control out.'

A mobile phone rang. It was Quadrille's. His jaw dropped. He dived into his pocket.

'It's the Commander.'

The two men looked at each other.

Angel's chest throbbed.

Quadrille put the phone to his ear and pressed the button.

'Yes, sir? ... Yes ... What! ... ' Angel could hear a voice speaking rapidly, but he couldn't make out what it was saying. Quadrille's face went white. Then he said: 'At a farmhouse, ten miles west-north-west of Bromersley ... Yes ... Straightaway ... 'Bye.'

Angel could see that something was very wrong.

'What's up?'

Quadrille cancelled the phone. 'Just a tick.' He switched on the mike and said: 'Control to flying doctor. Urgent. Go to a field at the south side of Friske police station in H for hotel 2 and pick up the surgeon and taxi him to control. We're in a parking bay on the road at V for victor 2. Out.'

'Roger, control.'

Quadrille switched off the mike and quickly turned to Angel.

'Yardley tricked him. He stopped the van. He said he needed to go in the bushes for a pee. He was gone a long time. The commander became suspicious and left the van

135

to look for him. He couldn't find him. When he got back Yardley had taken the van and left him stranded in the back of beyond. The commander couldn't phone before now. He's had to walk miles to a phone.'

Angel shook his head. It was hard to take in.

Quadrille added, 'He was mightily relieved when I told him that we were still with Yardley.'

'Where is he now?'

'Friske police station. Not far from Welham. That's where I've sent the chopper. He's joining us. It doesn't take long. He'll be here soon.'

Angel sighed and rubbed his chin. 'Is there any tea?'

*

The distant buzz of an engine, combined with the clackety racket of helicopter blades, drowned the gentle wail of the wind. The volume increased deafeningly as the ugly, yellow metal lobster bounded down from nowhere, skimmed the roof of the Mercedes and rested briefly with one rail on the tarmac and the other unsupported over the ravine. It hovered there precariously for five seconds then ascended rapidly and flew away in a cloud of dust and blue fumes, leaving behind a small man, holding the collar of his blazer over one ear, his hair flapping round in all directions. Boodle dashed up to the Mercedes, got in the front seat and closed the door. His face was white and his eyes flitted twitchily between the two men in the back seat behind him.

'Where is Yardley then?' Boodle said brusquely, running his hands through his hair to flatten it.

'He's up there. Up an unmarked road, sir,' Quadrille replied,

'Thank God. Is there a way out?'

Quadrille looked at Angel.

'Not by road.'

'Are the tracking devices working?'

'Perfectly.'

'Thank God.' Boodle sighed heavily. He pulled out a handkerchief and wiped his eyes and mouth. 'Yardley thinks he's smart. Huh! As if we could be shaken off as easily as that!'

'Michael knows the woman who lives up there,' said Quadrille.

Boodle brightened. 'Is she known? Has she a record?'

'No,' Angel replied decisively. 'There's nothing known. She's a widow, runs a small farm — on her own — as far as I know. Very respectable.'

'How does she fit in with Yardley then?'

'Don't know.'

'How old is she?'

'Dunno. Seventy-five, or eighty or more.'

'Mmm. What's her name?'

'Buller-Price.'

A mobile phone rang out. Angel recognized the ring. He pulled a face and dived into his pocket.

'I told them not to ring me unless it was urgent.' He looked at the LCD window and pressed the button. 'One of my sergeants.' He put the phone to his ear. 'Yes, Crisp. What is it, lad,' he said irritably. 'Have you nowt to do? I'm up to my eyes in it … Who? … Mrs Buller-Price?' he bawled.

He exchanged glances with Boodle and Quadrille.

'What does she want? … Hmm. Yes? … Have you got her number, lad? … Right, got it. Thank you.'

Angel's jaw dropped. He stabbed some numbers into the mobile and looked across at Boodle. 'You are not going to believe this. She has just phoned the station to ask to speak to me. She wants to see me urgently. Something about the security of the country.'

In unison, Boodle and Quadrille said: 'What?' There was a click through the earpiece.

'Mrs Buller-Price? Inspector Angel here,' he said excessively gently.

'Oh! Thank goodness, Inspector. Oh,' she puffed, sounding immensely relieved. 'Oh thank you for phoning. Oh dear! What a day I've had!'

Angela eyes focused straight ahead; his heart pounded away.

'What is it? Are you all right?'

'A space rocket,' she began, 'like the one that crashed here last week has just passed overhead. I think the invasion has started. I was in the bathroom looking through my telescope. I think it landed and something got out.'

Boodle gesticulated wildly for an explanation.

'Just a moment, Mrs Buller-Price. Hold on, please. Just need to … er … close the door.'

He covered the mobile with one hand.

'What's happening?' Boodle said frantically waving his hands in the air. 'What's Yardley up to? Is the van there?'

'I'm trying to find out,' Angel said. He returned to the phone. 'Hello there. Sorry about that, Mrs Buller-Price. Now I don't think it's anything to worry about. Are you all right? Are you there on your own?'

'Oh no, Inspector, no,' she replied firmly.

He squeezed the mobile. 'Oh? And who's there with you?' Boodle stared at him intensely.

'Oh, I'm surrounded by … er … friends.'

'Oh good,' Angel replied. 'Anybody I know?'

'Why yes. There's one here you know very well.'

'Oh yes? Who's that?'

'Schwarzenegger.'

' Schwarznegger?'

'You remember him, don't you?'

'Oh yes.'

Boodle's eyes shone like searchlights. 'Who the hell is Schwarznegger?!' he whispered loudly.

Angel covered the mouthpiece. 'It's a dog.'

Boodle looked blank. 'A dog?'

'Haven't you got a visitor, Mrs Buller-Price? A stranger?' he asked tentatively.

'No. No,' she replied vaguely.

'I tell you what,' Angel said in a confidential tone. 'As it happens, I'm not far away. I'll pop in and you can tell me what it is that's troubling you.'

'Oh. Yes. Could you? That is good of you. That would be absolutely super! I'll put the kettle on.'

'See you in five minutes then. Goodbye.'

'Goodbye, Inspector.'

He cancelled the mobile and stuffed it into his pocket.

'She says there's nobody there. I'll soon sort it out, face to face. I couldn't ask her about the van.'

'You can't go in there,' Boodle said. 'He's got one hostage. I don't want him to have two. An old woman is one thing, a police inspector is quite another.'

'Doesn't sound as if she's being held hostage.'

'He'll have a hammer at her head, or something. That's why she was babbling nonsense,' said Boodle, his eyes flitting nervously between the men.

'She didn't react as if anybody was there.'

'He's got to be there!' Boodle shrieked.

'There's only one way to find out.'

'Does that track lead anywhere else?'

'There's a television aerial mast at the top. That's all.'

'He could be there. He could be up there, right now. Digging out the gold,' Boodle said, his eyes blinking irregularly. Angel shook his head.

'Take the car up the track, drop me off at the farm. You proceed to the top and sus it out. If everything's OK, wait there. I will phone you in five minutes exactly and let you know what Yardley's up to. If anything goes wrong and you don't get my call, you can send in your team, the chopper, Kalashnikovs, the lot.'

Boodle sniffed and ran his tongue over his bottom lip.

Angel noticed that his left hand was shaking again.

Boodle looked at Quadrille. Quadrille returned the look. 'If Michael's willing to go in … ' he said, 'we shouldn't give Yardley any more time.'

Boodle sniffed and nodded.

'It's risky.'

Angel tapped Gawber on the shoulder. The engine purred into life.

Quadrille switched on the mike. He began instructing the chopper and the ARVs to take up positions close to the farmhouse to prepare for an assault.

The Mercedes took the slope easily and arrived at the lopsided sign to the farm in no time. Gawber pulled on the handbrake. Quadrille switched off the mike and turned to Angel.

'In three minutes, the ARVs and the chopper will be in position. One minute after that and we can be feeling Yardley's collar.'

Boodle rubbed his chin roughly several times, looked at Angel and nodded. 'Michael,' he said.

Angel opened the car door and looked at his watch.

'Phone you in five minutes — exactly.'

'Careful,' Quadrille called out as the door slammed.

The car continued up the hill.

CHAPTER TWELVE

He saw the rear of the white van projecting out of the barn next to the house. He looked round; there were no signs of Yardley or anybody else. It was surprisingly quiet, just the musical whistle of the strong wind. He made his way softly to the farmhouse door.

Suddenly a high-pitched bark followed by a multiplicity of other barks disturbed the quiet. Before he had the opportunity to knock the door opened and the big figure of Mrs Buller-Price appeared. Five dogs of various shapes, sizes and colours erupted from behind her, eager to investigate him.

'Steady! Steady! Quiet gang! Quiet!' she boomed. She looked up at Angel and smiled angelically. 'Hello, Inspector. You really are most kind. Come in. Come in.'

Angel stared into her eyes for any giveaway sign that things were not as they seemed. She smiled at him normally, glanced down at the dogs to make sure they were not being too much of a nuisance, then quickly back at him, still smiling and nodding happily. He could detect nothing wrong. He glanced back to see if anything untoward was happening. He did not want to be taken by surprise from behind. There was nothing there, only the cobbled yard, the barn with the white van sticking out and a bramble bush by the gate-post waving in the wind.

The dogs formed a circle round him and wagged their tails excitedly. Schwarzenegger was the last to arrive; he quietly lumbered across, sniffed Angel's shoes, then his hand, wagged his tail and returned to Mrs Buller-Price's side.

'Quiet gang! Quiet!' she bawled and peace reigned except for the smallest, ugliest dog who persisted. She stared down at him. 'Quiet, Bogart! Be quiet!' The dog gave four more challenging yaps and then fell silent.

'Got a new van, Mrs Buller-Price?' said Angel, nodding towards the barn.

The smile left her. She shook her head.

'No. No. Come in, Inspector. Come along in, and I'll tell you all about it. What a to-do!'

She turned and went into the house, Angel followed, stooping slightly through the door. The dogs dashed in behind, piling on to each other in the scrum.

'Sit down there, Inspector,' she said indicating a big easy-chair facing the fireplace. 'What a day! I'll just mash the tea.'

The dogs dropped down anywhere and instantly pretended to be asleep. Mrs Buller-Price went into the kitchen still talking.

'I made some scones yesterday. You must give me your opinion of them.' She reached out for a big round tin and noisily pulled off the lid.

Angel looked anxiously into the kitchen as he passed the door. He half-expected Morris Yardley to pop up from behind the door-jamb with a gun in his hand. He took the big chair. He was not happy. Everything looked terrifyingly normal. He looked round the small sitting-room, comfortably furnished with a huge old sideboard heaped with newspapers, letters and magazines. He could see the Farmer's Weekly, the Pig Breeder's Gazette, and Jersey Milk, heaped untidily in front of six seven-pound glass sweetie jars labelled Millington's Winter Mixture, a pair of rubber gloves, bottle of black rum and a glass. An assortment of large easy-chairs, each loaded with two or three cushions of various shapes and sizes, faced the big fireplace, which had a small fire glowing in it. Ten dusty blue rosettes as big as dinner plates with 1st Prize printed in the middle of each, hung limply from the mantelpiece. The room was untidy, dusty and warm, and he could smell cut flowers, dogs and freshly baked bread.

He listened out for any unusual noise. There was only the rattle of china from the kitchen and the howl of the wind down the chimney. He must keep his eye on the time.

'It was good of you to answer my call so promptly, Inspector.' Mrs Buller-Price called from the kitchen. 'It's been a perfectly dreadful day. And I've never stopped. I was up at five. I had to milk my Jerseys, and hump the churn up the lane.'

She returned with a tray and put it on a table. Schwarzenegger followed her in from the kitchen. 'There we are.' she said and flopped into the chair next to Angel.

'It was no trouble,' Angel said trying to sound casual. 'I was in the neighbourhood. You sounded troubled.'

Schwarzenegger circled twice and then settled down on the red tiled floor beside her.

Angel noticed that the dogs were relaxed and behaving perfectly naturally. He reasoned that if Yardley was still in the house they would be interested and unsettled, particularly the big Alsatian.

'Ah. Yes, indeed, Inspector, I am. The invasion has started, you know. Men, or whatever they are, from Mars have landed. Only half an hour ago a space ship zoomed over my roof and dropped something or somebody down the valley.'

Angel smiled. 'That was a helicopter. It's nothing to worry about.'

'Are you sure? There was another one of those crashed up there last week. Helicopter? What is it doing round here?'

'Probably army exercises.'

'There you are. The army. And the government are not telling us. I knew it!'

Angel knew he must find out about Yardley.

'Tell me. What's that van doing here? And where's the driver.'

'You might well ask. I'm the only driver round here, Inspector.' She passed him a cup of tea. 'Help yourself to sugar.'

'Thank you.'

'Ah yes. I'm very angry ... and put out, I can tell you. Well, my car, my Bentley, has been requisitioned by the American Army. It was taken by Lee Marvin and I have been lumbered with that tinny van.'

Angel's jaw dropped. 'Who is Lee Marvin?'

She shook her head impatiently causing all four chins to wobble.

'Oh, Inspector! Everybody knows Lee Marvin!'

'Oh, where?'

'At Lower Dalling.'

'Where's that?'

'It's in the dales.'

'Oh? Do tell me about it.'

'Ah yes. It's incredible. Yes. Well, I was visiting my cousin in Friske. The one who is the climber ... married to what's his name ... the naturalist ... makes those television programmes with ... er, never mind. Anyway, I was in the Bentley having seen her and taken my leave, and travelling from Friske to Lower Dalling and this van was stuck in the middle of the narrow road about ten or twelve miles from Friske. I couldn't get past it. I pipped my horn several times to get it to move. It didn't move. Eventually, I got out to see what was happening and then Lee Marvin came from behind some bushes and pushed his way into my Bentley. He said he was commandeering it. Naturally, I protested. He said I could have the van. He then turned my car round and drove off. I would have hit him but he was so quick. I wouldn't have let him see that I was afraid of him. Bette Davis was never afraid of him and I'm not. But I didn't want to be stranded out there.

'So I took the van, turned it round and drove it back here. I phoned you at the police station as soon as I could.

And I looked for a police car all the way back. Didn't see one. You can never find a policeman when you want one, can you? So I kept my foot down. I just wanted to get home. I've been here about an hour. And I'm tired out. Will I ever see my lovely car again?'

'I'm sure you will, Mrs Buller-Price. But where is this ... er ... Lee Marvin now?'

'Oh, I really don't know. He drove away and left me up there in Friske.'

Angel shook his head. 'Oh,' he said and looked at his watch.

'You're not going are you? You haven't had a scone.'

He searched in his pocket for his mobile. 'No. But I will make a phone call, if you will excuse me. We must start looking for your car.'

She beamed and lifted the cup to her lips.

He stabbed in Quadrille's number.

The phone was answered immediately. It was Boodle.

'What's happening?' His voice was squeaking. 'What is Yardley up to?' he snapped.

'He isn't here.'

'What?! He'd better be.'

'He isn't. He took Mrs Buller-Price's car.'

'What do you mean?' screamed Boodle.

'You know when he stopped, went in the bushes and you lost him? When he came back, he stole a car; he took Mrs Buller-Price's car, and left her with the van. Well, she took the van and drove it here.'

There was no reply. He knew Boodle would be livid as he adjusted to the news that his carefully worked out plan had gone haywire and that Yardley had absconded.

'Are you there?' Angel said.

There was silence.

'Hello,' Angel called.

Eventually Quadrille came on the line.

'Er. It's Oscar, Michael. We're coming in.'

Angel thought he sounded strange.

'Right.'

The line went dead.

Angel cancelled the phone and slipped it back into his pocket. He blew out a long sigh.

'I have some associates who've arrived outside in a car, Mrs Buller-Price, they're coming in. I hope that's all right?' He put his cup on the tray and went over to the door.

She beamed. 'Oh good, a tea-party.' She struggled to her feet. 'I'll get some more cups. How many did you say?'

Angel got up. 'I'll show them the way. Excuse me. Won't be a minute,' he said. He went to the front door, opened it and peered outside.

Boodle and Quadrille were running along the track towards him. He put up an arm and strode out into the yard to greet them. Boodle had a face like thunder.

'If Yardley isn't here, then where the hell is he?'

'The last we know, he was in Friske, sir,' Angel said.

'He could be anywhere by now!' Boodle boomed.

Angel knew that was true. Boodle saw the white van.

'Have you searched it?'

'No.'

He nodded to Oscar to look in the van. Quadrille crossed to the barn.

'Is it locked?'

Boodle turned back to Angel. 'Have you searched the house?'

'He's not here,' Angel said patiently.

Boodle's face went scarlet. His eyes stood out. He thought he would burst a blood-vessel.

A mobile phone rang. It was Boodle's. He yanked it out of his pocket out and stabbed a button with a finger.

'What is it now?' he yelled. 'What?!' he screamed. 'What? … Have you checked? … Stay there. Report to me if she comes back.'

He cancelled the phone, stared angrily at Angel but called out: 'Quadrille! Quadrille!'

The young man came round from the side of the van. His eyes opened wide.

'That was Simcox. Enchantra Davison has gone. She's given them the slip. The flat's empty. Her car is still outside the flat. She's been missing more than six hours!'

'She'll be with Yardley,' said Quadrille.

Boodle glared at him.

'Obviously!' he bawled. 'What's in the van?'

'The case is there, and all the new clothes and things, and the shoes, also some old prison clothes and personal things. But he's taken the money and the cigarettes. He must have stuffed them into one of those plastic bags!'

*

It was 4.45 p.m. when Quadrille stopped the Mercedes outside Bromersley police station. Angel and Gawber got out and the young man then sped off like an electric hare back up north to join Boodle at Friske police station. The commander had already been taken there by helicopter. The ARVs were also on their way north, and Angel expected Boodle would be co-ordinating a lightning search with North Yorkshire Police. He would desperately want to capture Yardley in daylight hours. It was essential to have him back in prison before he reached the gold and disappeared for ever!

Angel went straight to his office and closed the door. He was glad to be away from the heat of Boodle's rage. He pulled a small white paper bag out of his pocket and put it on his desk. He noticed the big words printed on it in blue: 'MILLINGTON'S WINTER MIXTURE.' He thought about it and frowned. In the bag was a scone Mrs Buller-Price had pushed into his hand on his way out; he had planned to enjoy it with a cup of tea. He reached out for the phone.

It was Ahmed who answered.

'Yes sir.'

'A cup of tea, smartish, lad.'

147

'You're back, sir? The super said he wants to see you as soon as you come in.'

Angel pulled a face. 'Aaaah…' He really didn't want to face the super just then. 'All right. Hold the tea.'

He trudged down the corridor and knocked on the door.

'Come in,' the superintendent called.

Angel opened the door.

Harker pointed to the chair. 'You didn't find the gold, then?' he said with a smile that would have made David Blunkett's dog throw up.

'How do you know, sir?' Angel replied wearily.

'Every copper knows that by now. We've had an email announcing Yardley's escape from Welham prison,' he sniggered.

Angel's eyebrows shot up. That was the story Boodle had put out, was it? He didn't reply.

'What happened?'

Angel relayed the facts as they had unfolded.

The superintendent sat there, attentive, nodding occasionally and grinding his teeth throughout. At the end, he merely smirked.

'What a mess,' he said. 'It was a daft plan anyway.' He sniffed.

Angel didn't remember him telling Boodle it was a daft plan!

'You want to thank your lucky stars you did as you were told.'

'What do you mean, sir?'

'Well, that you didn't drown another of his microphones. He had you pegged as a lad looking for an opportunity.'

'I don't know what you mean.'

'Don't be naive, lad. When you dunked your mike in the tea, he took it that you wanted your conversations with Yardley to be private, just between the two of you.'

Angel screwed up his face. 'I still don't understand.'

'You are thick, sometimes. He didn't trust you, did he? He knows you and Yardley have some secret history and he

148

thought the pair of you were cooking up your own private deal to organize his escape in exchange for a share in the gold.' Angel's mouth dropped open.

'He thought you were on the take, lad. Why do you think he sent in two 'gasmen' to run a metal detector over your house?'

'That was Boodle?'

'Course it was. That's why I couldn't do anything about it. You wouldn't have wanted me to set on another DI just to go through the motions of investigating it, would you? And what did you think they were looking for? Scratch cards? And you never did tell me what there was between you and Yardley.' Angel's jaw set like bell metal.

'I don't know Yardley, sir. I have never met him,' he said loudly. He felt heat generate in his stomach and climb relentlessly up to his face. It was some time since he had felt so angry. 'It's bloody outrageous,' he continued. 'I shall make a formal complaint. If you've finished with me, sir, I shall go and see the chief constable now. I shall bring a case against Boodle. There's too much of this, taking advantage of people, especially serving policemen and their families.'

'I shouldn't bother, Mike.'

'It's all right for you, sir. It wasn't your wife's privacy and your house that was violated.'

'You'll want witnesses, lad.'

'Well, I've got you.'

'Don't be daft, lad. Don't be daft! I've my back to watch, haven't I?'

Angel's face changed. He stared at the toothy alligator across the desk. What price loyalty? He couldn't believe what he was hearing.

'Best thing you can do,' the superintendent continued, 'is to get to that gold before he does.'

Angel shook his head in disbelief. Then he nodded. He wondered if he had correctly understood the way things were. If Boodle had been looking for an opportunity to get his hands on the gold for himself, then there would have been

149

little surprise that he might have thought Angel had the same idea. What a turn-up for the books?

'Come on, Mike. There's nowt you can do about it. I shouldn't have mentioned it. I thought you had worked it out. Let's get on to our own crime figures.' The superintendent shuffled through some papers in front of him until he found the one he wanted. 'Hmm. Yes. Now there's this chap Evan Jones. I've had a letter from Holloway probation office. They want to know if we've seen anything of Amy Jones. She's not clocked in since she was released a month ago. In the absence of any information from anywhere, the case officer seems to think she may have drifted back to her ex-husband. Alternatively, they think that as she was from round here originally she may have returned here. Take another look at Jones. See if there's any sign of her around his place. You never know. Give me something to write back. That Jones chap seems to be sailing very close to the wind. He's buying gold, isn't he?'

Trancelike, Angel said: 'Yes.' He was still thinking about the 'gasmen', and the loyalty of the alligator.

'Don't like the look of him,' the superintendent growled. Angel tried to shrug off the mood. It wasn't easy.

'If he's buying gold, it means he isn't stealing gold.'

'At the moment, we only know he bought the one bar.'

'That's more than eighty thousand quid! And according to the Inland Revenue, it seems to have been with clean money.'

'Yes,' said Harker, grinding his teeth. 'Exactly,' he said heavily. 'Exactly.'

'What are you getting at, sir?'

'Just supposing he's involved in fencing this stolen gold, and he's got access to these eight hundred and twenty bars. How's he going to turn it into cash so that he can spend it? I mean, he can't buy a house with four bars of gold, or a round of drinks with a pinch of it. A quantity like that, he'd have to sell legitimately, through bullion-dealers. And he'd have to sell it in small quantities, a bar or two at a time, not to arouse suspicion.' Angel realized what the super was suggesting.

'You think he's set up a laundering scam?'

The superintendent nodded. He stopped grinding, looked up and peered through half-closed eyes.

'Make sure he doesn't blow soap in your eyes, shoot you a line, and then hang you out on it to dry,' he snarled.

*

Angel arrived at the police station the following morning early, anxious to hear if there was any news about Yardley. He called in the communications room and read that there had been no reported sightings of him since his escape yesterday morning. Mrs Buller-Price's car had been found in good condition near to where it had been taken and a SOC officer had been over it and found nothing useful to the inquiry. Angel left the room and hurried down the main corridor. He followed the smelly plumber who was carrying a length of copper piping and a yellow plastic bucket. He arrived in his office and was fingering through the post when there was a knock on the door.

'Come in,' he called.

It was Gawber.

'Come in, Ron. Sit down.' He turned away from the letters. 'The super thinks Jones may have set up a gold-laundering scam. He's even suggested he might know something about this Bank of Agara job. Well, Jones got a receipt for that gold bar he bought in the Isle of Man. If we were to search his place and find one gold bar, he'd just wave that receipt at us.'

'Oh?' said Gawber, his eyes opening wide. 'And he can use that same receipt for a different bar over and over again.'

Angel nodded. 'Now, if he is running a laundering scam, we'd need to find him with more than one bar.'

Gawber shook his head. 'When those two men in suits turned his house over, it didn't look to me as if they had found anything interesting, and there wasn't a safe. We would need to look at his car-sales pitch. I expect there's a

151

safe in his office there. But we'd need something to justify a search warrant, wouldn't we?'

'Ay.'

There was a knock at the door. 'Come in.'

It was DS Crisp.

'What is it, lad?' said Angel irritably.

'I've caught Fishy Smith, sir,' Crisp said enthusiastically. 'I caught him meandering round Bromersley market.'

Angel's eyebrows went up. 'Oh. I'd forgotten all about him. Oh yes.' His jaw stiffened. 'I've a bone to pick with that evil little monster.'

'He's in cell number two.'

'Right, lad. I hope you didn't get too near. He'd empty your pockets faster than Gordon Brown.'

Crisp grinned. 'I kept my distance, sir.'

'Right. Have you searched him?'

'He's nothing on him that looks stolen, sir. His stuff is laid out on the counter in the charge room. Ed Scrivens is watching it for me.'

'Right, I'll come straightaway.' He turned back to Gawber. 'Don't go far away, Ron. I'll happen be wanting you to search Fishy Smith's pad.'

Angel headed straight for the charge room. Crisp followed behind him.

PC Scrivens was leaning against the counter. He straightened up when Angel appeared.

'Right, lad,' Angel said.

The constable went out and closed the door. Crisp nodded towards the few items on the counter.

'That's all he has, sir.'

There was an empty leather wallet, two pounds and ten pence in coins, a ring with two keys, a rabbit's-foot brooch, a little plastic model of a black cat and a small brown jar with a green screw-top. Angel poked methodically through them. He came to the jar. He picked it up, and unscrewed the lid. Inside was a clear greasy substance, like an ointment. It was almost empty. He sniffed at it. His eyebrows shot up. He turned and looked at Crisp strangely.

'What's up, sir?' asked the sergeant.

Angel held up the jar. 'What's this, lad?'

Crisp took it, sniffed at it. 'Smells like rubbing ointment. For colds.'

'It's menthol,' snapped Angel. He snatched the jar back. He put his nose over the jar again. 'Yes.'

Crisp shrugged, surprised at Angel's reaction.

'You rub it on your chest, sir.'

'I know what it's for, lad,' said Angel tightening the lid. 'What's he doing with it, that's what I want to know?'

Crisp looked blank and said nothing. Angel stuffed the jar into his pocket and turned back to him.

'He can have that stuff back. Bring it down to the cells. Follow me.'

Fishy Smith stood up as Angel and Crisp went into the cell.

'You can't keep me in here. I haven't done nothing wrong. I wasn't loitering with intent to do nothing. It's an interference with my liberty. I don't mind being bottled up when I've done something wrong but this is an infringement of my rights.'

Angel closed the cell door. 'Save it, Fishy. Save it. All that guff is wasted on me, you should know that by now. Let's get down to brass tacks. What have you done with my warrant-card and badge?'

Fishy's mouth opened and then closed.

'I don't know nothing about 'em.'

'Come on. Don't muck me about. When you were in last week, making a fuss in the charge room and I came up to speak to you, you took that opportunity to dip my pocket and relieve me of the leather wallet they were in.'

'Not me, squire. Must have been somebody else.'

'It was you and you know it.'

Fishy Smith looked away, smiled, shook his head a few times and looked back.

'Fancy the great Angel being dipped. I bet that stuff could be worth quite a bit out in the right hands. What a laugh, eh?'

'What did you do with them?' Angel bawled angrily.

'I haven't seen them. I don't do no dipping any more, Mr Angel.'

The inspector put his hand in his pocket and produced the jar of menthol ointment.

'Whose pocket did this come out of?'

'That? That? Huh. That's just ointment.'

'Whose pocket did you get it out of?'

'I didn't get that out of anybody's pocket. It's for my stuffed-up nose.'

'Your nose isn't stuffed up.'

'No. Not now. It's better, isn't it.'

'It's your head that's stuffed up. Stuffed up with the idea that you can pull one across me. Where did you get it from?'

'It's only ointment. I don't know. My sister gave it me.'

'Where did she get it from?'

'I don't know. A chemist's, I suppose. It's only a jar of ointment, Mr Angel. It's not exactly the crown jewels!'

'I need to see your sister.'

'No. Leave my sister alone. You can't. She's gone back.'

'Where to?'

'I don't know, do I? I'm not her keeper. Liverpool, I think.'

'You'll have to stop in here until we find her, then.'

'No. I remember. I bought it at the chemist's.'

'What chemist's?'

'I don't know what chemist's.'

'Did you buy it yourself?'

'Yes.'

'What did you ask for?'

'I don't know. I don't recall what I said exactly.'

'You're a liar. You lifted this from somebody's pocket.'

'No I didn't.'

'I'll let you into a secret, Fishy. This jar of menthol is evidence. The man you stole it from is a murderer. If he knows you've got it, he'll be after your blood.'

'Get off! What's a jar of menthol got to do with a murder?' Angel suddenly peered into his eyes.

'Ah. I see it all. You didn't steal it. It is yours. You must be the murderer.'

Fishy Smith didn't reply. His mouth opened wide. Angel turned to Crisp.

'Get a warrant to search this man's house while I charge him with the murder of Duncan McFee,' he said.

The man swallowed and his eyes opened up like two fried eggs.

'Hold on,' he yelled. 'Hold on. I found that jar of menthol in a bag in my step-sister's flat.'

Angel sighed. 'Now we are getting somewhere.'

CHAPTER THIRTEEN

He locked the car and went through the open office door. Olivia Button was at the desk, combing her long blonde hair. When she saw him, she quickly dropped the comb into her open handbag, deftly threaded her hair into an elastic band and pushed the little pedestal mirror into a desk drawer.

'Sorry about that,' she said with a sweet toothy smile. 'Can I help you?'

'Oh,' Angel began. 'I was looking for Mr Jones.'

'He'll be back in a minute. I'm sitting in for him. Is there anything I can do?' she offered delicately, flashing her big blue eyes.

Angel looked at his watch.

'It's his lunch hour,' she said. 'He's gone for a short run. He'll be back in a couple of minutes.'

'Won't he be staying out for lunch?'

'No. No.' She smiled. 'He'll be back. He'll just have a banana at his desk … with me. That's his lunch.'

Angel didn't think a run and a banana an adequate substitute for a pork pie and pint of Old Peculiar at the Feathers, but he was generously prepared to accept that in this modern world with its new found values, it took all sorts.

'How does he keep his strength up?' he asked with a grin. 'He's very strong,' she said, maintaining a smile. 'He says he's always been fit. He's exercise mad. He runs and he runs. There's not an ounce of fat on him. Always eats the right food. He's as strong as a bull. Now why are you so interested?'

'I'm Inspector Angel, Bromersley CID,' he said, then hesitated. 'I wanted to speak to him.'

Olivia Button's face changed. Her eyes got bigger, her mouth dropped open momentarily, then, as quickly, her face brightened and she smiled and sighed as a wiry figure in white shirt, shorts and shoes came running in through the open door, panting noisily.

'Four minutes and twenty seconds,' he gasped. 'My best yet.'

Angel turned.

Evan Jones pulled the sweatband off his head, wiped his forehead with it and blew out a long sigh.

'Ah. Oh? Hello, Inspector. What can I do for you?' he said in that sing-song way. 'Have you caught those men who broke into my house yet?'

'No. I want to see you about something else. It's private really,' Angel said looking towards Olivia. 'Perhaps we should go somewhere.'

'No. No,'Jones replied. 'That's all right. Olivia is all right. I have no secrets from her.'

Angel shrugged a shoulder.

'Well, it's about your ex-wife. It seems that since she came out of prison, she's not kept to the terms of her probation. In fact, she's not been seen since her release from Holloway on the sixteenth of March. I wondered if you had seen her?'

'No. No,' Jones said quickly and firmly. 'And if I never see her again, it will be too soon.' He looked at Olivia. She gave him a small, nervous smile.

Angel stared at him. His answer seemed conclusive.

'You've no idea where she is?'

Jones pointedly looked him square in the face.

'No idea,' he replied bluntly.

Angel paused, then he said: 'Right, sir.' He turned towards the door. He looked back. 'Thank you. If she should turn up, you'd let me know?'

'I don't think there's much chance of that.'

'Hmm. Thank you. Hmm. Thank you, Mr Jones.' Angel stood there, rubbing his chin. He looked at the Welshman through half-closed eyes.

'Something troubling you, Inspector?' said Jones daringly.

Angel turned back to the silver haired Welshman. He was slow to reply.

'Quite a few things, Mr Jones, actually,' he said ponderously.

'Well, what are they, man? Spit them out. I have nothing to hide.'

Angel nodded slowly. He turned fully round and took a pace towards Jones.

'All right. All right.' Angel sniffed. 'Firstly, I'd be curious to know the asking-price of your house on Creeford Road. "Orchard House", isn't it called? That's the only house you own, isn't it?'

Olivia stared at Jones.

Jones eyes opened wide. 'What sort of a question is that? It is the only house I own. What do you mean?'

'Well, you'll be putting it on the market soon, won't you?'

'Certainly not, man. I've only just finished decorating it, haven't I … and getting it how I want it. I expect to retire there in ten or twelve years' time.'

Angel raised his eyebrows deliberately and said: 'Oh.'

'If you're looking for a nice house, Inspector, you'll have to look elsewhere.' Jones sniggered.

Olivia moved closer to Jones. Her face showed her dismay.

Angel nodded. He could never have afforded a mansion like that.

'Yes. Right. It's not for sale, then?

'No. Was there anything else?'

'Ay. Are you planning a big social calendar of events and inviting all your friends and relations round this summer?'

Evan Jones laughed. It wasn't a genuine laugh.

'All my friends and relations? Huh! I have a cousin in a little god-forsaken place near Swansea. Haven't seen him for years. He's my only living relation, and I'll not be going down there even to his funeral. It's a certainty he'll not be coming to mine. And as for my friends? Huh. I haven't got a socializing, nosy-parkering, coffee-morning, cup-of-sugaring, Christmas-card-once-a-year, bunch of so-called friends.' He looked at Olivia and reached out for her hand. 'There! She's all my friends. I don't need or want any more.'

Olivia smiled and cosied up to him.

Angel looked at them holding hands. He said nothing.

'Anything else?' Jones said truculently.

'Yes.'

'What?'

'Do you eat meat?'

'Eh? What? No. I'm a vegan. That's no meat.'

'Chicken?'

'No.'

'Sausages?'

Jones pulled a face and shook his head. 'What is all this? I run a car sales business, not a butcher's shop?' he said edgily.

Angel glared at him. 'Well don't keep coming up with porky pies then!' he bawled and turned away. He put his hand in his pocket and pulled out his mobile. He tapped in a number and pressed the button.

Evan Jones and Olivia Button exchanged glances and then stared at him in anticipation.

'Ah, Ron. I want you to get a warrant ... to dig up a barbecue ... a barbecue, yes ... at Orchard House, Creeford Road.'

Jones's jaw dropped.

'Bring some men and picks and shovels. We'll meet you there.'

Thirty minutes later two policemen in yellow water-proof suits, armed with picks and shovels, were in the garden at the side of Evan Jones's house. They were lifting out the first shovel of soft earth, having removed the top of the barbecue and demolished two small brick pillars.

Angel stood next to Gawber at one side of the hole and Evan Jones, now in street clothes and wearing a raincoat stood, holding arms with Olivia Button at the other.

'What made you think to look here, sir?' Gawber said quietly.

Angel pursed his lips, then whispered: 'What man in his right mind would build a barbecue, if he's a vegetarian, doesn't entertain and is not tarring the place up to sell it?'

Gawber blinked. He looked away for a second then came back.

'I'd never have thought of that.'

Evan Jones looked distinctly subdued. Olivia Button hung on to his arm, her eyes looking down at the ground. She occasionally looked up, glanced at everybody's faces and then looked down again.

The two policemen worked quickly and efficiently, and after making a small pile of earth on the footpath, one of the constables, Scrivens said:

'I think we've hit something, sir.'

'What is it, lad?'

'A tin box, sir.'

'Dig it out, lad. Dig it out.'

The constables soon brought out a black metal box about fifteen inches square and ten inches deep. It had a handle at each end and it was locked. They lifted it out of the ground and put it on the footpath. Scrivens rubbed off the loose earth from the lid with his gloved hand. Angel looked up at Jones.

'Have you got the key, sir?'

Jones glared angrily at Angel, then he pulled out a bunch of keys, crouched on the path, unlocked the box, pulled open the lid and stood back.

Inside, Angel saw three brown-paper parcels laid side by side half-filling the box. He reached in and pulled one out. He tore through the paper to another wrapping of wax paper. Inside that was a gold bar. It was embossed on the top: JOHNSON MATHEY PLC, 9999, SERIAL NO. 22394297, 2003.

Angel looked up at Jones and shook his head. He then pulled out the other two packages, tore off the paper to check that they were also gold bars. They were.

'They are not stolen,' said Jones. 'I have hidden them to keep them away from my ex-wife. She's always on the prowl. She claims I owe her money, but I don't.'

Angel sniffed. 'We'll know all about that when we've checked the serial numbers. I hope you've got receipts.'

Jones pointed to the pile of rubble.

'You'd no need to make a mess like this.'

'If you had told us what was down here in the first place, we would have let you dig it out, but no. You said there was nothing here!' Angel turned to Gawber. 'Take charge of this gold, Ron. Give him a receipt.'

'Huh. I should think so,' Jones said indignantly.

Angel's eyes flashed. He turned swiftly back to the Welshman.

'Your troubles have only just started, sir. Your ex-wife is still missing, and I need to know what's happened to her!'

*

Angel arrived at his office the following morning at twenty-eight minutes past eight. He had just closed the door and was unbuttoning his coat when the phone rang. He reached over the desk to answer it.

'Angel.'

It was the superintendent.

'There's a telex from the fire department. There was a fire at Evan Jones's car site last night. Alarm came from a member of the public about twenty-one fifty hours. Looks like arson.

This might be the lead you are looking for. Anyway, sort it out, quick as you can.'

'Right sir.'

Angel dashed out of the office and in four minutes was at Evan Jones's place. He stopped the car in front of the office block and looked across at the scene. Behind the office was the roofless, doorless steaming shell of the old brick building Jones had been using as a store and workshop. Two fire engines were parked next to each other and six men in red-and-yellow uniforms were still directing two powerful jets of water into the building: one through the top where the roof had been, and the other through a hole in the wall where an upper window had been. A stream of black liquid trickled out of the doorway, under the thirty or so undamaged cars on the forecourt. It ran over the pavement, on to the main road, down the hill.

A fireman in waterproofs and yellow helmet standing at the rear of one of the fire vehicles saw him.

'Are you the police?' he yelled.

'Yeah.'

'Must watch the pressure. Come on up.'

Angel locked his car and trudged up the slope.

'This building here has been fired in four different places. Obviously arson. Must have been started about nine o'clock, last night. We got here about ten, there was quite a blaze. There were a few small detonations during our containment, we took them to be exploding petrol tanks.'

'Anybody inside? Anybody hurt.'

'No.'

'What's in there?'

'Thirty or forty cars: seem to be old cars chiefly. And old tyres.'

'Can anything be salvaged?'

'Shouldn't think so.'

'Hmm. The owner here?'

'In the office.'

'Right,' Angel said. He strode over to the old building and peered through the opening where the doors had been. He saw the steaming black burnt-out shells of cars and distorted metal; he noticed the sickly smell of burnt cellulose, smouldering rubber and petrol fumes, and the hissing sound of cold water meeting hot metal. It was not a pleasant experience. He turned back down the slope and made his way to the office. The door was ajar.

Evan Jones was sitting at his desk reading a heavily printed document. Olivia Button stood next to him, her hand on his shoulder. As Angel entered, Jones looked up. He wasn't his usual self. A strand of silver hair flopped across his forehead, his chin was bristly and the red bow tie was missing. In contrast, Olivia Button looked as crisp and clean as she always did.

'Oh. It's you. Come to gloat, have you?' Jones said in his best valleys accent.

'No,' Angel said. 'What's happened?'

'You can see what's happened. My warehouse has gone up. I doubt I'll be able to save as much as a jubilee clip.'

'What caused it?'

'Don't know. Build-up of petrol fumes, spanner falling on the floor causing a spark? Who knows?'

'Hmmm. What was in there?'

'My stock-in-trade, Inspector. Cars, car parts, spares, tools, tyres. Lots of valuable expensive equipment. Worth thousands.'

'Are you insured?'

'Yes, but not for everything. Got to wade through the small print.'

'Hmm. Where were you last night then, when this happened?'

Olivia Button unexpectedly replied.

'He was with me in my flat until about nine forty-five. We were having dinner together. It was a special cheese omelette and salad.'

Angel looked at her and blinked. Jones brightened at Olivia Button's forthright reply.

'That's right,' he added perkily. 'I left about nine forty-five to go home. I was on the stairs going to bed when I got a phone call from the police telling me about the fire.'

Angel sniffed. 'It was discovered at about ten o'clock. It seems it started about nine, so you two were together at the time?'

'Yes. We went straight from here after work.'

Angel sniffed again. 'The fire officer says it was arson. Have you any idea who might have started such a fire?'

'It's not arson,' Jones said tetchily. 'It's just one of those things.'

Angel shook his head. The Welshman had an alibi. He turned to go.

'Here, Inspector,' Jones called out. 'When am I going to get my gold back?'

'When the serial numbers have been checked.'

Angel left Jones poring over his insurance policy, and returned to the station. He went straight down the corridor. He passed the door to the gentlemen's loos, which was propped open by a yellow plastic bucket and from where sounds of water being pumped under pressure disturbed the usual sober quietness of the administration area of the station. He reached the bottom office and knocked on the door.

'Come in,' the superintendent called. 'Sit down,' he said, grinding his teeth. 'What about this fire? Did you see Jones?'

'He says he was with that lass, Olivia Button, and she confirms it.'

'Oh' Harker grunted and rubbed his chin. 'Is he insured?'

'Yes.'

'Ah. Do you think, when he gets the insurance money, he'll make a run for it?'

Angel shrugged. 'Don't know. Anything from the Inland Revenue?'

'Huh. It'll take them ages. If we could get anything hard from them, we could move in, arrest him on suspicion and take his house and that office place to pieces, brick by brick,' he snarled.

'He wants his gold back.'

'Ay,' the superintendent said and dismissed it with a wave of a hand. 'What did you find at Fishy Smith's pad?'

'Ron Gawber went over it, sir. Nothing helpful. A lot of 1940s furniture, old clothes, empty curry trays, fish and chip papers and Jubilee stout bottles.'

'I thought you'd be wasting your time. Another dead end.'

Angel glared at him.

'Well get on with it, lad! Do what you can.'

'Right, sir,' Angel said through gritted teeth.

He came out of the superintendent's office and stormed his way up the corridor. He saw Ron Gawber running towards him waving a piece of paper.

'Have you a minute, sir?'

Angel reached the office door. 'What is it, Ron? Come in. What's up?'

'I've just had a woman in reception making a complaint about a car travelling on the Wakefield road between Askham's roundabout and Jones's car-sales pitch. She says the driver was racing dangerously and nearly had her off the road.'

Angel slumped in the chair. 'So what?'

'It was nine o'clock last night. She got the car number, and it turns out to be a car owned by Olivia Button. Now isn't that Evan Jones's latest piece?'

Angel's mouth opened. 'Yes. Who's the complainant?'

'A Susan Tranter, sir.'

'Who? Never heard of her.' Angel pulled an ear. 'Hmm. Something fishy. I'd better see this Olivia Button. See what she's up to.'

'Did you want to see Evan, Inspector?' Olivia Button said from behind the desk in Jones's office. She was looking fresh and decorative, like a spiced kitten waiting for a chocolate mouse to surrender.

Angel smiled. 'No. I'm sure you can help me.'

'He's out running again. He'll be ten minutes or so.'

'It's you I want to see.'

'Oh?' she said, her eyes opening wide.

'Yes.' He sighed. 'We've had a report that your car was seen last night, being driven dangerously on the Wakefield Road between here and Askham's roundabout. At about nine o'clock.'

The big eyes opened wider. 'My car?'

'Yes. That little red Porsche. The one outside.'

'No, Inspector. It wasn't me,' she said adamantly. 'I put my car in my garage and locked it about six o'clock last night and I haven't been near it until this morning.'

Angel peered at her closely and rubbed his chin.

'Could anybody have borrowed it?'

'No,' she said adamantly. 'I have the only key.'

Angel gave her a straight look; there was something very funny going on, 'Are you sure?'

'I don't understand,' she said looking blank.

'Nor do I.' Angel decided to change tack. 'Mr Jones isn't much interested in the car business any more, is he.'

'Oh, he is,' she said eagerly. 'I don't know what you mean. He works all hours. Never away from this place. He enjoys his sport and his running, but that's all. He hasn't any other interests.'

'But if he came into money, he wouldn't be averse to packing all this in and say, emigrating, taking you with him, of course, would he?'

Her eyebrows shot up. She shook her head.

'He hasn't discussed anything like that with me.'

Angel decided he would try something else.

'Do you think he could have left your flat earlier than you said last night?'

Her face changed. She looked stunned.

'What do you mean?'

'Could he have left at say, nine o'clock?'

She hesitated. 'Oh no.' She licked her lips.

Angel stared at her. He said nothing.

There was a pause.

'Well, Inspector, it might have been a little earlier than I thought. I said a quarter to ten.'

'Oh yes?' he said gently.

'Well, I mean, we didn't have our eyes on the clock. It might have been a little earlier … say a quarter past nine.'

'Or even nine o'clock?' he suggested smoothly.

'Oh no. Not nine.'

'You see, Miss Button, if he left at nine o'clock, the garage is only three or four minutes away by car, he would have had time to drive there, start the fires and get home easily before the station phoned him.'

'Oh no. He didn't do that. He wouldn't do that. I'm sure.'

Angel shook his head. He took his leave, and drove back to the station with a lot on his mind. He wasn't very happy. He liked everything clear-cut. He had noticed lately that nothing was ever straightforward. Facts never seemed to be facts any more. They always seemed to be frayed round the edges. There didn't seem to be any black and white: everything was grey. Every statement was qualified. Everybody was lying. He met Gawber down the corridor and told him what had been said at Olivia Button's.

'I'll call on Susan Tranter and see what's going on,' said Gawber.

'Ay.' Angel sniffed. 'I'll come with you.'

CHAPTER FOURTEEN

Ten minutes later, the two policemen arrived on the Wadsworth Estate, built in the sixties and called Passion City by local wags. The estate housed more one-parent families than the chip-shop sold chips. The four huge blocks of flats had seen better days: they needed a fresh coat of paint, the lifts repairing, a crêche organizing and condom-vending-machines installing.

The policemen soon found Mickleberry Court and made their way to Susan Tranter's flat. They passed the kitchen window, splashed with pigeon muck and tapped on the door of number twenty-one. It was promptly opened a few inches by a woman. Angel recognized her immediately, and it wasn't Susan Tranter. His mouth opened and then closed.

'Well, well, well. Amy Jones. What are you doing here?'

'Who is it?' a younger woman's voice called from behind her and out of sight. Amy Jones's eyes shone like a panther's.

'It's for me. I'll deal with it,' she called back. 'What do you want, mister?' she said.

Angel put his hand up to the door.

Susan Tranter squeezed her nose round the door jamb. Her jaw dropped when she saw Gawber.

'Oh!'

Angel looked from the woman to Gawber.

'What's this?'

'I'm just visiting. Dropped in. For a coffee,' Amy Jones said quickly.

'That's the woman: Susan Tranter,' Gawber said. 'The woman who said she was nearly run off the road last night by that little red Porsche.'

Angel glared at her.

Amy pulled the door open.

'Oh. Leave her out of this, Mr Angel. This is between Evan and me. It has nothing to do with her.'

The younger woman ran into the back of flat.

'But it has everything to do with me,' Angel snapped, advancing into the room. 'Your friend is under arrest for wasting police time.'

'No! No!' Susan Tranter screamed and pulled at Amy Jones's arm. 'You said it would be safe. You never said there was no risk. That it was your husband. That it was just a laugh.'

Amy wrenched her arm free from the younger woman. 'Shut up, you silly cow!'

'Did she put you up to it?' Angel asked.

'She said it would be safe. That there was no chance of anybody finding out. She promised me a hundred pounds. I'm not going back to prison. I'll die.'

'Shut your mouth.'

'Tut-tut. Sit down on that sofa, the pair of you, and keep quiet.'

Angel reached for his mobile and tapped in a number. 'Ah Crisp. Bring a WPC to flat twenty-one, Mickleberry Court, to pick up two female prisoners. And hurry up.'

He cancelled the phone and pushed it back into his pocket. 'Right, Ron. You take the kitchen and I'll do in here.'

Susan Tranter stood up. Her bright eyes flashed at Angel. 'Here, what are you doing?' She stared down at Amy Evans. 'I'm not going back to prison for her or anybody else.'

'Sit down please.'

'What are you doing?'

'We're looking to see if you have any other surprises hidden away.'

'There's nothing. Why are you picking on me? What have I done?'

'Sit down, miss.'

Amy glared at her. 'Sit down, you silly cow.'

'He's picking on my family. His name's Angel, isn't it.'

'Sit down and be quiet, the pair of you.'

'No. I won't be quiet. Not in my own flat. He's picking on my family.'

Amy glared at her again. 'Sit down. You're making it worse.' Angel sighed. 'Will you sit down and shut up.'

Susan Tranter stuck out her jaw. 'No, I won't. He went over my brother's flat only yesterday and found nothing. And you'll find nothing here!' she bawled.

'Whose flat was that then?' asked Angel.

'Don't pretend you don't know. You're always chasing my brother, Arnold.'

Angel thought a moment, then shook his head.

'You've got the wrong bloke, miss.'

'No, I haven't.' She stared at Amy. 'Look, he's trying to get out of it.'

'Shut up,' Amy bellowed.

'You dragged him into the cop-shop for no reason at all,' Susan Tranter said. 'You searched him and then searched his flat. He said it was you. The big fat ugly one called Angel, he said.'

Angel smiled slightly. 'What's your brother's name again?'

'Don't pretend, Inspector. You know exactly who I mean. You're always pushing him around 'cos he's small. Arnold Smith. Well, he's my step-brother.'

'Yes.' Angel nodded knowingly. 'Fishy Smith. We know him.'

'There I told you, Amy. He can't deny it.'

'Sit down, miss.'

Eight minutes later, Crisp arrived with WPC Baverstock.

'Right,' said Angel. 'Cuff them. Charge this one with wasting police time and the other one with neglecting to observe a probation order.'

The prisoners were handcuffed and led down to the car. Angel caught Crisp by the sleeve on his way out.

'Keep them apart, lad. And don't let them out of your sight,' he added meaningfully.

Only two minutes after they had gone, Angel lifted up the dusty mattress of one of the two beds in the bedroom and found sandwiched between it and the base, a plain white polythene bag sixteen inches by twenty-four inches. It reeked of menthol. He sensed that he had found something important: the breakthrough, the clue he had been hoping for. His fingers shook as he pulled open the bag. He found a bunch of keys and a length of thirty feet of greasy sisal string. His pulse drummed in his ears. He was on the threshold of discovering the murderer of Duncan McFee.

*

'Ahmed, come in here,' Angel said and replaced the phone. He turned to Gawber. 'Ron, go up to that distillery at Slogmarrow, see Angus Leitch and find out if any one of the keys on this bunch fits the door to the ageing-room. Let's hope one of them does. Come straight back and tell me. I'll be down the cells, seeing what I can make of the Cheeky Girls!'

'Right, sir,' Gawber said. He took the keys and dashed off.

Ahmed came through the door. 'Yes sir?'

'I've arrested a woman called Amy Jones. Holloway probation is looking for her. Tell them we've got her here. They might want to send someone from the local office round to interview her.'

'Yes sir.'

'And if anybody is looking for me, I'm down the cells.'

'Right, sir.'

Amy Jones was in cell number one. Angel got the duty jailer to let him in. She was lying on the bunk looking at the door when Angel went in.

'I thought you'd forgotten about me,' she said chirpily, sitting up.

'No,' Angel said sombrely. 'We've found a plastic bag containing a bunch of keys and some string under a mattress in a bedroom at the flat. Is it yours?'

'Don't know what you are talking about. It's not my flat. She was only letting me stay a few nights there while I found my feet,' Amy said smoothly.

Angel stroked his chin while he considered what to do next.

Men were usually smarter than women at defending themselves in cross-examination: although more dishonest, they were always more positive, whether lying or telling the truth. Men's lies were therefore usually easier to isolate, detect and analyse, whereas women were far more devious and would try to confuse the questioner with half-truths, insinuations and convincing intricate false trails. He was thinking he would be better off recording any further interview with Amy Jones, which was, strictly speaking, the requirement these days. He made the decision.

'Right,' he said. He stood up, went out and closed the door.

Amy Jones's jaw dropped. In her experience interviews always lasted longer than that. She leaned back on the bunk, lit a cigarette and blew a blue cloud of smoke towards the door.

Angel peered through the observation slot of cell number three at Susan Tranter. She was sitting sedately on the edge of the bunk fidgeting with a handkerchief. He let himself into the cell.

'You know, I don't know what I am doing here, Inspector. I've done nothing wrong. Just because I let Amy Jones stay with me, it doesn't mean that I am tarred with the same brush. She's a bad lot, I know. I demand to see a solicitor. I am entitled to that, I know. I am not going back to prison again. No way. I've served my time and that's enough. You've no right keeping me in here. I should be out leading a normal life. It isn't as if I have done anything wrong. Tell me. What am I doing here? Go on. Tell me.'

'You know why you're here,' Angel said patiently. 'You told my sergeant a tall story about a woman driving a car dangerously — '

'That was her. She made me do that. She said it was a joke … on her ex-husband.'

Angel shook his head. 'Well, let's see what we can do. There's a plastic bag containing keys and string under a mattress in your bedroom in your flat.'

'I don't know anything about it,' she said, her bulging eyes staring at him. 'She must have brought it with her. I don't know anything about it. She's not going to blame me. I expect she's told you it was mine.'

Angel wasn't prepared to be put off. 'It's very important for you to tell me how you came by it.'

'I don't know anything about it. You've got to believe me, Inspector. I wouldn't lie to you, now would I?'

Angel said: 'Did you say your brother came round to see you yesterday?'

'Last night. Comes round regular.'

'Did he come round the week before?'

'I expect so. I do his washing. Every week. I always done it.'

'Did he go in the bedroom.'

'He changes in there. Puts his clean stuff on. Look here, what's this got to do with anything?'

*

Angel picked up the phone and pressed a button.

'Ahmed … I want Fishy Smith bringing in urgently … Get communications to put out a general notice. I want everybody looking for him. It's in regard to his step-sister. She is in the cells under arrest … Right, lad.'

He replaced the phone. There was a knock at the door. 'Come in.'

It was Gawber with a triumphant look on his face.

Angel smiled. 'Ah! You've found a key that fits?'

'Yes, sir.'

Angel sighed. 'At last! Now we've to find out how the bunch came to be in the possession of Amy Jones and Susan Tranter. They won't talk. They admit nothing. They want to see their lawyers. I bet that one of them read the leak I gave to the Bromersley Chronicle about the 'menthol murder' and the missing keys, that she stumbled across that bag of stuff, and worked it all out. They must have been blackmailing the murderer. Amy Jones has a history of that sort of thing. If I could only find a link between either or both of them, and Angus Leitch, I would have enough for a conviction.'

Gawber looked surprised. 'How was it done, sir?'

'It's something to do with the menthol ointment and the sisal. It's time we went back to the scene of the crime. Bring that bag of string with you.'

Angel drove determinedly up to Slogmarrow, through the gates and round the block to the ageing-room. He parked up and they went through the door and up the steps to Angus Leitch's office. The young man was in a white coat and sitting at his desk writing.

He made to get up as Angel and Gawber came through the door.

Angel waved him down. 'Just need to have another look round, Mr Leitch.'

'That's fine,' the young man said with a smile. 'I have to go out, as it happens. Can I help you with anything?'

Angel looked through the office window and pointed outside.

'Ay. Won't keep you. That overhead crane out there. Is it easy to operate? Could I work it?'

Leitch rubbed his chin. 'Ay. All you do, is activate three switches. Each switch has three positions: all marked. Easy as pie. The controls are on that board by the door. I must warn you that the hook and balance weigh more than a hundred-weight, so keep them high so that they don't hit anything as you move it around.'

'Thank you.'

'Must go.' Angus Leitch took off his white coat, threw it on the chair and rushed out of the door. 'Goodbye.'

Angel looked out of the office window to the vats below. He suddenly had an idea. His eyes glowed with excitement. He dashed downstairs. Gawber followed. Angel went to the switchboard and flicked a switch.

The crane motor was heard to start and the cable rolled, up taking the hook with it up to the ceiling. Angel then moved the crane motor over the vat where the laird's body had been found.

'Look Ron,' he said. 'Go up there, to Leitch's office, open that window and throw the non sticky end of the string out to me. Keep hold of the other end.'

Gawber dashed up the steps.

Angel lined up the crane motor over the vat carefully and then lowered the hook.

Gawber opened the window and threw the string out of it. It didn't drop, it stuck in a tangle, dangling in mid-air six feet below the window.

'You'll need to fasten something heavy to it. Try a spanner off the bench behind you,' said Angel, with a twinkle in his eye.

Gawber grinned. 'Ah. I'm with you, sir.'

A minute later a spanner fastened to the string dropped on to the distillery floor with a rattle. Angel went over to the string, released the spanner and tossed it back on to the floor where it had been found the morning after the murder. Then he lowered the hook on the overhead crane to a position low enough to where he could tie the string to the link above the weighted hook. He positioned the hook over the inspection door of the storage vat, then he returned upstairs to the office.

'Right Ron. Pull that string tight. Sit in the chair. Thread it through the desk drawer handle and pull it.'

Gawber pulled the string fastened to the crane hook and weight through the window. The rough string snagged on the window bottom.

'You need some lubrication, Ron.' Angel said knowingly. He pulled out of his pocket the jar of two per cent menthol in white paraffin and placed it on the desk.

Gawber smiled.

'Now tie it off on the drawer handle.' Angel said, pointing to the desk.

When Gawber had made a simple knot, he turned to Angel.

'And that's how it was done, sir?' he asked.

'Yes. The murderer then sat in the dark and waited. McFee let himself into the room with his own keys and left the bunch in the door. He did his rounds. He tasted a small drop of the gin at each vat. When he reached this last vat and was in the critical position, the murderer released the string, and the crane hook and weight careered through the air delivering him a mighty blow to the back of the head, knocking him into the vat.'

'And some crack on the head that would have been! Just as Mac said.'

'The murderer then threw the end of the sisal through the office window, closed it and went downstairs. He lowered the crane and unfastened the string off the hook. He drove the crane hook well away from the scene, closed the inspection door of the vat and gathered up the string. When he reached the door, he found Duncan McFee's bunch of keys in the lock. He didn't want to go back and he didn't want to leave them there. It might have aroused suspicion before he had time to cover his tracks, if anybody had seen them in the lock, so he put them in the bag he had brought with the sisal and the jar of ointment and walked nonchalantly home.'

'That explains the spanner, the keys, the smell, everything!'

'It doesn't explain what the stuff was doing in Susan Tranter's flat.'

'When we find that out, we can arrest him.'

*

He picked up the phone. 'Angel.'

'It's Crisp, sir. I'm in reception. I've got Fishy Smith. Where do you want him?'

'Ah!' Angel said, his eyebrows raised. 'Bring him straight down here.' He replaced the phone. He stood up and went round and opened the office door. He could hear the protestations as he came down the corridor.

'I don't know why he's got it in for me. Ever since he lost his passport and his tin badge with his photograph on it, he's been after me.'

'It's just round this corner.'

'I know. I know. Don't rush me. Dang me, I've been here often enough.'

Crisp and Fishy Smith appeared round the corner. Fishy Smith saw Angel and pulled a face.

'I don't know nothing about your photograph and badge, I've told you.'

Angel nodded at Crisp. 'Right lad, I'll take it from here.' He turned back to the pickpocket. 'It's not about that, Fishy. Come on in. It's about your step-sister, Susan Tranter. Sit down there.'

'What about her?'

Angel closed the door and moved round to the desk. 'She's in trouble.'

'What? Huh! Up the duff? It's about time at her age.'

'Nothing like that. She's been arrested. She's down here in a cell.'

'Eh? Well, she's not done anything, honest. Our Susan is as straight as a die. She has no need to do anything bent.

177

She's got a big, posh job as housekeeper to a big wheel up at the distillery.'

A coin dropped into a slot in Angel's head. He felt the flutter of a Red Admiral in his chest but he tried not to get excited.

'She gets a wage now, every week, regular as clockwork,' Fishy continued. She's no need to do anything hookey.'

Angel beamed. He tried to stay calm.

'I thought so,' he lied. 'And which gentleman is she doing for?' he said, trying to speak gently and slowly. He was as dainty as a fisherman tickling a trout.

'Eh? I don't know. There's a few of them.'

The Inspector spoke with the charm of an angel. 'You see, Fishy, it's all to do with that bag with the bunch of keys, the string and the jar of menthol ointment you took out of it.'

'Well, I mean even if she's nicked them, they're not worth a quid all in, are they! What will she get? Seven days at the most. Community wotsit.'

'Well, you see, if we could find out who owned them, and speak to the owner, maybe they wouldn't even want to press charges for such a trivial amount. Not worth the solicitor and the time, eh?'

'Sounds fair enough.'

Angel leaned forward. 'So what did you say was the name of the man she works for?'

'I don't know his name, Mr Angel,' said Fishy Smith, shaking his head.

The policeman licked his lips.

'But you could ask Susan.'

'Yes,' said Fishy Smith glumly. He pulled a face and rubbed his neck. 'He was in the paper. There was a full page about the distillery. There was a picture of him, you know. She pointed him out to me.'

'Did she? Which paper?'

'The local rag.'

'The Bromersley Gazette?'

'Yes. Last week, wasn't it?'

Angel shuffled through the pile of stuff on the corner of his desk and soon pulled out a copy of the appropriate paper. He remembered the article and the photographs. He quickly found the pictures of the four retiring directors next to a picture of Angus Leitch, as a possible new CEO. He showed it to Fishy.

'That's him. The one at the end. Nice chap, she says he is.'

Angel looked closely at the picture. 'You sure it is him?'

'Yeah. Positive. She's doing five mornings a week for him.'

Angel reached over to the phone. 'Ahmed … Find DS Gawber. And find Scrivens. It's very urgent. I want them to go up to Slogmarrow, to make an arrest.'

CHAPTER FIFTEEN

'Put him in the interview room, Ron. I'll follow you down.'

'Right, sir,' Gawber said. 'This way, sir.'

The prisoner looked at Angel, then turned and made his way sullenly down the corridor behind DC Scrivens.

'Has he been cautioned?' Angel enquired.

'Yes sir,' Gawber said.

Scrivens opened the interview room door. 'After you, sir.'

'Ay. This way, sir,' Angel said. 'That's it. Sit down there.' He leaned over the table, pushed a tape into the recording machine and pressed the button.

'I've been expecting this, Inspector Angel,' the old man said, shaking his head. 'It's a relief really. Yes. It's been on my conscience ever since I saw his staring eyes looking up at me through the spirit. By then it was too late. But I knew I had to continue to try to get away with it. Mmm. But I almost came to you and gave myself up when that ghastly woman and her friend found the bag with McFee's keys, the string and the menthol in it, and began to blackmail me. You knew about that?'

'I'd worked it out, Mr Fleming. What I don't understand is why you chose to take such an extreme step?'

180

'It was his birthday, you know. The following day. Yes. He would have been fifty. Only a young man. Fifty! He was having a party! He'd invited me to it. It wasn't right for him to enjoy another birthday, when he wouldn't let me enjoy mine! And I'm eighty. Eighty!' he said, the corners of his mouth turned down. 'You know, Inspector, it was exactly thirty years ago, when I was fifty, that McFee's father deliberately stood in the way of me getting on to the board, which made it far too late for me ever to have the opportunity of making chairman. When he was about to be fifty, he was already chairman! It was a case of like father like son, but I wasn't letting a McFee get away with it twice. Oh no! His father had stood in the way of my progress towards the chair, now he was standing in the way of my retirement. I simply had to do something about it. He wouldn't let any of us on the senior board retire. Time was going on.'

'But he couldn't stop you retiring,' Angel said.

Fleming's grey eyes flashed. 'No. But he would have paid out only the absolute minimum. I had been wanting to go for nigh on fifteen years. It was always the same. Wait until next month, next year. We were victims of our own success. We are in for a bumper year, he'd say ... and so on. Somebody had to do something. While he was enjoying his birthdays, I was dreading mine. We'd all signed service contracts. We were paid only a small basic salary while we were working, then after we retired we were to receive those accumulated earnings and the interest on them, and a golden handshake at the chairman's discretion! How much discretion do you think it would have been if I had gone against him? I have a son, daughter-in-law and grandson in Florida. I had hoped to spend the rest of my days in a sumptuous flat overlooking the sea there, which they had prepared for me. I had to do something. I was desperate. My heart is not so good. I didn't expect to survive another British winter. I don't suppose I will now.'

Angel had heard enough. He shook his head. There was enough on the tape for the CPS to close the case. He looked up at Gawber.

'Take him away, Sergeant. Take him away.'

*

Angel was in a cheerless mood when he reached home that evening, even though he had solved the murder of Duncan McFee. He felt sorry for old man Fleming and he tried to console himself with the simplistic view that criminals have to be caught and stopped, whatever justifications are claimed for committing the crime. He talked to Mary about this; she tried to cheer him up, and had prepared finny haddock for tea, which, with brown bread and butter, went down a treat. He then wandered into the garden. The sun was still shining, it had been warm all day; the lawn was dry enough to make cutting it easy, so he dragged out the mower from the little shed and finished it in an hour. He had time to strim the edges and do the paths before flopping in the chair in front of the television to watch Bad Girls, sup two bottles of German beer and toddle up to bed.

It was 8.28 a.m. the following morning, Friday, when he arrived at the office as usual. The evening's relaxation had served him well, and he was absolutely bursting with get-up and go! He threw off his coat and sat down at his desk, determined to launch an all-out effort to find the gold and Yardley before Boodle and his cohorts did. There were two lines of enquiry he hadn't had the opportunity to explore. One was interviewing Martin Taylor, the bank employee who was the inside man who had provided the intelligence to the robbers, and who was now serving time in HMP Hallas End, and the other was searching Enchantra Davison's flat.

He reached out and picked up the phone. 'Ahmed … Get me Hallas End prison. I want to speak to the governor … I'll hold on.'

Eventually he was put through to the assistant governor. He had hoped to make an arrangement to see Martin Taylor that morning, however, the earliest time he could visit him was the following Monday, 25 April. He replaced the phone and pulled a face. Even though he had stressed that the matter was urgent, there was some unexplained reason why it was not possible to see Taylor any earlier. He reached out for the phone again.

'Ahmed ... Tell DS Gawber I want him, then let me have that last known address you found for Enchantra Davison and a street map of Birmingham ... Right.'

Gawber knocked on Angel's door.

'You wanted me, sir?'

'I've got to find the gold before Boodle does, and I've got to find Yardley. If we find one, t'other won't be far away. I want to take a look at Enchantra Davison's flat; there might be something Boodle has missed.'

Two hours later they were in Birmingham. Angel was driving and Gawber navigating.

'This is Sokell Road. We want Montpelier Buildings,' Gawber said lifting his head out of the A to Z. 'It's on the left ... along here a bit, I think ... Turn here. Number forty.'

'Right,' Angel nodded. He drove up the short drive, round the bushes and across the front of the block and parked next to a small blue car. He looked up at the three storey block of modern, red-brick flats with small balconies which stood back from the road and overlooked dedicated parking-spaces beneath them.

'It looks as if number forty's on the first floor.'

'Any sign of Boodle's men ... or anybody else watching the place?'

'No sir.'

They went up the thirteen stone steps at the double, and along the balcony area, past four windows displaying pretty floral curtains, and four scrubbed-down doorsteps to number forty. Angel knocked on it boldly, just to make sure, and dived in his pocket for his skeleton keys. Gawber kept look out. It took Angel three minutes to turn all five levers, not one of his best performances. The lock clicked and the door opened.

Fortunately nobody in the street below seemed interested. They pushed straight inside and closed the door quickly. It was a pleasant enough one-bedroom flat, with sitting-room, kitchen and bathroom. There was very little furniture. It was plain and cheap; and the wardrobe, drawers and cupboards had very little in them. Enchantra Davison had made an excellent job of emptying the place without Special Branch noticing.

The two men systematically searched every drawer and every cupboard. They moved all the furniture and lifted the edges of the carpets. Gawber unscrewed the fancy polished fastenings from the boxed-in bath and removed the long side to look underneath it. They pulled out the cushions from the three-piece suite and ran their hands down the sides. Angel took off the back of the television set to see if anything had been deliberately hidden or had accidentally fallen through the grilles. Nothing. They put everything back as it was and, two hours later, Angel stood in the middle of the room and surveyed the scene.

'Well, Ron,' Angel said. 'Boodle's men did a good job. If there was anything here, they've found it. Let's go. Will you see to the dustbin? I'll take a look in her car. That'll be the blue one.'

They left the flat quietly and repeated the business with the skeleton keys to lock the door. They flew past the four neighbouring flats and down the steps. Gawber disappeared round the back of the building. Angel crossed over to Enchantra Davison's car and tried the doors. They were locked and the windows fully wound up. He took a retractable metal tape out of his pocket, pulled out a foot's length and slid it in the gap in the door. There were a few people walking past on the pavement about six yards away. He was pleased that they were not interested in his activities. He had to manoeuvre the metal strip in the gap several times before he felt the pressure of the lock mechanism, then he gave it a smart tug, the button on the door jumped up and he was in.

Gawber appeared. 'We're too late. The bin's been emptied.'

Angel pulled a face. 'Huh!' That was another line of information closed. He leaned across the car and unlocked the door opposite. 'Check that pocket in the door on that side, will you, Ron?'

Gawber opened the door and dug into the cavity; he found a duster. Then he ran his hand along the shelf under the radio. There was nothing there.

Angel opened the glove compartment. He pulled out a 1999 AA book, an empty packet of Capstan full strength cigarettes, a gilt-coloured lipstick-holder called 'Honeymoon Orange', a tyre-pressure gauge and half a roll of Trebor Extra Strong mints. He glanced at the items, then pushed them back in and slammed the door. He crouched down and looked across the car floor. It was pretty clean. Under the seat was something; it looked like a discarded tissue. He reached for it and brought it out. It was a screwed-up, empty paper-bag. He straightened it out. A few dry crumbs dropped out. It had obviously at one time held a sandwich or similar. It was six inches by six inches. His mouth dropped open when he read the words printed on it in blue: Millington's Winter Mixture.

*

Although it was ten minutes to five when Angel and Gawber arrived back in Bromersley, Angel could not possibly have deferred calling on Mrs Buller-Price until the next morning. He dropped Gawber off at the end of Church Street, which was only sixty yards from the station, and drove purposefully on the moors road to the Buller-Price farm. He was trying to work out what he was going to say to her; the words weren't coming easily. He really had thought it was a coincidence that she should have been in North Yorkshire the same day as Operation Midas, and that it had been pure chance that Yardley had commandeered her car! That was obviously all hokum! She had deliberately deceived him and he was very angry.

He passed by Tunistone and then turned off the main road up the steep hill to the lopsided sign, along the cart track, through the yard gate until he arrived at the farmhouse. He pulled on the handbrake and switched off the engine. The dogs had heard the car arrive and pandemonium broke out as the farmhouse door opened and the huge figure of Mrs Buller-Price appeared framed in the opening. The dogs pushed roughly past her through the doorway into the yard, barking and yelping with excitement.

When she saw that it was Inspector Angel who had caused the dogs to get excitable, a big smile appeared on her face, her eyes twinkled and she put her hands together in front of her with delight.

'Just in time for tea, Inspector.'

The dogs surrounded him noisily in welcome.

'Come along troops,' she called heartily. 'Let the Inspector by.' The dogs immediately lost interest except for one small, ugly, little one who yapped a bit longer to get the last word in, then dashed into the house. Schwarzenegger padded silently up to him, sniffed his hand and shoes, wagged his tail lightly twice and wandered through the front door.

'Come along in, Inspector. The kettle is on.'

Angel followed her into the house.

'Make yourself at home. Find a chair you like. It's very nice of you to call.'

'I'm not really on a social call,' said Angel, trying to establish some distance between them. He couldn't ignore the way he had been grossly deceived by her and he intended that she should become well aware of it. 'It's business. Very much business,' he said coolly.

'Oh?' she said, detecting the frost. She turned to him and raised an eyebrow. 'Business, is it? Well, you can still have a cup of tea and a fairy cake, because, dear Inspector

Angel,' she added with a beaming smile, 'whatever the business is, I'm determined not to fall out with you.'

She flounced off into the kitchen. Angel shook his head.

'Please don't walk away from me when I'm talking,' he bawled.

'Temper. Temper. I'm just mashing the tea and putting the cakes on a plate,' she called back from the kitchen. 'Sit down in that big chair by the fire. The one you like. I won't be a minute. Then I will give you my full attention, I promise.' She appeared at the sitting-room door with the tray in her hands. 'There we are.'

Angel made to stand up.

'Stay where you, Inspector. I told you I wouldn't be long. I'll put it on this little table here, between us. There. Now. Yes. Let it mash for two and a half minutes. I'll watch the clock.' She dropped into the chair opposite him. 'Now whatever is this business? I hope it's not tedious. I do hate stocks and shares. And I am hopeless at percentages. I know that twenty per cent is a half, but that's all.'

Angel stared straight into her face. 'It's about you giving a scone to Enchantra Davison the last time you saw her,' he blurted out in rapid fire. He felt that if he hadn't spat it out there and then, she would never have given him the opportunity.

Mrs Buller-Price's jaw dropped and her mouth stayed open for five seconds, while her eyes tried to find somewhere innocent to look.

'Oh. How did you know about that, Inspector?' she eventually managed to say.

'There's lots of things you had better start telling me, and it had better be the truth, the whole truth and nothing but the truth!'

She put her hand to her mouth. 'Oh dear.' But she recovered quickly. 'I have never told you a lie, Inspector. I may not always have told you the whole truth, but I have never told you a lie. I cannot tell lies. Why, I would never, ever be able to share another bowl of strawberries and ice cream with the Archbishop of York if I had told a lie. Oh no. No.' She pursed her lips and shook all four chins.

'I need to know the whereabouts of Morris Yardley and the gold, and I need to know it now!' roared Angel.

'Time's up. Tea's mashed,' she said.

Angel glared at her.

She picked up the teapot lid, stirred the tea round vigorously with a spoon and replaced the lid. She sighed, then said: 'I have no idea where Morris is, Inspector, or the gold.'

'Or Enchantra Davison?'

'She's with Morris, almost certainly. That was their intention.'

'Oh? There was a plan then?'

'Oh yes.'

'You'd better tell me what it was.'

'It was not my fault you put a thingie in the van and followed me all the way back here, you know. Morris said that it had been agreed that the van would not be bugged. You didn't keep your word, Inspector. It was very naughty of you.'

'Oh,' Angel said. 'How is it you know Morris Yardley?'

Mrs Buller-Price smiled sweetly as she lowered the teapot.

'I have known him over fifty years, Inspector. It will be fifty-one on Boxing Day. That's his birthday.' She passed a cup of tea to Angel. 'There's sugar and milk. Help yourself.'

Angel took the cup and thoughtfully stirred the sugar in for a few moments. Then, suddenly, his mouth dropped open. He immediately put the cup down on the table in front of him.

'Don't tell me you're his mother,' he said.

She nodded proudly. 'He was born years before I had ever met dear Ernest Buller-Price. But don't ask me who the father was; I was sworn to secrecy in a limousine outside Claridges two weeks before he was born.' She paused for a moment, then added: 'I know now I didn't press my case hard enough. If I had been more grasping, I think I could have kept my baby, got a villa in the Mediterranean, and a title.'

'A title?'

'Yes. Lady Duchess Victoria Millington. How does that sound?'

Angel sniffed. 'A bit over the top, don't you think?'

She laughed and all four chins shook.

'Where does the name Millington come in, then?'

'It's my maiden name, Inspector.'

'Of course.'

'You are not eating. Have a fairy-cake.'

'Thank you. Of course. Millington's Winter Mixture'.

'The sweetshop in town. Yes. Founded by my grandfather in nineteen hundred and six. He used to make boiled sweets at the back. He created 'Millington's Winter Mixture'. They were posh cough-sweets, you know. After my father and mother died my dear sister, Elizabeth ran the shop until she died last October. That's how I came by the jars,' she said, pointing to the six large glass bottles of sweets on the sideboard.

'And the printed sweet-bags?'

'Elizabeth must have ordered millions. Still, waste not, want not.'

Angel realized they were moving away from the point. He was determined not to be taken in as usual by her olde worlde charm.

'Where is Morris Yardley now?' he said impatiently.

'I don't know.'

'You said there was a plan.'

'Yes. A plan to get him out of prison. He knew the judiciary would never grant him his freedom for gold. But if they thought they could trick him into believing that they would, he could see a plan that might work.'

'Where is he now?'

'I don't know. He wouldn't tell me his plans in case you arrested me and tortured me.' She gave a small smile.

He stared at her with his poker face.

She looked back into his eyes.

'And the gold?'

'All he would say was that it was somewhere safe.'

Angel shook his head.

'Have you seen him since he escaped?'

'No.'

'Have you been in touch with him or him with you, by phone or in any other way, since his escape?'

'No. He'll keep out of the way while that man Boodle is hunting him. I'm certain of it. He'll disappear into the night, and nobody will ever hear from him again. He knows how to disappear,' she said, looking thoughtfully down at the plate of fairy-cakes. Then she added sadly, 'More's the pity.'

Angel shook his head. He felt sorry for the old lady.

She munched into another cake.

He sighed. 'It's a very serious matter, you know. You colluded with him to exchange vehicles, and then you drove the van that was monitored back to Tunistone, creating a false trail to fool the police. You were aiding and abetting the escape of a prisoner. It's a very serious offence.'

Mrs Buller-Price's eyes opened wide.

'I didn't know you'd put a thingie in the back and that you were following me. I didn't intend to lay a false trail. I didn't fool the police intentionally or unintentionally. I didn't see any police cars in my mirror. In fact, there wasn't a single police car or a bobby on the beat that I could have reported the matter to on my way home. And I did have to come home. I couldn't dawdle about up there with five Jerseys to milk and animals to feed.'

Angel knew this was right.

'Nevertheless,' he said sternly. 'I will have to consult the Crown Prosecution Service and see exactly what charges they will want to bring against you. By rights, you should come back with me and be formally arrested. However, if you give me your promise not to leave the area, I won't insist on it.'

Mrs Buller-Price blew out a big sigh.

'Oh, I do. I do,' she said earnestly. 'I do most solemnly swear it. On my best Girl Guide uniform. The one I was wearing when the Queen Mother pinned the badge on me, for being the best cook in our pack at frying a sausage on a candle I had made from goose-grease and a toilet-roll middle.'

*

Angel arrived home late, tired and mentally spent. Mary could see from his face that all was not well. She asked him what was wrong and he told her about the trip to Birmingham, the finding of the crumpled sweet-bag with scone crumbs in it, and how it had led him back to Mrs Buller-Price and so on … She smiled sympathetically, but he didn't really believe she understood how he felt, and he was too wound up to explain how desperate he now was to find Yardley and the gold, ahead of Boodle. He sat in the chair and chewed it all over and over again, like a duck with an elastic band. By 8.30 he was asleep.

Next morning, Saturday, he got up late and spent the day doing nothing in particular. Mostly, he sat tense in the chair looking at the television screen but seeing nothing; he shrunk into himself as he visualized Boodle chasing up and down the country, questioning everybody who had had the slightest connection with the robbery: their friends, their known acquaintances and so on. However tenuous the lead, Boodle would be there, whipping his men, ploughing through records of contemporary cases to see if he could come up with some link or idea that would lead him to Yardley and the gold.

Mary served up tea and they watched television — well, Mary watched television. Angel's only unexplored accessible lead was Martin Taylor. If anyone knew where Yardley might be or where he might have stashed the gold, it could be him. It was infuriating that he would have to wait until Monday before he could interview to him.

The television screen went blank as Mary pressed the remote. 'It's eleven o'clock,' Mary said and she yawned.

Angel yawned.

CHAPTER SIXTEEN

Sunday morning was hell. He got up late and spent the first hour trying not to get under Mary's feet. She wanted to be in every room at the same time! He eventually managed to get dressed, putting on his sports jacket and flannels, and saunter down to the newsagents where he bought a paper. He came back, and noticed with satisfaction the smell of meat roasting and the warmth of the oven as he passed it. Mary was doing something dangerous with a carving knife and a turnip on the worktop; he took a bottle of German beer from the fridge, opened it and went into the sitting-room.

'Anything you want to do, love?' he called out. 'Do you want to go out somewhere?'

'No.'

He wasn't surprised or disappointed. He put the beer down on a coaster and picked up the newspaper. He opened it up and at the bottom of page two there was a little piece comprising five short paragraphs. As he read down the column, his blood ran cold.

GOLD ROBBER FOUND HANGED
Martin Taylor, 42, a prisoner at Hallas End jail was found at 6.10 am yesterday morning dead

in his cell. He had been hanged by a rope contrived from strips of material torn from a towel and suspended from an air-grate in the wall. He was serving ten years for armed bank robbery. Foul play is not suspected.

Martin Taylor had been security manager to the Bank of Agara and had been the source of information to the gang who robbed a security van outside the bank of gold bars worth £66m in April 2003. None of the gold had been recovered.

It is understood that Taylor had had a high-ranking visitor from Special Branch yesterday (Friday) afternoon. It was not known whether this had had any bearing on his state of mind.

A prison spokesman said Martin Taylor, from Fulham, London was not a known depressive and had not been on suicide watch.

Footnote: The leader and the only other known survivor of the gang, Morris Yardley, escaped from high security Welham prison on Tuesday last and is still on the run.

Angel's jaw dropped.
'You can set the table,' Mary called from the kitchen.
He didn't hear her.

*

It was Monday, 25 April. Angel arrived at the station at 8.15 a.m. and burst into the communications room to learn the latest news regarding the search for Yardley and the recovery of the gold. There was a piece in the Police Gazette about the death of Martin Taylor, but there was nothing new or helpful. He came out of the room with a face like an undertaker's cat and charged down the corridor, just missing the plumber as he was feeding out a blue plastic waterpipe. He stopped briefly, stared at the man, shook his head impatiently, stepped over the pipe and proceeded to his office. The plumber straightened up, stared after him, took the unlit stub end of a cigarette out of his mouth, muttered something, then put it back in again.

Gawber came up the corridor. They met at Angel's office door.

'Come in, Ron,' said Angel, as he hung his coat on the hook. 'I've been making some rough calculations. That gold will weigh about half a ton and take up the space of about four hundred house-bricks. Where might Yardley have put it? I mean, it's got to be somewhere. He couldn't just shove it in his back pocket.' He sniffed and flopped in the chair. 'We're not looking where it is, Ron.'

'No sir.' Gawber frowned. 'Could it be concealed in a car ... say, the boot and some on the back seat?'

'Might do. I don't know if the car would move though.'

'A heavy-powered one might.'

'I don't think you'd get four hundred bricks in a car.'

'No. P'raps not.'

Angel couldn't any longer avoid saying: 'Heard about Martin Taylor?'

Gawber nodded. His face spoke volumes.

'Very sad. Tragic. No need for a trip to Hallas End then. I suppose the high-ranking visitor from Special Branch would have been Commander Boodle?'

'Who else?' he said waving his arms. 'We've got to find Yardley and the gold soon, before he does! They have to be somewhere.'

Gawber nodded.

'Ay,' Angel said, rubbing his chin roughly. 'There's nothing more I can do about it. Let's get on with something else.'

'Yes sir. I have checked the serial numbers of Evan Jones's gold bars and they are definitely not stolen. I've seen the receipts. He bought them quite legitimately.'

'Oh,' Angel said coolly. 'That's a profitable business.'

'Can he have his gold back now then, sir?'

'Not yet. The super's expecting magic from the Inland Revenue. Ask him?

194

'Right.' Gawber made for the door. When he opened it, Ahmed was there, about to knock.

'Come in, lad. What is it?'

Gawber went out and closed the door.

'About holidays, sir?'

'Holidays?' bawled Angel.

'Yes sir,' Ahmed said boldly.

'What about them?'

Ahmed's face brightened. 'Well sir, I've been wanting to mention this to you for some time. Most bank holidays fall on Mondays: Easter Monday, May day, Spring bank, August bank and so on. All Mondays.'

'Yes lad, so what,' said Angel, testily.

'Well I don't work Mondays, sir, as you know. So I don't get them off. I work regular Saturdays instead.'

'Yes, lad. Well if you are not working on Mondays, how can you possibly have them off?' said Angel, deliberately missing the point. 'What do you want? Do you want to work Shrove Tuesday, Sheffield Wednesday and Maundy Thursday instead?' he bellowed mockingly.

'No sir,' Ahmed protested. 'As I don't work those Mondays … '

Suddenly, Angel jumped to his feet. He stared straight ahead, trancelike, and appeared to see nothing. His mouth was wide open.

Ahmed was surprised. He wondered if the inspector was all right. Something very strange had happened to him. It wasn't clear what it was. His face was white. The blood had drained away. Something had changed him. Ahmed didn't know what to do. Then Angel began to mutter.

'Maundy Thursday … Maundy Thursday. Yes. That's it!'

Ahmed stared at him. He was worried.

'Are you all right, sir?'

The blood was coming back to Angel's cheeks. His eyes began to shine. A bell had rung! A penny had dropped! Or something.

'Maundy Thursday,' he said. 'Yes. Of course. If Maundy Thursday was on 17 April, then I know where the gold is!'

'Are you all right, sir?'

Angel didn't hear him.

'Hey! Ahmed,' he bellowed. 'Ahmed! Where the hell are you?'

Ahmed blinked. 'I'm here, sir.'

'Oh,' Angel said surprised. 'Well stay here. Stop dodging about the place!'

'I haven't moved, sir. I've been here all the time.'

'Well, listen. It's obvious, lad,' said Angel, excitedly. 'Obvious! If Maundy Thursday was on 17 April, then I know where the gold is! I need a diary. Have you got a diary for 2003? Have you got a diary? Quick! Quick! One that will show us.'

'I've got this year's, sir. On my desk. I'll fetch it.'

He turned to the door, opened it and ran down the corridor to the CID office. Angel followed. They arrived at the office together.

There were twelve officers in the CID room: some working at computers, some on the phone, some talking.

Ahmed picked up a red A5-sized book from his desk by the door and began slowly turning over the pages. Angel snatched it from him.

'But will it show us, tell us, when Maundy Thursday was, two years back?'

Angel turned over the pages rapidly. He looked at the back and then the front and then threw it on the desk.

'That's no good!' He turned to the other people in the room. 'Listen up everybody,' he bellowed. 'Quiet please!'

There was silence. Everybody stared at him.

'This is very important. Very important! Has anybody here got a diary for 2003?' he bawled. Everybody looked blank. 'Anybody here got a diary for 2003?' he repeated. 'Or can say when Maundy Thursday was … You see, if Maundy Thursday was on 17 April 2003, then I know where the gold is!'

There was more silence.

'Nobody?' he yelled.

A few small voices muttered: 'No sir.'

Angel darted out of the room and then came back.

'Ahmed!'

'Yes sir?'

'Find DS Gawber, DS Crisp and DC Scrivens, and send them to my office pronto.'

'Yes sir.'

'And for god's sake, find me a diary for 2003!' he bawled.

Ahmed shook his head in confusion. Then nodded. 'Erm — yes sir.'

'And hurry up. It's vitally important. You see, if Maundy Thursday was on 17 April 2003, then I know where the gold is!'

'Yes sir. Yes sir. I heard you the first time!' Ahmed stammered, not quite sure what to do.

Angel dashed out of the room calling back over his shoulder:

'I'll be in the super's office!'

'Right sir.'

Angel raced down the corridor to the office at the far end. He pushed open the door and burst straight in. The superintendent was at his desk. He looked up angrily and snarled.

Angel didn't notice the snarl.

'Horace, if Maundy Thursday was on 17 April 2003, then I know where the gold is!'

'What's that?' Harker growled, and spat out a nail.

'Have you got an old diary for 2003?'

'What? Erm … erm … erm … '

'Or a calendar?'

'What? Somewhere, no doubt. Let me think?' He rubbed his bony chin. 'Let me think. What's the matter, lad?'

Angel groaned impatiently, then he said:

'All I want to know is what date Maundy Thursday was in 2003? That's all. If it was 17 April, then I know where the gold is.' As an afterthought, he said, 'And Yardley will be standing right in the middle of it!'

The superintendent blinked, then quickly pulled out a drawer at the bottom of his desk and began rummaging about in it.

'I'll want an ARV. At least one,' Angel went on. 'Six men. And some picks and shovels. Where's that diary? Have you got one, Horace, or haven't you? A calendar will do if it's for 2003.'

Ahmed appeared, breathing heavily at the superintendent's door. He had a book in his hand; it looked like a diary.

'This is 2003, sir,' Ahmed said tentatively.

Angel turned and saw him. He looked at the diary he was holding. His eyes flashed. He snatched it and glanced at the cover. 'This is it, lad! This is it!' He zipped through the pages to April. 'Tenth, fourteenth ... seventeenth ... Here it is! Maundy Thursday. Feast of the Passover! Yes!! Yes! It is!' he shouted. He shoved the diary back into Ahmed's hands.

'Come with me, lad.' He charged up the corridor to his own office. DS Gawber, DS Crisp and DC Scrivens were waiting for him. They stared at him apprehensively. 'Right lads. I want an ARV straightaway. Will you see to that, Ron. Have it out front in five minutes. Travel in convoy behind me. Bring your own car. No sirens. Right?'

'Right, sir,' Gawber said and dashed off.

Angel turned to Crisp. 'Now, lad, I want six uniformed men and a big van. The riot van'll have to do. And you bring your own car. And be ready out front in four minutes. And tell everybody, no sirens.'

'I'll do what I can, sir,' Crisp said and turned to go.

'That's not good enough!' Angel bawled angrily. 'Do what I bloody well tell you!'

Crisp muttered something and was gone.

Angel turned to DC Scrivens. 'Now lad. Go to the stores. Draw six picks and six shovels and get them to the front of the station to go in the riot van immediately. All right?'

'Yes sir.'

'You've got three minutes.'

'Wow!' yelled Scrivens.

'And get yourself a place in Gawber's car.'

'Sir,' he shouted and was gone.

Ahmed looked very nervous.

'Now lad. How many wanted pics of Yardley have you in CID?'

'Erm ... about twenty, sir. I think.'

'Fetch them and make sure every one in this task force has got one. Right.'

'Yes sir.'

'Go on then. Scatter!' he bawled and waved his hands in the air.

Ahmed ran off, looking very serious.

The superintendent bustled into Angel's office, putting on his raincoat.

'I don't know what madness this is, Michael!' he said, sourly. 'But I'm coming along.'

'Right, sir.'

Harker pointed a long, skinny finger at Angel's face. 'But it's your show.'

'We're leaving in two minutes. From the front. Meet you there in one. Going to fetch my car round.'

'Where are we going exactly?' asked Harker busily buttoning up the coat and adjusting the collar. 'Where is the gold? And what the hell has it to do with Maundy Thursday?'

Angel had gone.

The super looked round.

'Michael? Where are you?' He looked out through the office door. 'Grrr!'

The task force was duly assembled at the front of the station; considering the speed at which it had been called together, it was in remarkably good order. There were five vehicles altogether. Angel arrived and parked his car at the head of the convoy. The riot van was next in position with six burly uniformed PCs with picks and shovels at their feet.

The ARV was a black Mercedes with four marksmen in bulletproof vests and helmets, and behind them were Gawber and Crisp in their respective cars.

Ahmed was still pushing photographs with descriptions of Yardley on the back through the vehicle windows into any pair of hands that didn't have one. There was a hubbub of animated chatter and the clunk of vehicle doors being hastily closed. Angel walked rapidly down the line.

'Follow in convoy. No blue lights. No sirens. Let's go!' he yelled to each of the drivers.

He reached his car and jumped in. Ahmed followed and slammed the door, then the superintendent came running down the steps and got in the front passenger seat.

Angel started the engine and the convoy pulled away.

He drove along Church Street to the roundabout, travelled three quarters of the way round it and then turned off towards the old part of town.

'You didn't say where we were going,' the superintendent said.

'Just a minute, sir,' Angel said as he changed gear. He glanced towards the backseat. 'Ahmed.'

'Yes sir.'

'Keep your eye out behind. Make sure we all keep together.'

'Right sir,' Ahmed replied.

Angel glanced at the superintendent as he changed into top gear.

'To answer your question, sir.'

'Ay,' Harker said. 'About time.'

Progress was very satisfactory. They were making about 20 mph through the town centre. Suddenly, they were at the traffic lights. They had just changed to red.

Angel applied the brake.

Three big black foreign cars and a black van, all with tinted windows and CD plates sailed past the front of the car bonnet like a fleet of sailing-boats.

'Did you see that lot,' Angel said.

'Ay,' The superintendent sniffed impatiently.

'What's a convoy of CD cars doing trooping through Bromersley? Wonder what country they are from?'

'Who cares?' the superintendent snarled.

The lights changed. Angel let in the clutch. They moved on fifty yards.

'Ahmed. Everybody still with us?'

'Yes sir.'

The superintendent cleared his throat, very loudly.

Angel glanced at him and changed gear.

'Oh. Yes sir. I'm sorry. I was saying, erm … the robbery was on Maundy Thursday, 17 April 2003.'

'I know that, don't I?' the super sneered. 'I know that. By god, you've made enough fuss about it. Tell me summat I don't know.'

'Well, the day after Maundy Thursday is Good Friday. That's a holiday. And it was a holiday on Easter Sunday, Monday and Tuesday following as well.'

'Ay,' said Harker. 'So what?'

'We're going to Morris Yardley's aunt's shop, better known as Millington's sweet-shop.'

The super's eyes opened wide. 'Oh? Used to get boxes of candied peel and all sorts of fancy chocolate and Christmas novelties from there.' He sniffed. Then he added, 'What are we going there for?'

Angel looked in the driving mirror. He could see the riot van nicely positioned behind him. He changed up to top gear again.

'Well, sir, the few days following the robbery of the gold in London, Millington's shop, here in Bromersley, would have been closed for the Easter holidays. Now, if you remember, the shop used to flood sometimes, say after a heavy downpour of rain, because it was below pavement level.'

'It did. I've seen it,' Harker said, suddenly becoming almost human. 'I remember an old woman, Miss Millington, serving me on duckboards in wellingtons.'

'Yes. Well, Mrs Buller-Price told me that her sister had had a drain put in two years ago. Now that would have been the time of the robbery: April 2003. Also, I remembered Morris Yardley was an experienced bricklayer; it was his trade for thirty years. Now he would have needed a safe place to hide the gold, wouldn't he? The newspapers were then full of news of the robbery. Everybody was looking for him. The Met and all forty-three police forces were on red alert. It occurred to me that with the shop being closed for the Easter holiday, it must have seemed to him a golden opportunity (if you'll excuse the pun) to bring the gold away from the heat in London and hide it in Bromersley under a new floor, whilst putting in a drain for his grateful old aunt!'

The superintendent's jaw dropped.

Ahmed had been earwigging and his eyes shone like a B707's landing-lights.

'I'm sure the gold is there.' Angel said, pushing up the indicator switch. 'It's the obvious place.'

The super rubbed his bony chin. 'Yes. Hmmm.'

'The imminent demolition of the shop would explain Yardley's urgency to get out of prison and move the gold before it was buried under the new Multimass supermarket.'

'Or dug out by workmen levelling the site, and shared out among themselves,' the super added with a sniff. 'Hmmm. Hmmm. And that means there's a strong case against the woman, then.'

Angel changed down and turned left into Albert Street.

'I don't think Elizabeth Millington knew. Anyway, she's dead of course. Died six months ago. And I don't suppose her sister knew either. Anyway, the shop is still standing, with thirty or so other buildings — I remember — all boarded up, awaiting demolition to make room for the big new Multimass store, petrol station and car park. And there are eight-hundred and twenty gold bars under the floor.'

Ahmed's face was a picture of wide-eyed amazement.

Angel turned the corner into Victoria Street.

'We are nearly there.' the superintendent said. 'Have you decided how you are going to play this, Michael?'

'Yes sir. We'll be with the quiet mob at the back door, while a brass band plays at the front.'

The superintendent wrinkled his nose. He seemed to approve.

Angel followed the bend round in the road and there it was: a partly cleared stretch of seven acres of land that had once been mixed residential and business property, on the fringe of Bromersley town centre. In the middle of the site was a row of twenty-four stone-built houses, and two small retail shops, all empty and boarded up with chipboard. The fascia above the window of the far end shop could still be read: ENDERBY's HIGH CLASS BAKERS. The nearest shop had a big faded wooden sign saying MILLINGTON'S SWEET SHOP. The roads, pavements, lampposts, foundations and sewer grates could still be seen. That morning, it was deserted. There were no cars, no vehicles, no demolition equipment, and no signs of life. No Yardleys. No children playing. Even the birds were giving it a miss.

Angel pulled on the handbrake, put his hand through the window and signalled the convoy to stop, then he got out of the car and walked up to each vehicle to give the driver his instructions. He returned to his car and led the Mercedes ARV and the riot van into the cleared area round the derelict streets to the back door of the sweet-shop. The sergeant leading the ARV had had instructions to make a rapid entrance, using whatever force was necessary, arresting any occupants, securing the premises and reporting back to him ASAP.

Meanwhile, DS Gawber and DS Crisp pulled away and let their cars roll quietly downhill to the front door of Millington's shop. They were to wait two minutes exactly and then bang on the door and kick up a racket.

Angel stopped at the back of the shop and got out of the car. The superintendent and Ahmed joined him.

The armed men went straight into the building. He saw that no force to gain entrance had been necessary: the back door had already been torn off its hinges and thrown on to some flagstones.

In seconds, men's voices called from inside the house.

'All clear upstairs.'

'All clear downstairs.'

The ARV sergeant poked his gun and his nose out of the back door.

'It's all clear, sir. There's nobody here. We haven't checked it for explosives.'

'That's all right. Thanks, lad.' Angel turned to Ahmed. 'Nip round to the front and tell DS Gawber and DS Crisp, we're in.'

'Yes sir.'

Angel and the superintendent pushed their way into the ramshackle remains of the big, old kitchen with the black fireplace grey with dust, the torn wallpaper showing six different floral patterns and the open door revealing wooden stairs leading to the upper floor. There was very little light. He brushed past a man who banged his elbow with his gun.

'Sorry sir.'

'Can I get in the room that was the shop?'

'Straight ahead, sir. Though that middle room and then through the door at the opposite side of it.'

'Right, thanks.'

The superintendent said: 'Can't see anything, Michael.'

'No sir. Stick with me.'

They lowered their heads and descended precariously down two steep internal steps into the old shop. Angel's eyes were becoming adjusted. The ceiling was unusually low, just as he remembered it. Light leaked in round the edge of the boarded-up window. He could see the old wooden counter pushed back against the wall. The floor was uneven and like a freshly ploughed field. There were piles of fresh soil and chunks of concrete unevenly strewn across the floor. It smelled like a sewer and the air was cold and damp.

The superintendent sniffed. 'We're too late.'

Angel pulled an angry face but said nothing. He could smell something burning.

On the dusty shop counter Angel could see a balance scale, a short handled pick, a vacuum flask with its stopper out, a plastic screw-top cup half-full of coffee, two empty plastic sandwich packets, and the lid off a sweetie jar with a cigarette still smouldering in it. He stuck his little finger in the coffee. 'Still warm,' he muttered. He picked up the improvised ashtray and took it across the uneven shop floor to a shaft of light peeking through the edge of the boarded window. He peered closely at the smouldering tab end. It was no surprise to him to read the printed words: Capstan Full Strength.

CHAPTER SEVENTEEN

It was a week later when Ahmed dashed down the corridor to Angel's office from reception with an official-looking cream coloured envelope in his hand. He knocked eagerly on the door.

'Come in.'

Ahmed bounced noisily into the room, panting.

'Steady on, lad. Steady on. What's up?'

'This has just come for you by hand, sir. Ed Scrivens said a foreign chap in a top hat in a Rolls Royce brought it. He had to sign for it, in three places! Looks very important. I brought it straight down.'

'What?'

Angel turned the envelope over and looked at the address. It had the letters CD stamped in red on both sides, and some writing in Arabic along the bottom of the face side. He frowned.

'Must be my refund from the Inland Revenue,' he quipped. 'Let's have a look. They didn't have to send it "special delivery".' He ripped into the envelope and unfolded the single thick yellow typewritten A4 letterhead. 'Hmm. It's not from the tax office, Ahmed. P'raps it's a special offer: probably twenty quid off a new wheelchair. Let's see.'

He read:

From the office of the Head of Police and Judiciary,
Ministry of the Interior,
Dongo El Mitsoshopi,
Agara.
April 29th 2005.
Dear Inspector Angel,

I don't suppose you ever expected to hear from me, but I want to thank you for the decent, mostly fair and honest way you have dealt with me. My mother was right, for a copper you are not bad. She had always said that you was. Now I am writing to you because, regrettably, I won't be able to visit her in the UK for the next 20 years or so, as there aren't any extradition laws between them and the UK. (But she can come over and visit me here, and I'd look after her and give her a right good time). In the meantime, I would be grateful if you would continue to keep an eye on her for me.

Coming to Agara is a colossal sacrifice, but all in all, life isn't looking too bad. My lady friend, Enchantra is with me and we hope to get married very soon and settle down in this lovely hot climate. I've been appointed Chief of Police and head of the judiciary for which I feel I am well qualified.

When I arrived here, I spoke with the King about the RAF flying over the Mitsoshopi desert. I had heard about the UK government's difficulty from the newspapers. The King has now phoned the PM and sanctioned the flight path, so that has all been sorted out. By the way, I have also persuaded the King to do something for you as a thank you. He has agreed to award you the golden Scimitar of Agara. It will be coming to you direct from the Minister of Culture with a letter very soon. It's worth about £10,000, so if you don't want to wear it you can always flog it at Sothebys.

With best wishes,

Yours truly,

Morris Yardley Esq.,

Chief of Police and head of the Judiciary.

Angel pulled up outside the farmhouse, got out of the car, walked up to the door and banged the knocker. The door opened and Mrs Buller-Price filled the doorway. A torrent of barking dogs piled out. She smiled at Angel and waved her hands about excitedly.

'Come in. Come in. It's so nice of you to call. Now you dogs be quiet. And get out of the way. Mush! You know the Inspector by now.'

The barking and leaping stopped, except for Bogey.

'Quiet! Bogey! Quiet!' she bawled and winged a copy of the Farmers' Weekly through the air at him; he dodged it expertly and ran off. 'It's lovely to see you again.' she said brightly. 'I'll just put the kettle on, it's coffee time. And I've got some lovely fresh cream buns. Made them last night.'

She went into the kitchen, plugged in the kettle and pressed the switch.

'Why don't you sit down, Inspector. In there. I'll bring this through in a jiffy.'

He nodded, turned and came back into the sitting-room.

'Sit wherever you like,' she called.

He lowered himself into the easy-chair facing the fire and looked down at the assortment of dogs already snoozing on the carpet in front of him. He took a long white envelope out of his inside pocket, looked at it, and put it back again.

Mrs Buller-Price leaned in from the kitchen.

'Is that the letter from my son?'

'What?' he said in surprise and then: 'No,' he replied quickly.

'He phoned me, you know,' she said waving her hands in the air. 'What a delight to hear his voice and to know he's all right. The line from Agara was as clear as a bell. Told me where he was. With Enchantra. I am glad Morris is settling down. And she's such a nice girl.'

Angel shook his head pensively.

'We had a near miss with your son, last Monday.'

She arrived with the tray, placed it on the little table, found a rubber ball in her chair, put it on the sideboard and sat down.

'Yes. He told me. Must let the tea mash for two and half minutes. I'll watch the clock.'

'You should have informed me, you know. When did he phone you?'

'Saturday morning, eleven o'clock. He said he had written to you the day before. He read a copy of the letter he had sent to you over the phone. Anyway he didn't tell me anything you hadn't already worked out.'

'You'll know all about the gold then?'

'I was amazed. My dear sister Elizabeth would have been dumbfounded if she had known. What's that in your pocket, then, Inspector? Come on. You can tell me about that.'

Angel slowly reached into his pocket and pulled out the long white envelope.

'I am afraid I have brought you the summons,' he said quietly.

'Oh,' she said, shaking her head very slightly. 'Oh. What's it say?' She straightened the cups, saucers and spoons. 'Would you read it to me?'

Angel sighed. He held the envelope in his hand and said:

'Well, I needn't read it, really. It's simply a document from the court directing you to attend before a judge at Leeds Assizes, on the tenth of May at ten a.m., to face a charge of aiding and abetting the escape of Morris Yardley from Her Majesty's prison Welham on the nineteenth of April. That's what it amounts to.'

She sucked in a length of air, and her lips quivered. 'Oooh! I don't like the sound of that.'

'We need to organize a solicitor for you,' he said gently.

She opened a round tin on the tray and lifted out the buns.

'I can see old Mr Rubens. He's been very good to me and my husband over the years. He does all Michael Parkinson's stuff and Dickie Bird's. He'll see me all right, Inspector. Will you be there?'

'I'm afraid I'll be giving evidence against you.'

'Oh?' she said with a pout.

'But you knew that.'

Her jaw quivered, shaking all her chins.

'Will I have to go to prison?'

'That's a matter for the judge. In view of your age and the circumstances, it is unlikely.'

'I can't possibly go to prison,' she said, shaking her head. 'Who would look after my animals? And what about the milk for Windsor Castle? The Queen would never forgive me.'

'You'll probably get a hefty fine.'

'Oh,' she said, looking very troubled. 'How much?'

'That's up to the judge. But it might be quite punitive,' he said evenly. 'The judge will see it like that, I'm afraid.'

'Oh dear.'

She shook her head.

*

It was Monday morning, 9 May. A week had passed and it was the day before Angel had to attend the Leeds Assizes, Regina v Victoria Buller-Price, to be heard in front of Justice Erin Skool-Friedlaker.

Angel was in his office, reading through his deposition when the phone rang. He reached out for the handset.

'Yes?'

It was the superintendent.

'I've heard from the Inland Revenue.'

'Oh yes, sir.'

'They have looked into the status of Evan Jones; everything appears to be in order. He can have his gold back.' The phone clicked and went dead.

Angel shook his head and replaced the handset. There was a knock at the door.

'Come in.'

It was a smiling Ahmed. He was waving a sheet of A4. 'What you got, lad?'

'I don't think you'll have seen this.' Ahmed placed the paper on the desk in front of him. 'It's just come down the wire.'

'Oh ay?' Angel said, looking down at it. It read:

Press statement released Prime Minister's Office,

10 Downing Street, London SW1.

0946 hrs 9 May 2005.

Distribution all news agencies.

Security category: U (unrestricted)

Commander awarded OBE

Downing Street has just announced the award of an OBE to Commander Peregrine Boodle (56) of Sheridan Walk, Chelsea, London for unstinting diplomatic work in securing peace in the Middle East.

End of press release.

Angel smiled, shook his head and rubbed his chin.

'Thank you, lad. Now there's a thing.'

Ahmed beamed.

'Has the super seen this?'

'No sir.'

There was a knock at the door.

Angel frowned. 'See who that is, lad.'

Ahmed opened the door.

The plumber in the blue overalls was standing there with the unlit cigarette-end in the corner of his mouth. He was holding a yellow plastic bucket. He looked across at Angel. 'Here. Can I have a word with you?' he said.

Angel screwed up his eyes.

'Me?' he queried. 'Ay. What is it?' He stood up.

The plumber shuffled into the room. Angel turned to Ahmed.

'Take that press release down to the super's office, lad,' he said. 'Tell him I sent you. You never know. It'll soon be Christmas, he might smile.'

Ahmed went out grinning, and closed the door.

Angel wrinkled his nose and peered at the man with the bucket.

'Now then, what can I do for you?' he said.

The plumber placed the bucket on Angel's desk.

'I think it's more like what I can do for you,' he replied.

'Oh,' Angel said, glaring at the location of the bucket and considering what he might do about it.

'Yes. I've been four weeks trying to unblock yon gents' lavatory, without disturbing the granite wall at the front of this station your chief constable is so proud of. And I've just this very minute managed it. I got this out, what's been causing the blockage. And by the look of it, it belongs to you.' He tipped the bucket slightly towards him. Angel peered into it and saw an open leather wallet, with his badge and his warrant card, showing a photograph of him, floating in an inch of clear water at the bottom.

His jaw dropped. 'Oh.' He couldn't think of anything to say. 'Oh.'

'I've rinsed them, the best I could. Where do you want them?'

Angel looked vaguely round the office.

'Well, just put the bucket down there,' he said pointing to the floor by the door.

'No. Can't leave it. I want the bucket back.'

Angel was about to speak, when there was a knock on the door.

'Come in,' he called. It was Ahmed.

'Ah,' Angel said, smiling. 'You weren't long.'

'He wasn't in, sir.'

'Well, take this bucket off this chap, go down to the boiler room, put the contents out to dry.'

'If I don't get the bucket back, I shall stick it on the bill,' the plumber said challengingly.

'And make sure you give him his bucket back soon as you can,' Angel said irritably 'Right sir.'

The plumber handed the bucket to Ahmed and sniffed loudly.

'I'll be working in the gents' lav,' he said and wandered out of the room.

Ahmed peered into the bucket.

'Oooo look, sir. It's your ID stuff, your warrant card, your badge — '

'I know. I know,' snapped Angel.

'Ah? Does the super know about this?'

'No.'

'Shall I tell him, sir?'

'No,' Angel growled.

Ahmed's eyebrows shot up.

'Right sir.' He turned to go. 'Does the chief constable know, sir?'

'No!' snapped Angel more loudly.

'I thought — '

'Never mind what you thought.' Angel waved his hand angrily. 'Just do what I tell you.'

Ahmed looked surprised. 'All right, sir.' He turned back. 'You've got a visitor. In reception.'

'Oh? Who?'

'Mrs Buller-Price.'

Angel groaned. 'Ooooh. Mrs Buller-Price? This is very unorthodox. It's the court case tomorrow. She really shouldn't be speaking to me.'

'Shall I say you're not in?'

'No, no. I'd better see her. She'll naturally be worried. On her own. You'd better show her in here.'

'Right, sir.'

Ahmed took the bucket and closed the door.

Angel wondered what she could possibly want so near the trial. She would naturally be apprehensive; he would do what he could to alleviate any nervousness. He gathered together the papers he had been working on, squared them off and put them neatly on the corner of the desk; he straightened his tie and buttoned his coat. He was ready to see her.

There was a knock at the door.

'Come in!'

Ahmed opened the door. 'Mrs Buller-Price.'

Angel stood up and smiled.

'Come in. Come in.'

The old lady sailed in wearing a big smile, a weatherproof coat and hat and carrying a big leather shopping-bag.

'Ah, there you are Inspector,' she said, loudly. 'How nice to see you again.'

Ahmed went out and closed the door.

She looked round the room. 'Is this the torture chamber, where you get all your confessions?' she said with a girlish giggle.

He smiled and pointed to the chair.

'Please sit down. Now what brings you here?'

She dropped the leather bag by her feet and slowly lowered herself into the chair, carefully placing her stick on the floor beside her. Then, in a confidential tone, she said: 'I'll tell you. It's my day in court tomorrow, isn't it.' She shook her chins. 'You said that the fine was likely to be substantial.'

Angel nodded. 'I am afraid so.'

'Well look here, Inspector, to save all that trouble and time-consuming business of me appearing there, perhaps I could plead "Guilty". Hmm?'

She dived into the big leather bag, and swiftly pulled out something heavy wrapped in a spotlessly clean yellow duster.

She placed it on the desk in front of him. 'And do you think you could ask the judge to take the fine out of that?'

Angel turned back the corner of the duster to reveal a bar of gold.

THE END

YORKSHIRE MURDER MYSTERIES

Book 1: THE MISSING NURSE
Book 2: THE MISSING WIFE
Book 3: THE MAN IN THE PINK SUIT
Book 4: THE MORALS OF A MURDERER

Don't miss the latest Roger Silverwood release, join our mailing list:
www.joffebooks.com/contact

FREE KINDLE BOOKS

Please join our mailing list for free Kindle crime thriller, detective, mystery, romance books and new releases! www.joffebooks.com

Thank you for reading this book. If you enjoyed it please leave feedback on Amazon, and if there is anything we missed or you have a question about then please get in touch. The author and publishing team appreciate your feedback and time reading this book.

Our email is office@joffebooks.com

Follow us on facebook www.facebook.com/joffebooks

We're very grateful to eagle-eyed readers who take the time to contact us. Please send any errors you find to corrections@joffebooks.com

Printed in Great Britain
by Amazon